9A-2B

A Death Worth Waiting For

Shaun Beattie

ACKNOWLEDGMENTS

My grateful thanks go to Judith who patiently put up with my interminable ramblings about this story during the years and months it took to write, and for her insightful comments and suggestions. Thanks also to Alexander who helped develop and improve parts of this tale. Thanks also to Blake our dog for putting up with being ignored for hours on end. Finally thank you to my great grand uncle Michael Wilkinson, who's emigration to Canada and subsequent death at Wellington Colliery in 1884 inspired this work.

Chapter 1

The church bells were tolling seven o'clock. Father
Étienne locked up the presbytery, checking the door
carefully before placing the well-worn iron key in a
pocket in his ancient Ulster coat. As he walked away
from his door, he reflected that he had few possessions
anyone would wish to take and only carried out this
unnecessary ritual partly from habit, but mostly to avoid
the wrath of his housekeeper the formidable Madame
Vernier. In his 76th year, a tall bespectacled man with a
full head of snowy white hair and a neatly trimmed
beard, straight backed but with a slight limp, he walked
purposefully into an icy cold January night along the
frost coated cobbled streets towards Rue Des Lingots
and his unexpected liaison with his friend Michel
Londres.

He had known Michel for many years, in fact Étienne
was one of the first people Michel encountered when he
had arrived in Honfleur all those years ago. How many
years was it now? The cleric tried to recall the day of that
chance meeting 14 or 15 or maybe 16 years earlier. He
had been strolling along Quai de la Quarantaine near the
harbour area when Michel had approached him and
speaking in an unfamiliar French accent asked where he
might find work and a place to stay. Étienne recalled
how he had been instrumental in helping Michel find
both work and accommodation at the very shop in Rue
Des Lingots which a few years later, Michel would buy
from its owner Monsieur Guillaume. Although they had

become good friends over the years, Michel had never spoken much about his earlier life, and had quickly changed the subject when Étienne broached upon it, but now tonight it seemed all that was about to change. A few hours earlier Étienne had received a note from Michel asking him to visit after seven that evening. There had been a sense of urgency about the communication, but little detail other than Michel required his assistance and all his questions about his friend's past would be revealed.

Few people were abroad as Father Étienne hurried past the picturesque Église Sainte Catherine, said to be the largest wooden church in France, its familiar chestnut shingled roof now entrancingly sprinkled with a light covering of snow. He approached Michel's premises in Rue Des Lingots. The dimly lit shop was closed, its unshuttered windows already shrouded with the evening's frost, and with the expectation of discovering his friends long concealed story, Father Étienne knocked more firmly on the door than was necessary.

As he waited for Michel to come to the door, Étienne pondered on what could have been the catalyst for his friend's sudden desire to talk about his past. His life appeared to be quite uncomplicated. Michel had no family as far as he knew. He had always lived alone and aside from himself, Michel appeared to have no particular friends. He ran his business efficiently, cheerfully passing the time of day with his customers. He seemed very much a man of habit for on the same day every week he frequented the same cafe in the Vieux

Bassin, where on fine days he would sit outside savouring his coffee as he studied the passers-by and watched the activity on the boats at their moorings. Étienne doubted Michel suddenly needed his spiritual guidance, for although he occasionally attended his church on Sundays, he was not a believer, he did not take communion.

Michel greeted him warmly as usual, but Father Étienne sensed Michel was far from his customary self. The shopkeeper quickly locked the door and ushered Étienne towards the spiral staircase which led to his living accommodation, picking up a bottle of wine from a shelf on their way through the shop. In the sparsely furnished living room a lively fire burned in the grate, Michel poured two generous glasses of wine and the two men reclined on carved armchairs at either end of the hearth.

Michel began, 'Well old friend, thank you for coming to see me tonight. We have known each other so many years and you have been patient with me, and though I am sure you have had many questions about my past, you have never pried or complained when I ignored your gentle probing. As you are well aware I have lived in Honfleur these past fifteen years or so, most of them quite uneventful. I have generally become accepted as Honfleurais, and I suppose most people would see me as a fairly unremarkable member of the commune, but before I came here my life was far from unremarkable. Folks know me as the reserved shopkeeper Michel Londres, but that is not my real name. I have held my past close for good reason, but a few hours ago my former life caught up with me, and that is why I asked you to come here this evening . You see, I am a man with a veiled past, you could say a man with some history, a man who has had to be ever watchful, a man who has a story to tell, and tonight Étienne my friend I shall tell that story. So where should I begin? I suppose I should start with my childhood for it sets the scene for what was to follow.'

My family lived in the northeast of England in Sheepwash, a small village at the lowest bridging point of the river Wansbeck. My parents had settled there soon after their marriage so my father could take up work nearby. He was a carpenter by trade and used his skill doing jobs for local tradesmen and our neighbours, supplementing his income from time to time working on houses the mine owners were building for their workforce. I was the second of four children, my elder brother John, three years older than me, then there was William, two years my junior and finally along came my little sister Sarah. I had a happy and mostly carefree childhood, at least in the early years, until I encountered Reverend William Wildblood my school teacher, who told me his vocation was to instil Christianity and discipline into my godless life.'

I speak of the Reverend Wildblood and my early schooling for they introduce key players into my storey who would go on to have no small part in determining the path my life would take a few years later. School was in the village of Bothal, some two miles walk over the fields from my home, there being no school in the village of Sheepwash at that time. The Reverend

Wildblood was both Rector of the Church of St. Andrew's and also Head Master of the village school. There can be no doubt that Reverend Wildblood was a man of God, for he told us so frequently, but he was also a bully as far as small children were concerned and used older children who followed his inclination as a means of ensuring discipline.

My early nemesis was the leader of these bullies Albert Charlton. Albert was almost six months older than me, and about two years younger than my brother John. John had no truck with Albert and his cronies, and he acted as my protector during my early schooldays. John was a bright lad, who worked hard at his studies and by and large avoided any censure from Rector Wildblood due to his diligence. However, I was not so lucky. I was bright, but easily distracted and as a consequence I frequently received punishment from the good Rector. Albert resented me because I was popular with my classmates and sufficiently competent at my studies that I was usually able to answer the Rectors' questioning when he couldn't. When my brother wasn't around, I suffered frequent beatings for 'showing off' as Albert called it, but one incident in particular seemed to infuriate him, and after that day Albert needed little excuse to make my life even more difficult.

To understand the significance of the event I must describe to you the game of conkers for I think it is not played in these parts. In England schoolchildren play this game conkers using the seeds of Horse Chestnut trees. The contest takes on huge importance each autumn and to possess a champion conker is a very prestigious achievement. The game is played by two combatants, each with a conker threaded onto an old bootlace or string. Each player in turn, takes three consecutive swings at their opponent's conker, which is held out perfectly still dangling on the full length of its string, in an attempt to shatter it or detach it from the bootlace. The process is repeated until one conker breaks or becomes detached from its bootlace, the player with a remaining laced conker is declared the winner, even if it sustains damage, and the victorious conker gains a point. A conker begins life as a nones-er, meaning that it has not yet beaten an opponent, when a nones-er breaks another nones-er then it becomes a ones-er, and if it was a ones-er then it becomes a twos-er and so forth. If the winning conker beats a conker that has had previous victories, then that winning conker adds the score previously earned by the losing conker, as well as gaining the score from that game, so for example a twos-er beating a fives-er becomes an eights-er. Oh, and there is one other rule that is important for my tale, should a player drop his conker or have it knocked from his hand, the other player can shout 'stamps' and can immediately stamp on the fallen conker; but should its owner first shout 'no stamps' then the fallen conker is saved and can be retrieved. I tell you this Étienne so that you can begin to understand the magnitude of the event I am about to describe.

Albert was the conker champion of our school; it had been so for three years. This particular day he was especially boastful, he had achieved many victories and he claimed his conker was a ninety-fives-er. It was his great ambition to possess a hundreds-er and victory over my nines-er stood in his way. The school yard was tense with anticipation as the momentous game commenced. Albert was to strike first. I stood stock still, not daring to flinch, as three mighty blows hammered down on my conker, but it stood firm against the onslaught. Then it was my turn. Nerves and the expectant crowd got the better of me and I missed my first swing. My second swing was a feeble glancing strike, but my third attempt hit hard without seeming to do any damage to either conker.

Albert grinning broadly, prematurely savouring an expected victory, resumed his onslaught. Once again, my conker survived three vicious blows almost intact, except for losing a small piece of shell revealing the nut underneath. The playground crowd fell silent as I prepared to swing my conker. My hesitant swing just lightly tapped his conker; Albert taunted me growling, 'You'll have to do better than that runt, if you want to beat me.'

Shutting out the expectant crowd and summoning all my concentration I aimed for Albert's conker will all my might. There was an almighty thud followed by a yelp of pain as my conker crashed onto Albert's fleshy knuckles. I was first to react and shouted 'stamps' followed by Albert's 'you bastard, no stamps.' I jumped on Albert's conker crushing it with my boot as permitted within the rules of the game, but my triumph as the proud victor, boasting a hundred and fives-er, was short lived, simultaneously with cries of 'cheat,' fists reigned in on my unprotected body. There was little I could do to protect myself from Albert, his rage visibly rising like milk heating in a saucepan. Unable to fight back against a much stronger opponent, I fell to the ground and curled up in a ball, as his brutal kicks pummelled into me. This playground hiatus eventually attracted the attention of Reverend Wildblood. His sonorous voice rang out across the playground, 'You boys stop! I say stop!' The schoolchildren now silent, parted like the Red Sea, and Reverend Wildblood stood before us.

'Well Charlton, Wilkinson, explain this outrageous behaviour.'

Albert recounted the conker game, then to save face added that I had cheated by deliberately hitting his knuckles so causing him to drop his conker and then I compounded this injustice by stamping on his conker even though he had clearly shouted no stamps. I mumbled my version of events, but it was clear from Wildblood's expression that he chose to believe Albert. Wildblood was about to dismiss Albert and issue my punishment, when a gentle timorous voice spoke out, 'Reverend Wildblood excuse me sir,' interjected a diminutive Mary Scott, 'Michael's telling the truth, he beat Albert fairly and Albert attacked him out of rage.'

So, you see Étienne, that fateful day by playing an innocent children's game, I unwittingly made an enemy who was to be largely responsible for the course my life was to take a few years later. Mary also had an ill-starred role in my story, but I will speak more of her in a while.

Fortunately, my childhood was also enjoyable, my elder brother John and I, sometimes accompanied by my younger brother Will, spent many happy hours roaming the local woods and fields and fishing on the nearby river. Indeed, in my youth the river and my future fate were inexorably linked. The first story I will tell you Étienne, occurred a year or so after the conker episode. It was summer, my brother John and I were at the river. We had been fishing since dawn, hoping to catch the early rise, but as often happened, the trout did not share our enthusiasm. As we sat drinking some cold tea in an old, abandoned stone walled sheep shelter near the riverside, which we had made into our den, we decided to venture downstream. We walked further than our usual self-imposed limit, exploring territory that was fairly new to us. Faintly, carried by the slight summer breeze, we could hear the sound of music. Adventurers that we were, we decided to find the source of this unexpected phenomenon.

The music soon ceased but we decided to carry on to see if we could discover it's origin. As we rounded a bend in the river, we saw in the distance a ramshackle stone cottage close to the riverbank. Near the cottage was a small rickety looking jetty with a green painted rowing boat moored to it. As we approached the tumbledown building, we observed an equally bedraggled old man sitting on a bench outside the cottage with a cornet placed over his knees. This was the source of the music.

Being curious but cautious boys, we walked warily towards the old gentleman. He appeared to be asleep and totally unaware of our approach, but to our surprise he called out in a not unfriendly way, 'Good morning young masters, what can old Jacob be doing for you today?' He stood up and walked towards us. He was well over six feet, but old age had caused him to cultivate a slight stoop. He wore a dark knitted woollen hat and jersey, a mysterious eye patch covered his left eye. He smiled enthusiastically on noticing our fishing rods, and said, 'Aye but it's a grand morning for the fishing is it not?'

My brother John replied that we were exploring the river bank looking for a likely spot to catch a trout or two but had had no luck so far. The old gentleman then offered to show us a promising trout pool just a few yards further downstream. Old Jacob watched us for a while then gave us both some advice on improving our casting technique and offered us a couple of his own trout flies which he said may well improve our luck. Sure enough, after a short time I hooked and landed a fine trout and soon after John was the proud captor of a brace of handsome fish.

Jacob invited us to breakfast and being ravenous after our early morning exploits, we eagerly accepted his invitation. The interior of his cottage appeared quite dark to us after being outside in the bright sunlight, but once our eyes adjusted to the dimness , it revealed itself to be surprisingly clean and tidy. It was sparsely furnished with just a couple of oaken captain's chairs and two stools arranged around a large wooden table. An oak storage chest stood underneath the window and a welcoming fire burned in the kitchen range. Jacob set to work cleaning the fish and soon had our trout, supplemented with a couple of his own, sizzling in a pan and presently we were feasting on fried trout and crusty bread washed down with strong sweetened tea. This chance encounter between us and Jacob Armstrong turned out to be the beginning of a firm friendship, a friendship that would unwittingly contribute to my later misfortune.

We visited Jacob regularly over the next two years or so, both together and singularly, and I believe he delighted in the role of a kind of honorary grandfather. I mentioned earlier that it was the sound of music that led us to find Jacob Armstrong. Jacob was the owner of an old cornet which he played occasionally during the course of our visits. He offered to teach us to play, an offer that John declined after a few abortive attempts, but one which I enthusiastically accepted. It transpired that Jacob had spent some time in France in his youth and it was there he acquired and learned to play the instrument.

After a fishing expedition one fine but chilly early October afternoon, Will, John, and I returned to Jacobs' cottage where the old gentleman soon provided us with a warming hot drink. As we sat by his fireside Jacob began to play his cornet. We had always been curious as to how he obtained it and where he had learned to play. So, that afternoon John asked how the instrument came to be in his possession. Jacob smiled to himself and recounted how as a young man he had been billeted in Paris. He had been assigned to be the servant of an officer and it was this officer who taught him to play. I asked Jacob about Paris and what he was doing there. It transpired he had been in the Coldstream Regiment of Foot Guards Second Battalion and had been part of the British occupation forces of Paris following the war with

Napoleon. John and I often speculated as to how Jacob had lost his eye, our childish imaginations foolishly fancying or perhaps hoping that he had once been a swashbuckling buccaneer, and although we never found the courage to ask him directly, henceforth we assumed his injury occurred during his time in the army.

At first, he was reluctant to talk about his military experiences, but with our encouragement Jacob soon warmed to the task and told us his battalion fought in the most important battle of the whole war, Waterloo. It was here, he recounted that the Second Battalion, along with the Light Company of the Scots Guards, held Hougoumont Farm against overwhelming odds. Of course, we knew of the battle of Waterloo, and we were thrilled to hear about it from someone who was actually there.

Jacob told us how Hougoumont farm secured the Allied right flank and holding it was key to Wellington's plans. Sixteen thousand French troops attacked the farm all day, but they were unable to capture it. At one stage the French troops even came charging through the main gates, however the British guardsmen counterattacked and successfully pushed them back. In the struggle the gates were damaged, but Lieutenant Colonel MacDonnell's men forced them shut and Sergeant Graham of the Coldstream Guards dropped the locking bar in place earning the honour of being described by Wellington as 'the bravest man in the army.'

For the rest of the day Hougoumont was subjected to a sustained attack by the French 6th and 9th Infantry Divisions. Jacob related that during the course of the afternoon ammunition was running low, and he had volunteered to accompany Sergeant Fraser of 3rd Scots Guards, back to Major Generals Byng's position for supplies. When they returned bringing back a much needed waggon load of cartridges, the main farm building was burning fiercely, and the farm buildings were heaped with British dead and wounded.

'It was a hellish sight boys, but the French were undaunted and continued their attack. Their dead and wounded littered the nearby fields and woodland. Even though we prevailed, we'd suffered greatly too lads, for by the close of the day we had lost well-nigh 500 men dead and wounded, out of our force of 2,000 troops. Although I never heard him say it myself, I was told Wellington said afterwards that the outcome of the Battle of Waterloo hinged on us closing them gates at Hougoumont, and he'd declared, '*No troops but the British could have held Hougoumont, and only the best of them at that.*' It was later on, well after the battle was done and dusted, I was part of a detachment walking the battlefield looking for casualties, when I came across this here cornet lying in the mud, next to the body of a French Infantryman.'

It must have been a depressing scene Étienne, all those men from both sides taken in their prime, but such is the folly of war. My friend you must wonder why I am telling you this story of Jacob Armstrong, all will become clear soon. To continue; now Jacob had finished his tale and he got up and went to the oak chest beneath his window, after rummaging around for a short while he returned to the fireside clutching a small canvas pouch. Opening the pouch Jacob produced a silver object, which he handed to us to view. 'This here medal', he said, 'is the medal issued to every man who took part in that campaign'.

As I viewed his medal, examining the head of the Prince Regent on the front and, the figure of Victory depicted on the reverse, little did I know the impact this object would have on my future life.

Chapter 2

The following winter was one of great sadness for us as we had our first experience of the death of someone close. Jacob had been taken ill in early January with I think pneumonia. Towards the end of the month his condition suddenly deteriorated and sadly for us he passed away. His daughter Hannah, who lived nearby, took charge of the funeral arrangements and on a wintry, wet and windy afternoon later that same week Jacob was laid to rest in the churchyard at Cambois. The following week Jacob's son-in-law came to visit us. He told us he and Hannah had been clearing Jacobs' cottage as the Duke of Portland's agent was eager to install a new tenant, and they had come across a will. Jacob had bequeathed to my brother his fishing equipment and his decaying rowing boat, and I had been entrusted with his cornet and waterloo medal.

The next day, John and I walked to Jacobs' cottage to collect our inheritance. The rowing boat with its flaking green paint had surely seen better days. It would require a lot of work to make it watertight. Nonetheless, John and I decided to try to row it upstream and beach it closer to our house, where John and father could work on it. So, with John rowing assisted by the incoming tide and me bailing out, we eventually made landfall close to Sheepwash Bridge. Not much of significance happened to us in the aftermath of Jacobs' death. John had left school by now and worked with father, although he had an ambition to go into business. For a while I became the centre of attention among my classmates as they all wanted to see the Waterloo medal, which I had taken to wear on a chain about my neck. Albert dismissed the medal as a fake and continued to be my tormentor at every opportunity. However, as winter eased into spring and spring in turn made way for summer, father, John and I succeed in restoring old Jacob's rowing boat.

Autumn that year was exceptionally wet. Rainfall had been much higher than was usual and as a consequence the land was saturated and since mid-September the river level had been rising steadily. John had hauled his boat high up onto the bank and frequently went to check on it, anxious it didn't get washed away by the ever rising floodwater. It was now almost mid-October and if anything, conditions seemed to be getting worse. One night after tea John asked me to go with him to check up on his boat. It was another wild and stormy night, but I reluctantly agreed. As we approached the mooring, we could see the water level had risen sharply since our last visit and it was still rising rapidly. Debris was stacking up against the arches of the nearby bridge and the wooden part of the bridge was groaning ominously.

I should tell you Étienne that this was not a healthy bridge. It was an ancient stone bridge but a storm some four years earlier had damaged part of a weir upstream and stones from the weir carried by the surging water had undermined one of the four medieval arches causing part of the bridge to collapse. This part of the bridge had been temporally repaired with a wooden structure and it was from this wooden area that we could hear loud creaking noises caused by the wood struggling against the powerful floodwaters.

As we stood gazing at the rapidly rising floodwater, we became aware of a horseman approaching. He was galloping along the road from Pancake Row, clearly heading for the Thieves Bank Road on the far side of the river. As the rider came upon us John, to my surprise, ran out into the path of the horse and snatching at its bridal forced the startled animal to veer from its course. The astonished horseman no doubt believing he was to be the victim of an audacious attack began to swing his riding crop at John but as he did so there was a tremendous cracking noise almost like thunder or an explosion and to my horror the wooden section of the bridge collapsed into the surging waters of the Wansbeck.

Whether John saw some indication of the impending demise of the bridge or whether he had some sort of second sight I do not know, but I do know that had he not intercepted the speeding horse both horse and rider would have been inexorably swept away by the torrent. As the gentleman regained his composure following John's sudden appearance, he dismounted and thanked John most heartily. He introduced himself as Sir James Alexander. His name was familiar to us although we had never met him; he was a local magistrate and entrepreneur. Sir James waited for us to introduce ourselves which we did self-consciously not being used to conversing with people of his social standing.

'Well master Wilkinson,' he said addressing my brother, 'I shall expect to see you at my house tomorrow morning at 10 o'clock sharp, where you will hear something to your advantage by way of saving me from the river.'

I didn't accompany John to the big house as we habitually called it, but the next afternoon when I returned home from school John had a smile as broad as a rainbow spread across his face. He had met Sir James in his drawing room where to his great surprise and delight he was served coffee. Sir James had asked John about his family and discussed his education and his ambition in life. Finally Sir James thanked him again and by way of a reward not only gave him £35, which at that time was more than six months' salary for many, but offered John a position in one of his various businesses as an apprentice clerk, an offer which John gratefully accepted.

So once again Étienne another event occurred that not only played a substantial role in helping John achieve his ambition to go into business, but in an incidental and unforeseen way it was to have a bearing on the path my life was to take a couple of years later.

Life was comfortable if uneventful over the next few years. John settled into his new position and I on leaving school, like many of my school friends, took a job in the local colliery. Albert was also employed at the colliery, but our paths seldom crossed at work. However, when the opportunity arose, I still suffered from Albert's taunts and practical jokes but as I was now at least a head taller and stronger than him, the risk of beatings had subsided. It seemed to all the adults that Albert had mellowed as he grew up. He worked hard at his job and was well thought of by the older men on his shift. However, his former school mates were well aware of his aggressive nature and explosive temper, and most went out of their way to avoid him. Albert lived with his mother and father and elder brother at the far end of Pancake Row three doors up from a hostelry called the Shakespeare where he spent much of his leisure time.

My former defender and school mate Mary Scott returns to my tale at this point. Her father George Scott managed the Shakespeare Tavern assisted by his wife Harriet. Mary on leaving school helped out in the kitchen and sometimes served at the bar. Mary and I had remained friends from our schooldays. I had always looked out for Mary from the day she stood up for me against Reverend Wildblood, but I had not seen her very often since leaving school. Much to everyone's surprise Albert seemed to have developed a romantic interest towards Mary and it appears she did not discourage him. On the contrary, rumours reached me that they were to become engaged. I decided, in the arrogance of my youth, that he was not the man for her and that at the earliest opportunity I would try to persuade her against this ill-conceived match, given his temperament and penchant for bullying and her innate good nature and sense of fair play.

A couple of weeks later I made one of my rare visits to the Shakespeare determined to speak with Mary. The tavern had a dark and gloomy but reasonably clean interior, and what natural light shone through the grimy windows appeared to radiate onto the bar just where Mary happened to be standing. I went up to the bar and spoke with Mary and asked her if she could come outside where we could have a more private conversation. She finished putting away a couple of tankards and after telling her father she was going out for a few minutes, we left together. As we walked along Pancake Row down towards the river, I expressed my concerns about her relationship with Albert. She listened patiently to my pleas for her to break off her engagement but insisted that he had changed and aside from his occasional moodiness and irritability, he was kind and considerate towards her. She informed me he had great plans to make something of himself, to move away from Sheepwash and she wanted to go with him. I told her this was all nonsense, she could do much better for herself than Albert and that he would never amount to anything more than a colliery labourer. Our discussion became quite heated at this point, she slapped me about my head shouting that I was jealous of her happiness, and she never wanted to see me again, as she stormed off home towards the Shakespeare, I shouted back that she was a silly girl and that she would be sorry, and went off for a walk along the river bank reflecting on our squabble.

I hadn't walked very far when I was suddenly set upon from behind. My attacker was Albert Charlton. Albert grabbed me by my jacket lapels and pulled me towards him intending to head-butt me on the nose. I pulled free with one arm and managed to forestall his blow, Albert was enraged shouting at me 'to keep away from Mary if you know what's good for you.'

I told him there was nothing going on between me and Mary, but I could see there was to be no reasoning with him and prepared to defend myself against his next ferocious assault. Albert ran at me with his arms swinging wildly, I stepped to one side to avoid an intended punch and landed a blow on the side of his head. As Albert stumbled, he caught hold of my waistcoat tearing off the buttons as he went down. I walked towards him and he grabbed my legs knocking me to the ground. I got up quickly and caught him as he was rising and we again struggled, wrestling to the ground. I could see that in spite of his bluster Albert was tiring and as we broke free, I jumped to my feet and with my head down charged at him, I caught him an unguarded blow in the stomach, leaving him gasping for breath as a result. At this point I thought it wise to be off and left Albert scrambling around in the sand on the river bank. As I ran off, I heard Albert screaming after me, 'you'll be sorry for this Wilkinson, do you hear me? I'll make you pay for this, you see if I don't.'

As it was late February and the daylight hours were still short, it was almost dark when I got home. John hadn't returned from work yet, but my mother and father, who were sitting by the fire with Will and Sarah, noticed the state I was in, so I had to explain about my encounter with Albert and what had led up to it. We settled down to our evening meal and as the night wore on, I began to put the altercation to the back of my mind until John came home when I had to repeat the whole saga again for his benefit.

I had been in the habit of doing a bit of poaching at the river and about 9 o'clock I decided to go out and check on my salmon net as I knew the bailiff would be in the Shakespeare by then. I asked John if he wanted to come but he said he was too tired and was going to bed. It was a fine but breezy night. As it was only a few days before the full moon I was able to find my way along the riverbank easily, for the intermittent moonlight lit my way as the breeze blew the clouds across the sky. My journey to the river was uneventful and so was my poaching, my net was empty. I reset the net then watched a couple of otters swimming around and playing on the riverbank for about half an hour or so before returning home.

I was roused early the next morning by John shaking me quite vigorously, 'Michael quick wake up,' he shouted, 'Michael, its Mary, Mary Scott is dead! Come on get up there isn't much time.'

'What's happened John? What do you mean Mary is dead? She was fine yesterday when I left her.'

It was still quite dark, but as was his habit before setting off for work, John had taken our dog Ralph out for a walk, and he had come across a commotion in a little alleyway close to the Shakespeare Tavern. For some reason he had stayed in the shadows, observing the scene play out in front of him. He described how he saw the constable arrive and heard someone in the throng say that it was Mary Scott who had been found dead, in the alleyway a few minutes earlier.

'Oh my God John how can this be? She looked fit and well when I was with her yesterday.'

'Well folks are saying she's been murdered Mike, strangled or stabbed what I heard.'

'No that can't be true John, who would want to kill poor Mary?'

'That's the thing Mike,' said John, 'they're saying it was you that did it.'

'That's ridiculous everyone knows that we were friends, why would they say I killed her?'

Well people are saying they saw you arguing with Mary yesterday and you threatened her. But that's not the worst of it, they're saying your Waterloo medal and some buttons were found next to her body.'

'Well that certainly can't be true, I have the medal right here.'

I went over to pick up my waistcoat from the floor where I had left it the night before. The chain had snapped a few days earlier, so I had placed the medal in my waistcoat pocket for safe keeping, but as I searched the pocket there was no medal to be found. 'Oh my God, it's not there, but how could my medal be with Mary?'

'John what am I to do now? You know I didn't murder Mary.'

'Of course, I do, but people are saying you did, so we need to get you away from here for a while so we can come up with a plan to prove your innocence. You remember the disused sheep shelter near the river we used to use as a den when we were kids? You could hide out there till we come up with something.'

I quickly dressed and grabbed a few spare items of clothing and sneaked out of the house creeping unseen down to the riverside then stealthy I made my way to the old sheep shelter. John had told me he would come to me when he could get away and would bring some food and drink, but I realised I would be in for a long wait as he would have to go to work before he could bring any sustenance.

I passed a long and bitterly cold day in that sheep shelter, not daring to light a fire in case the smoke was observed. It was about seven o'clock that evening when John arrived. He lit a candle and produced some food which I ate ravenously and washed it down with water which he had also supplied. He said the constable had been to our house looking for me and father had told him that he thought I had gone to Bedlington, a town 4 miles away, to visit an old friend. This was a notion that John had given him, and father had no reason to doubt it. John said things were looking bad for me as a number of people had seen Mary and me arguing on the day of her murder and in their eyes that made me guilty. John told me he had come up with an idea and if I was agreeable, it would mean staying in the sheep shelter for a few more days until he could arrange things.

John's plan was that I seek the help of his employer and benefactor Sir James Alexander. John was certain he would be sympathetic to my case and would be a great ally in proving my innocence. I wasn't as confident as John for I was well aware that my waistcoat had missing buttons after my fight with Albert, my Waterloo medal had been found with Mary and witnesses said they had seen us arguing and heard me threaten her. How could anyone believe I was innocent? I was certain all I could look forward to was a trip to the gallows as a punishment for a murder I did not commit. In my desperation a thought came to me. 'John, do you remember a while ago you told me your work involved arranging passage to America and Canada for emigrants? Well, I believe that could be the answer to my dilemma.'

John tried to talk me out of it, insisting that Sir James was my best hope, but I was adamant this was the only path to take. Étienne you must remember I was just a young man then and not as wise as I am now, but in the foolishness of my youth I grasped at that idea. Looking back, it probably wasn't the best thing to do, but at that time it seemed to me to be the only way out of my predicament.

The following evening when John arrived with provisions my resolve to get away was intensified by the news he shared. My brother recounted that, depending on who was telling the tale, he had heard Mary had been either strangled or hit on the skull from behind with a heavy object, but worse from my point of view was the revelation that Mary's father had told the constable that she had been looking after her younger brother and sister that night as was customary. She had put them to bed sometime between 8 and 9 o'clock, and when her mother had looked into the back room sometime after half past 9 there was no sign of Mary. She must have sneaked out of the back door and was not seen again until her body was discovered early the next morning. I was both extremely saddened and alarmed to hear this report. I had no one to vouch for my whereabouts until nearly midnight for I was out of the house at that time checking on my nets.

John looked grave and continued his tale, 'the constables are searching for you Michael, they've been back to our house a couple of times and rifled through your things. They found your waistcoat with the missing buttons under your bed and said some similar buttons had been found beside Mary's body. They told father to keep you there if you return. Most of the villagers don't believe you could be the murderer, but others are saying you must be guilty because you've disappeared. Albert is the most vocal in condemning you, but something about his manner doesn't ring true, I wouldn't be surprised if he is mixed up in this affair somehow.'

Again, I told John that all I could see before me was my inexorable doom if I remained trying to prove my innocence and I should flee to America as soon as possible. I had almost £3 of savings at home, and I asked John if that would that be enough to pay for my passage?

'No, not nearly enough, more like £5 for the crossing and possibly another £5 or so for railway fairs, food, and supplies, and for accommodation in Liverpool while you wait for the steamer.'

Eventually John conceded defeat and agreed he would not only arrange my passage, but also use his own savings to pay for it. Of course, Étienne I vowed to pay him back, but realised it would likely be quite some time before I would be able to fulfil my promise. My course of action was set and now all I had to do was to spend a few more days holed up in the dreary sheep shelter, avoiding discovery, while John made the necessary arrangements for my journey.

Chapter 3

The next day was bitterly cold, with heavy intermittent snow flurries breezing in from the North Sea adding to my discomfort. I hadn't slept much, and I spent the day freezing cold and hungry, pacing around the shelter in a vain attempt to keep warm. I had disguised the entrance with branches and fashioned a crude roof, but this did little to keep out the cold. When I wasn't pacing, I huddled against a wall shivering, wrapped in a woollen blanket John had smuggled away from home. My hideaway was in a remote spot and unlikely to be visited by anyone in winter, but even so I was too scared to light a fire for fear that I be discovered. After what seemed to be an interminably long day John arrived. He had rowed down the river from Sheepwash and moored his boat fairly close to the sheep shelter, leaving it well-hidden under a large overhanging willow bush. He was a little earlier than had been his habit, for which I was most grateful. He quickly set to making a small fire to boil some water for a most welcome cup of tea, saying if anyone ventured by he would rush outside to reveal himself as the author of the blaze.

'Here Mike, get this tea down you,' he said passing me a lukewarm drink. 'Sorry I haven't brought much food, but the constable's been watching our house, so rather than go back there tonight, I came here straight from work. Still, I managed to get a loaf of bread, some cheese and a couple of apples from the shop across the road from my office just before it closed. I told our parents

I'd have to work late and then I'd stay the night at a friend's house near work, so they'll not miss me.'

I savoured the tea as if it were an elysian nectar, and hungrily tucked into the bread and cheese as John shared his news. 'Your passage to Philadelphia's all set and paid for Mike, at a cost of £4.10s., and you'll be sailing from Liverpool in four days' time.' John handed me a confirmation letter which he said I would need to present at the Shipping Agent's office in Water Street Liverpool to collect my ticket for embarkation.

'It seemed safer to make the travel arrangements in a name other than yours, so it's all arranged under the name of Mike Wilson, a miner from Tynemouth. I hope that's alright. I thought seeing as it's a town we know passably well, having spent time there with our grandparents before they died from the smallpox, you'd be able to answer any questions about the place if asked.'

Never having travelled far from my home, I was feeling apprehensive about the journey I was about to undertake, but my fear of discovery and a summary trip to the gallows far outweighed my anxiety of travelling. The night was cold but thankfully without further snow, and we settled down in our cheerless shelter to await our departure time which was to be 4 o'clock in the morning. John was well acquainted with arranging travel for emigrants through his clerking work for Sir James Alexander, and as we huddled together under the blanket, he gave me valuable instruction about what to expect on my journey to Liverpool docks and how to go on at the shipping office. We discussed what John would tell our parents about my departure. I scribbled them a brief goodbye note, little thinking as I did so that I was never to see them again. Our conversation helped pass the time and eventually I must have fallen asleep. John woke me just as the distant church clock sounded its fourth chime.

'Mike come on wake up, it's time we were off. I'll check outside and see if the coast's clear while you get your gear together.' Moments later John reappeared, 'Right Mike let's get going. Luckily for us the sky's cloudy so that should help us travel unseen up the river.'

We cautiously crept from the sheep shelter, made our way down to the river and silently clambered aboard the concealed rowing boat. We paddled upstream without incident, silently passing under Sheepwash Bridge, which was one of the few places on our journey where a passer-by may have been able to observe my escape. The only obstacle to our passage was the weir at Bothal Mill. We rowed towards the bank opposite the mill where the river ran more slowly. We quickly jumped out, and with a little effort dragged the boat up over the weir, getting a little wet in the process. Again, we were fortunate that we were not observed, but one of the miller's dogs must have heard us for it began to bark. Whether anyone was roused by the barking, I do not know for we were paddling rapidly upstream away from the commotion. There was another mill and weir just outside Morpeth, but we decided not to risk going that far. So just before a bend on the river, about 500 yards downstream from this weir, we made for the riverbank. It was now almost 6 o'clock and time for John and me to part company.

Holding my arm tightly, as if this very action would reinforce his words, John remarked solemnly , 'Mike take care and good luck, write to me when you can.'

I promised I would write when I reached Philadelphia. He smiled forlornly and said, 'you'll be needing this for your journey,' thrusting a purse containing £30 into my hand. I thanked him knowing I would need the money and it would be futile to refuse his generosity, then we hugged and parted, me heading on towards the lane that led to Morpeth and my destiny, and John back to the river.

As I approached the main thoroughfare into Morpeth there were a few other early risers making their way into town. It happened to be market day, which was a stroke of fortune, as the town would be busy, and this would serve my anonymity while I waited for the train. Some handcarts passed me by, their thrifty owners taking their produce to the market place, eager to bag a prime location. They were soon joined by a shepherd driving a few sheep to the animal market which was also in the centre of the ancient town. Morpeth was a place I had often visited, so I was confident of my route to the station. I walked through the town, trying to adopt a nonchalant gait, my cap pulled down low in an attempt to hide my face, and I studiously avoided making eye contact with anyone who passed me by just in case I was recognised.

I had never travelled by rail before, so I was thankful for the instructions my brother had given me the previous evening. As John told me, I looked for the ticket office and bought a third class ticket to Liverpool. As I handed over the 4s.8d the ticket seller informed me I would have to change trains at Newcastle. Thankful I had successfully completed the transaction I left the ticket office and asked a station porter how long I would have to wait for the next train to Newcastle? He informed me there was a train at half past eight; it was now about five past seven . Lest I was spotted, I lurked in the shadows on the draughty platform rather than seek the warmth of the waiting room.

Eventually a steam engine roared its way into the station. Porters and other railway staff were suddenly swarming around seeing to their appointed tasks, and an assortment of passengers decanted from the waiting room onto the platform to bord the waiting train. Remembering John told me the third class carriages were painted dark green, I headed to the nearest one, climbed on board and took a seat on the side closest to the platform. As I sat there gawping out of the window waiting for the train to depart, I saw a constable walking along the platform heading towards me. Panicking I jumped up then realised he probably hadn't seen me and feeling embarrassed, pretended to be looking for something in my pockets, keeping my face turned away from the window. Mercifully, he continued walking along the platform. On calming down I realised he probably hadn't been looking for me, but the incident reminded me to be more watchful. Then there was a slamming of doors, a loud whistling, followed by a cloud of steam and the mighty North Eastern Railway Company engine set off.

Even though I had lived some 15 miles north of Newcastle I had never been there, so as the steam train approached the city, I was astonished to see so many houses and workplaces huddled together and all capped by great clouds of smoke issuing from the workings of industry and the hundreds of domestic coal fires burning away. The train slowly pulled into the vast cathedral like station and shuddered to a halt. On leaving my train I found I had well over an hour to wait for the next train to Liverpool, so I ventured out of the station to have a quick look around the neighbourhood and find somewhere to have a cup of tea and a bite to eat.

After a welcome repast and feeling refreshed, I returned to the station to find platform 3 and my train to Liverpool. This was my second train journey, but I confess other than getting on at Newcastle and arriving at Manchester I remembered little about the journey, apart from the uncomfortable wooden seats and the guard checking my ticket, for being exhausted after my earlier adventures I slept most of the way. On arriving at Manchester, I again had to change trains and after a brief sojourn I was soon on my way, this time bound for Liverpool Central Station travelling courtesy of the Cheshire Lines Railway Company.

Liverpool I was told was the second city of the British Empire. The people there spoke with an accent I found difficult to understand at first, and I believe they had some trouble understanding me as I often had to repeat myself. Nonetheless, anxious about finding my hotel, I asked a newspaper vendor for directions to Whitman's Brunswick Hotel in Clayton Square, which he informed me was just a three or four minute walk from the station. Emerging from the Central Station I found myself in the impressive Ranelagh Street. My instructions, which I followed diligently, were to turn west along Ranelagh Street and walk but a short distance to the junction with Cases Street on my right and then going up that street for two hundred yards or so I would find myself in Clayton Square. Thankfully, my guide was correct and there in front of me was my hotel.

I had never set foot in a hotel before, so I gingerly made my way up to the front door. I took a deep breath and grasping the large brass handle, opened the door and entered a dimly lit foyer. Clearly the foyer had seen better days, though it was clean and smelled strongly of furniture polish, the décor and furnishings looked quite shabby and neglected. I approached the reception desk nervously and rang the bell as instructed by a sign. There was a shuffling noise coming from behind a door on the other side of the desk, followed by a cough then a man about five feet two inches tall emerged and came ambling towards me. He had thinning dark hair combed over his head in an attempt to hide his baldness, bushy side whiskers, staring dark eyes and a large mole to the left of his chin.

'Good evening, how may I help you?'

 I responded sheepishly that I had a reservation and almost gave my real name but quickly corrected myself and said, 'in the name of Wilson, Mike Wilson, from Tynemouth.'

The man pushed the register towards me, and as I signed, feeling self-conscious about using my assumed name, he said, 'you're in room 18, it's on the first floor. If you want you can get an evening meal at 7 o'clock tonight for an extra 2 shillings, and breakfast is at 7.30 in the morning, and you're not permitted to have visitors in your room.'

Anxious to extricate myself from the balding clerk, I scurried off to find my room. It was small and sparsely furnished. Without getting undressed, I lay on the bed and reflected on my day. I soon drifted off to sleep and slept soundly at first for a good few hours before wakening around three o'clock in the morning. The events of the past week were coursing through my mind and though I eventually nodded off again, they kept returning and disrupted my sleep for the rest of the night. I awoke early the next morning and after a vigorous wash and a hearty breakfast, I paid my bill and left the hotel to find the emigration agent's office in Water Street.

Coming from a small village, I marvelled at the grand and not so grand buildings and hustle and bustle of this city, noticing the purposeful stride of some people and the ambling gait of those with time on their hands. Presently I arrived at number 17 Water Street, the offices of Richardson Spence & Co, Agents for the American Line. I entered the office and joined a lengthy queue. The young man behind the desk dealt with the would be emigrants and their enquiries efficiently and politely and eventually it was my turn to approach him. I handed him the letter John had given to me. The young clerk read it quickly and looking up at me said. 'Your departure is in two days' time, be at the Prince's landing stage at 10 o'clock on the day of sailing; your passage will be forfeited if you don't present yourself and your baggage at the landing stage on Wednesday at 10 o'clock sharp.'

As he handed me my ticket, I asked him about suitable places to stay while I waited for my departure, the Whitman's Brunswick Hotel being too expensive for my pocket. He gave me a card that had printed on it, the addresses of hotels and lodging houses used by the American Line. He also recommended that I should visit an emigrant's outfitters shop to purchase some necessary supplies for my voyage and gave me another card with the name and address of an outfitters printed on it together with a suggestion of recommended purchases for the well-equipped traveller. I thanked him and bade him good morning and set out to find appropriate accommodation and the outfitting store.

I decided to seek out the emigrants outfitting store first and asked a young lad for directions to the shop at 7 James Street near St George's Dock. He offered to guide me there for a penny, so transaction agreed we set off and in no time at all I was in front of a green painted shop, with dirty windows, proudly bearing the name 'David Davis' in dull gold lettering. In one window stood a dusty notice proclaiming, 'wholesale price clothes and equipment for sailors and emigrants.' The floorboards creaked noisily as I walked towards the counter where a stout shabbily dressed man with a bushy ginger beard and side whiskers wearing what I imagined was a seaman's hat, stood chatting to his wiry assistant.

On the counter at one end, were piles of striped blankets and at the other end lay an assortment of tin pans, cups, plates, and cutlery. On the wall behind the shopkeeper was an array of shelving stacked with an assortment of canned foods, various sizes of glass jars and cardboard boxes containing goodness knows what. Other shelves were piled high with folded seaman's pullovers, stout trousers, jackets, canvas waterproofs and boots. The shop was a curious place; in the body of the emporium were other aisles of shelving stacked from floor to ceiling with various supplies and seafaring equipment, all in no apparent order.

I explained to the shopkeeper I was taking passage on an emigrant boat in a few days' time and needed essential supplies for the Atlantic voyage. A smile, or maybe it was a smirk, flashed across his heavily bearded face and he winked at his associate. In no time at all he had convinced me I needed to purchase a tin mug, plate, knife, fork, and spoon followed by a seaman's pullover, a jacket, two pairs of dark blue woollen socks, a shirt and one of the black and red striped blankets. He then persuaded me I should need a towel and soap for my voyage. He looked down at my badly worn footwear and recommended I try on a pair of strong nailed Derby watertight boots at the knockdown price of 5s11d. Finally, he convinced me I would need a stout canvas bag in which to transport my new possessions. I left the outfitters with an uneasy feeling I had been duped into buying items I wouldn't really need and suspecting I had been grossly overcharged, the price of my newly acquired goods being £2-19s-6d, substantially more than I had ever before spent in one transaction.

On leaving the shop with my purchases stowed safely in my travel bag, my task now was to find shelter for the next two nights. It had started raining heavily while I was in David Davis Outfitters so trudging away from St George's Dock, I had an unwanted opportunity to test the waterproof qualities of my new jacket. There were five lodging houses on the list the American Line clerk had given me. Having no knowledge of which might be the best for my circumstances I decided to start at the top and work my way down if the first establishment proved unsuitable. I set off to find John Tobin's lodging house which was located at No. 8 Dublin Court Carlton Street. After about ten minutes or so I'd almost reached Carlton Street when a lean fresh faced young man approached me.

'Good morning, you looking for lodgings Master?' he enquired, I replied I was looking for Tobin's lodging house.

'Well, there's a coincidence, I work for Mr Tobin,' he said in a friendly manner, 'here let me take your bag and I'll show you the way.'

I handed my heavy bag to him and just as I was about to thank him for his kindness, he pushed me over and ran off at great speed, in the opposite direction to Tobin's, taking all my newly acquired possessions. I jumped up intending to race after him but just as I did so a tall dark haired man dressed like a dock worker tackled him, knocking the fellow to the ground then following up with a vicious kick. The thief, who had now dropped my bag, scrambled to his feet and ran off cursing as he did so. My rescuer picked up my bag and brought it over to me.

'I take it you're new to these parts,' he remarked speaking with an Irish accent, 'you'll need to be wary of the runners, they'll have the shirt off your back as soon as look at you given half a chance. They're a bad lot. Many's the travellers been robbed by them scoundrels. You'll be wise to steer well clear of them.'

I thanked the Irishman for his assistance and asked him about the runners.

'They're a mean bunch of thieves and confidence tricksters, who prey on emigrants like yourself. They come up to you all smiley and helpful, like that fella, gain your trust, then quick as a blink of an eye, they'll be off hell for leather with your stuff, and you'll not see any of it again unless you pay them a hefty ransom. I wouldn't linger around here if you know what's good for you for the runners are rife in these parts.'

I told him I had little choice as I was seeking John Tobin's lodging house.

'I'd keep well clear of that place unless you've a liking for being fleeced or worse. You'd be better off going to Sterne's Hotel in Paradise Street. The owners are protestants but they're trusty and it's reasonably priced and passably clean.'

He gave me directions and set me on my way with the warning to keep my possessions close.

Sterne's Hotel was just as the Irishman said it would be, neat and tidy and moderately priced. I booked a bed for two nights at a cost of 2s per day including breakfast and an evening meal. My room, which I shared with another emigrant, was fairly basic, a small well-worn rug part covered the wooden floor to the side of a bunkbed, a set of drawers and a wash stand with a basin and jug were also provided. My roommate was a Dutchman who spoke no English except for the word please; however, we managed to communicate satisfactorily by using facial expressions and gestures.

The next two days passed slowly, as I spent much of the time in my room venturing out only for meals and occasionally to stretch my legs and take a breath of air. Eventually Wednesday morning dawned and after eating a generous breakfast, I paid my bill and departed the hotel in ample time to arrive at the Prince's landing stage before the 10 o'clock deadline.

There must have been a crowd of over two hundred people milling around the dock. The emigrants comprised of a host of nationalities including Germans, Danes, Swedes, and Scots to name but a few. All clutching their worldly possessions horded in carpet bags, suitcases, trunks or brown paper parcels of various types and sizes, as they waited for some kind of direction from the American Line employees. Towering above everything was the largest ship I had ever seen, the SS Pennsylvania, a two-masted steamship with a central red painted funnel. This handsome vessel was to provide my escape and become my refuge for the next twelve days.

Chapter 4

The crowd began to move incrementally towards a gangway labelled 'Emigrants. Some were shouting final farewells to the relatives and friends they were leaving behind and others like me, were singletons or family groups with no one on the dockside to share parting goodbyes or to wish them bon voyage. All were burdened by an array of boxes and baggage which they heaved up the walkway onto the ship. I took my place amongst the shuffling throng, advancing inexorably closer towards the SS Pennsylvania and my unknown destiny. At the head of the gangway an official checked my ticket and directed me to a hatchway with accommodation for single men; families and women traveling unaccompanied were sent in other directions. Clutching my luggage, I trudged after my fellow travellers down a stairwell along a corridor then down another stair and eventually entered a dimly lit stateroom about 16 feet square with bunk beds for 8 passengers. The room had been recently painted and the floor was freshly scrubbed, towels and bedding were provided, and there were hooks on the walls ready to receive items of clothing. A small porthole offered a glimmer of light. I threw my baggage on to a lower bunk near the door and was about to sit down when I heard a genial voice saying, 'I'd be taking the top bunk if I were you, for then seasick folk can't throw up on you.' I looked up to the top bunk opposite and saw to my surprise the Irishman who had recovered my luggage the day before.

'So, if we're to be companions I may as well introduce myself, I'm Sean Padraig O'Brien from Kilmacow County Kilkenny, and you may call me Padraig for Sean's me ould da's name, and you'll be called?'

I introduced myself as Michael Wilson from Tynemouth and feeling more confident about my new identity told him I had been a miner in Northumberland and was going to America to make my fortune. He told me with a broad grin that was a coincidence as he had intentions of doing the exact same thing. Then he added he was also to be chaperoning his sister Isabella who would be joining the Pennsylvania when it called at Queenstown the next day. Our conversation was suddenly interrupted by the boisterous arrival of more cabin mates. Four men entered our stateroom laughing loudly at some incident they found amusing and addressed us in a language we didn't understand saying *'Guten Tag, meine Herren Wie geht es?'* They had no sooner thrown their gear onto the bunks and begun to settle down when two more men entered. The men were both tall with strikingly blue eyes, longish blond hair, and short beards. They introduced themselves, as they claimed the bunks below us, as brothers Aaro and Eska Järvinen from Finland bound for Canada. Save the newcomers none of our other cabin mates had any English.

Presently the Pennsylvania had taken on board its consignment of steerage passengers and preparations were underway to feed this multitude while the ship waited for the First Class and intermediate passengers to embark later that afternoon. At midday, the steward rang a bell to summon us to lunch. Clutching my tin plate, mug and cutlery and accompanied by my new acquaintances I duly headed to the dining room which was to be found in the centre of the deck with our staterooms opening on to it. Tables let down from their housing in the ceiling, filled the dining area and were neatly set with cutlery and heavy white porcelain plates. Feeling slightly embarrassed, and not a little angry with David Davis Outfitters, I stuffed my dining accoutrements into my jacket and took my place at a table alongside Padraig O'Brien, Aaro and Eska.

I was surprised by both the quality and quantity of the food which was served to us by stewards as we sat at the table. First on the menu was a soup which the stewards poured into our mugs from containers that resembled watering cans. This was followed by a serving of beef and potatoes in gravy with a thick slice of bread. The midday meal proved much the same each day with the only difference being the type of soup and variety of meat or fish served and the numbers of people partaking. When the meal was over the stewards cleared away the dishes and the tables were raised, so clearing the floor to provide a recreation area for the sated passengers.

Next on the agenda was an examination by the ships' doctor. The doctor was set up at the far end of the room and it was nearly two hours before my companions and I reached the head of the queue. At length, when it was my turn, the portly monocled doctor looked me up and down asked me to show him my teeth then peered into my eyes, asked me to take a deep breath and cough and finally nodded at a steward who stamped my ticket. I believe I was then declared fit to travel. While all this transpired the First Class passengers boarded and were escorted to their comfortable cabins and staterooms in the upper decks, well away from the noise of the ship's engine and from us less fortunate steerage voyagers.

There was a noticeable change in the vibration of the ship, no doubt caused by the engine being made ready to depart and soon after that a warning bell sounded. Passengers rushed to the dockside deck, some to wave a last farewell to loved ones on the quayside, others to bid goodbye to their homeland and others for a last look at a city that had been their temporary home. As I stood on the deck I saw the last gangway raised and my final link with England severed. I say to you my dear Étienne; I felt a pang of sadness and anxiety not knowing when or indeed if I would see my family and my home again. I stood on the deck for some time as Liverpool faded into the distance and the ship headed down the Mersey past what I was told were the lights of New Brighton on the port side, and out into the Irish Sea. I remained on deck not wishing to return to the stale air of the stateroom, and presently saw the lights of Holyhead in the distance before Padraig persuaded me to return below. Later as was the custom the stewards served supper and soon after that I returned to the airless stateroom and settled on my bed. Remarkably in spite of all the noise of strange accents, shouting, arguing, singing and crying I slept soundly and was up early the next morning in readiness for breakfast at 8 o'clock.

Not long after I'd finished eating my new friend Padraig sought me out and vigorously shaking me by the shoulder, shouted excitedly, 'won't you be coming out on deck Mikey me boy, there's something you need to see.' I followed him with less enthusiasm and looking out into the mist he pointed, 'there, you see on the horizon? God's own country, – look there man, you see it?'

I replied I did, and watched Padraig become more and more excited as the land of his birth drew closer. Soon the vista became clearer, and Padraig drew my attention to the lighthouse at Roches Point seemingly guarding the entrance to Cork harbour and Queenstown beyond. Before long we passed Roches Point on the starboard and steamed into the harbour, rounding Spike Island and docked at Queenstown quayside. There was a bustle of activity on the quay, with thirty to forty emigrants waiting to board and anxious relatives saying farewells. Eventually the gangway was lowered and the new arrivals were set to embark.

Padraig was leaning over the shipside rail anxiously looking out for any of his family. 'There me ould folk,' he said to me, and waving frantically he shouted loudly, 'Da, Ma, over here, its Padraig.' They saw him and waved back shouting in return, but I couldn't make out what was said. Then Padraig exclaimed. 'look, there's Ciaran me brother with Bella, Dara and Orla and look there's Uncle Nail and Aunt Rosa, they're all here to see Bella off.'

Indeed, it seemed half the residents of Kilmacow had descended on Queenstown to say goodbye to Bella, as Padraig reeled off even more names of friends and neighbours. By the by the Queenstown passengers were allowed to board the Pennsylvania and Padraig got close enough to speak briefly with Bella before a steward directed her to the single ladies' staterooms and no doubt her cursory examination by the ship's physician. Within the hour the ship was underway again with the southern Irish coast being on view on our starboard side for some while. The sea remained reasonably calm as we passed the Fastnet Lighthouse, standing proudly on its rocky island outcrop, our last glimpse of the Emerald Isle.

It wasn't until later that afternoon that Padraig was reunited with his sister. It appears they had much to discuss as I didn't see him again until he returned to his bunk later that evening. Padraig seemed restless when he returned and finding me awake and willing to listen, revealed why he was travelling to America.

'Me big sister Maureen and her husband Brendan O'Flahavan, I never warmed to the man, left Ireland for America about eight years ago. They moved around a bit and finally settled in a place called Port Clinton not far from Philadelphia. They opened a store and a lodging house, and had two boys , Nail and then young Padraig. They were doing well for themselves, till July last year when Brendan was killed in an accident with a horse and cart. Maureen wrote home to me ma and da asking the family for help with looking after the boys and running the business. Soon as she heard, Bel up and volunteered to travel to America to help. Well, I was working in Liverpool and what man would let his wee sister go all that way by herself, so I decided to go with her, and here we are. I think that's enough of me bletherin' for one night. You've heard some of my tale Mikey boy, and maybe tomorrow you'll tell me a wee bit of yours, and if you're lucky perhaps I'll introduce you to my little sister.'

That evening finding our stateroom too hot and oppressive for comfort, Aaro and Eska and the Germans decided to sleep on deck, so when I awoke the next morning, I was hardly surprised to find I was alone in the cabin. The bell was sounding for breakfast, and I hurriedly made my way to the dining room and found a seat beside Eska. There were noticeably fewer passengers at the tables this morning, no doubt because of an increase in the sea swell after a couple of days of almost calm weather. I was just finishing my coffee when Padraig came over to join me. 'Mikey me boy hurry up,' he exclaimed impatiently, 'I want you to be meeting me young sister, come on now look lively, and brush your hair.'

I hurriedly finished my drink, ran my fingers through my hair, and duly followed Padraig to the far side of the dining room. 'Bella,' he said with a mischievous twinkle in his eye, 'this fine fellow is Mike Wilson me English friend, but don't hold that against him.'

Bel was quick to pick up on Padraig's mood and said, 'so this is the gullible young English lad you so bravely rescued from the Liverpool runners?'

I smiled at Bel self-consciously, and I could feel my face reddening though whether through embarrassment or bashfulness, I could not be sure, for Bel was most beautiful young woman I had ever seen. I remember meeting her as if it were yesterday, she was wearing a dark blue dress with a shawl across her shoulders held in place by a silver and jade shamrock brooch and I tell you Étienne I was quite mesmerized by her glowing brown hair and sparkling eyes the colour of a cyan sky. So enchanted, I could only mumble and stutter and said something totally banal along the lines that I was pleased to make her acquaintance.

Étienne my dear friend you and I have debated many times about whether one's destiny is predetermined and inescapable or whether as you maintain, man has freewill. Who is to know for sure? But if for once you could accept the mythology of old Norse legends and believe in the three Norns, who spend their time weaving a tapestry of fate where each thread on their loom is the destiny of a person's life, then I contend that those Norns contrived to bind my lot to this brother and sister and henceforth shape the path my life was to take. Now Étienne, enough of my philosophy, let me fill you glass and please take some more bread and cheese and I shall continue my story for I still have much to tell you.

Chapter 5

The voyage settled into a monotonous progression of long days and stifling nights interspersed with various meals which provided our highlights. Padraig especially had become increasingly restless having been used to an active routine in Liverpool where he had worked as a stevedore until a few days before joining the ship. On the fifth or sixth evening of our voyage Padraig, who had been noticeable by his absence at supper, suddenly bounded up to me with that customary twinkle in his eye and his habitual enthusiasm returned.

'Mikey me boy,' he said grinning, 'Are you game for a bit of an adventure?'

It transpired Padraig's disappearance had been due to him exploring the ship. Curious to see what the upper decks were like, he had sneaked past the stewards and gained entry to the first class saloon. There he had ventured into the smoking-room and made the acquaintance of a passenger by the name of Cornelius Brady. Padraig explained that Brady had vouched for him when a steward realising he was from steerage, had tried to eject him. Padraig said Brady told him he was bored with the company of the business men and tourists in first class and was apparently happy to find distraction in the company of an honest working man. The two men had enjoyed swapping stories; Brady had bought Padraig a couple of drinks and suggested he return another time. Later when a steward escorted

Padraig back to steerage, he told Padraig that Brady was in fact Captain Cornelius Brady and quite a hero. The previous year when the SS Atlantic had got into difficulties off the coast of Nova Scotia Brady, then the ship's third officer, had personally taken a line ashore and fastened it to a rock thereby saving over 250 lives. Padraig enquired, 'So what do you think then Mikey, are you up for a jaunt tomorrow night to meet the great man and see how your betters live?'

We had been blessed with moderate weather so far, but during the night the wind increasingly strengthened from the west and the seas became heavier. Many of our fellow passengers succumbed to sea sickness but fortunately Padraig and I were spared. There were very few passengers at breakfast or dinner that day and the smell of sickness was pervasive. Around five o'clock Padraig got Aaro and Eska to distract Mr Williams the steerage steward, while he and I made our way up the barred ladder that led to the upper decks. We climbed quickly unobserved, and stealthily reached the spacious deck reserved for the saloon passengers. The seas were quite turbulent, so we crossed the deck cautiously as the ship rose and fell with the motion of the waves and entered the warmth and luxury of the saloon. Padraig indicated a well-dressed fellow sitting with his back to us, and said, 'There he is Mike, Mr Brady the man I told you about.'

On hearing us approach Brady turned and seeing Padraig signalled for us to join him. Cornelius Brady was well-groomed, with neatly trimmed dark brown hair, dark but warm eyes, a strong nose, and a full beard without a moustache. 'Sit down lads,' he said, waving to the steward to leave us be, while asking him to bring over some drinks.

We spent a convivial few hours in conversation with Cornelius Brady and while we were aware of the motion of the ship as it soared and tumbled on the implacable seas, unnoticed at least by Padraig and I sitting in the comfort of the saloon, the weather conditions had seriously worsened. The purser came into the saloon and in a conversation with Brady said there was a mighty gale blowing from the North West causing the ship to strain excessively and the high waves had swept everything movable from the decks. Moments later an enormous wave swept over the starboard beam damaging the social hall wall and flooding the saloon.

Fortunately, few people were in the social hall at the time, and no one was injured. Brady, Padraig, and I did what we could to right the damage, while one of the waiters went off to inform Captain Bradburn the Pennsylvania's captain. The waiter returned with the ship's carpenter, and he quickly set to making repairs to the badly damaged social hall wall. Satisfying himself that he was no longer needed, Cornelius Brady went along to the officer's companion way to speak with Captain Bradburn, while Padraig and I went to assist the carpenter. Around midnight Brady returned and began helping us in our task. Not long after, another frightful wave lashed across our starboard side putting the ship in a critical situation as it was placed in the trough of the raging ocean.

Brady looked concerned and declared 'This is one of the most violent storms I have ever encountered lads and I'm fearful of the ship going over, for never have I felt a worse shock. I believe we are at the very centre of a raging hurricane, be prepared for the worst for I fear the ship may well break to pieces.'

We looked at each other grim faced but persisted with our work continually battling to stay on our feet as we carried out the repairs. Enormous wave after wave buffeted the straining ship and Williams suddenly appeared shouting to Brady, 'Captain, the waves have stoved in the forward hatchways and water is pouring through, gushing into steerage.'

Brady immediately set off running down the saloon companion way towards steerage. Padraig, no doubt worried about Bel, abandoned his work, and charged off after him, and I hastily followed. When we arrived in steerage, we found the greater part of the crew and passengers there, and most were in a state of panic. Padraig and I found Bel who though looking anxious was calmly trying to comfort a agitated mother and her two wailing children. She reassured Padraig that she was alright and then we became aware of the drama that was unfolding.

Brady realising the immense danger the vessel faced, ordered that the lower hatches be taken up on deck and used to secure the upper hatches which had been washed away by the earlier surging waves. Brady formed the crewmen and other willing helpers, including Padraig and I, into three teams to carry out the work. While these events were unfolding, Charles Rivers the third officer was lamely leaning against the pump well looking wretched and bewildered, apparently detached from the activity going on around him. Brady noticing the ineffectual third officer angrily shouted, 'are you not a ships officer Mr Rivers, why the hell aren't you doing anything to help save the ship?'

The cowering man merely shrugged his shoulders and in a despondent tone said, 'Yes sir I am but what can I do? What do you want me to do?'

An exasperated Brady curtly replied, 'Go man, get yourself off after the work parties and make sure those damned hatches are secured with all possible haste.'

Brady then ordered Mr Brennan the steward, to go to Captain Bradburn and inform him of the instructions he had given. Brennan returned presently saying he had been unable to locate the Captain and feared he may have gone overboard. Brady went up on deck and in spite of the tempest safely reached the after wheelhouse where he found the quartermaster Mr Murphy at the helm. The quartermaster told Brady the Captain had left to go to the bridge a short while earlier. Brady went back out on deck and looking towards the bridge was shocked to see that the wooden bridge house had been destroyed by the furious waves and realised that Captain Bradburn and any men with him must surely have been swept overboard with the bridge house wreckage.

While Brady was making this grim discovery, the work teams had set about their task with a stoic determination. Padraig and I assisted some crewmen struggling to take the lower hatches up onto the deck. Getting the hatches in place was a difficult task with the shrieking wind and the tempestuous ocean doing their best to prevent us. The fearful waves frequently thundered over us sending more water down the still uncovered hatches. I was knocked off my feet by one of the more powerful breakers but quick action by Padraig who grabbed at my arm to save me before the racing torrent could wash me away. Presently our hatches were secured without injury or loss of life, and we returned below decks glad of a respite from the storm. Shortly afterwards Brady reappeared below decks and with a stern expression on his face, disclosed to the purser and ship's doctor the fate that had befallen Captain Bradburn. Mr Sweetland the first officer, Mr Ross the second officer and two other men had also been swept away.

Mr Blake the first assistant engineer, cried out, 'for pity's sake Mr Brady take charge of the ship for I fear we are all doomed if you do not.'

The other senior men unanimously concurred with Mr Blake and anxiously looked at the steely faced Brady.

'I believe I've already taken command Mr Blake. Now get about your duties and with God's help and our diligence we'll save this ship. Now get off to the engine room and set the engines to dead slow ahead.'

The storm was still causing the Pennsylvania serious strain and Captain Brady made off for the wheelhouse to take charge there. After an hour or so the ship appeared to change course and came up head to the sea. We noticed that the Pennsylvania seemed to cease labouring so heavily as the ship changed direction. We didn't see

Captain Brady for many hours after that for, he remained in the wheelhouse, resolutely steering the imperilled ship through the worst of the storm. Below decks we spent an anxious night, people were soaked, no one could sleep, many were sea sick and many were praying that we would survive the night.

Fortunately, their prayers were answered for around 6 o'clock in the morning it was apparent the worst of the tumultuous storm had subsided. Captain Brady had saved the Pennsylvania. The cruel storm continued for the next few days as Captain Brady and the crew skilfully navigated the Pennsylvania away from the worst of the weather. Brady's seamanship in guiding the steamer through the hurricane had of necessity taken the ship well off its planned route adding at least four days to our expected arrival in Philadelphia.

As we drew closer to our destination the feelings of anticipation and excitement amongst the steerage passengers became almost tangible. I however was experiencing different emotions, I had been so absorbed with escaping from England that I had never considered what I might do on reaching Philadelphia and this lack of forethought was playing deeply on my mind. Three days before we were due to dock those three Norns of legend weaved their threads again. During supper that evening Padraig and Bel were discussing their future with their sister when Bel suddenly enquired, 'and Mike what will you be doing when we reach America? We've heard nothing of your plans.'

 They both looked at me grinning expectantly, as I sheepishly replied that I hadn't really got any plans but expected I would soon get a job somewhere in Philadelphia.

'I see,' said Bel, 'and what sort of job will you be looking for then Mike?'

I was about to reply when Padraig looking at Bel with that impish sparkle in his eye said, 'are you going to tell him, or should I?'

Bel continued, 'we've been discussing your future Michael and we've decided you should come to Port Clinton with us if you've got nothing better lined up. You can lodge with us and work at me sister's place until you get fixed up with something more befitting your talents.'

'There, it's all agreed,' said Padraig not waiting for my consent, 'let's have a cup of tea to celebrate.'

So with my immediate future decided I was almost able to relax and enjoy my final days on board the SS Pennsylvania. I say almost able to relax, for a niggling voice in my head continued to raise concerns about entering America, fearing that somehow the American authorities may have been informed that a wanted murderer was on soon to arrive in Philadelphia.

After the turmoil of the storm the rest of our voyage was mercifully uneventful, until one afternoon Eska came charging into our stateroom shouting excitedly, 'Aaro! Aaro! Olen nähnyt Amerikan, olemme melkein saapuneet,' to his brother, who jumping up from his bunk, started clapping Eska on the back as the brothers engaged in a crazy jig.

Smiling broadly Aaro looked at us and said, 'my friends Eska has just told me he has seen America.'

We all rushed up on deck and sure enough in the far distance was the dark silhouette of the American coastline. There was an air of excitement amongst the passengers as they gazed toward the distant land. The sighting of the American shore had lifted the mood of the emigrants and there was a good-humoured ambiance in the dining hall that evening as travellers discussed their future plans over supper. The buoyant mood continued at breakfast the following morning, but there was now also a sense of impatience with people eager for the voyage to draw to an end.

As the coastline drew ever closer, we rounded Cape May Point and entered Delaware Bay. Padraig asked Mr Williams the steerage steward how far it was to Philadelphia?

'Well, you see that lighthouse starboard. That's Cape May lighthouse, so I reckon we've still got over a hundred miles to go. It could take us anywhere between six and twelve hours to get to Philadelphia, that's if the river's clear of ice and there's were no undue delays at the Lazaretto quarantine station for the mandatory health inspection.'

Later that day we rounded Pea Patch Island and a couple of hours after the ship anchored off Tinicum Island to await its quarantine inspection. The tug boat bringing the Lazaretto physician and the quarantine master tied up alongside the Pennsylvania, and the Lazaretto officials boarded. As was the practice the Pennsylvania's crew and passengers were all required to muster on deck and Captain Brady had to affirm the state of health on board by listing the number of passengers who were well and sick. The eventually physician was ready to begin his examinations to confirm the captain's health assessment.

The waiting queue seemed to diminish incredibly slowly, and I became increasingly nervous as I stood in line, imagining that my description had been telegraphed across the Atlantic, and at any moment I would be discovered and be taken away by the quarantine party. When my turn came, I pulled my cap down low over my face as a precaution against identification, but I need not have worried as my examination was quickly completed without incident. While the examination of passengers was continuing, the quarantine officer and his team were looking at the general state of the ship's quarters, hold and cargo. Eventually , the inspection was over, and the ship was given a clean bill of health. The Lazaretto physician and quarantine master returned to their tug taking three passengers with them whom they intended to quarantine in the hospital on Tinicum Island. Two hours after leaving the Lazaretto, the Pennsylvania docked at Pier 53 Washington Avenue, and I had arrived in America.

Chapter 6

There was a bustle of activity in the Pennsylvania's steerage accommodation of as upwards of 200 souls packed up all their worldly goods ready for disembarking and the next stage of their exodus. Most passengers would spend little time in Philadelphia as like us it was to be merely a staging point in an ongoing journey. The landing stage was in an area filled with factories, warehouses, grain elevators, and various refineries all linked to the Pennsylvania railroad. Padraig and I said goodbye to Aaro and Eska as we collected our baggage and headed up onto the deck. We soon found Bel and the three of us waited until the gangplanks were opened to allow disembarkation. Eventually the barrier was released, and we exited the ship to be directed straight into the large immigration station building for customs inspection.

As we queued at customs my previous anxiety returned and Bel noticing my condition asked me what was wrong. Without revealing my whole story, I told her that shortly before I left home, I was involved in some trouble but not of my making, and I was worried that I could be arrested by customs. Bel and Padraig exchanged a quizzical look and Padraig said, 'look Mikey I don't know what you did but I know you're a decent lad, the important thing is to stay calm. When you answer their questions be confident and polite and try to smile. Tell them you're our English cousin going with us to Port Clinton to work for a widowed relative, and if asked we'll back you up.' I smiled and thanked them and hoped I could hold my nerve.

The immigration station was a huge room with a number of officials sitting at tables processing would be immigrants. Anyone who appeared unwell or failed to satisfactorily answer their questions was detained. Bel had already passed through customs, and I was next. I approached the table and scrutinised by the middle aged official, I put down my luggage. The man was about 45 years old with steely grey eyes that seemed too small for his large oval hairless face. He looked me up and down and asked where I was from, what was my occupation, had I been unwell recently and where I was going in the United States? He appeared to be satisfied with my answers, and I heaved an internal sigh of relief as I collected my bags and made to walk over to Bel. 'One moment sir,' he said, my heart missed a beat, and I resisted an urge to bolt, I turned around and he said smiling, 'welcome to America.'

Padraig joined us having passed his customs interview and we made our way to the money exchange where we swapped our remaining pounds for U.S. dollars. We headed downstairs to the railroad ticket office. I purchased a ticket to Port Clinton, and re-joined Bel and Padraig, who had bought ongoing tickets with their passage. I looked around the railyard and spotted a telegraph office and excusing myself from my companions I went inside and composed a short note to my brother addressed to his office, '*Arrived in P. All well. M.*' I rejoined Bel and Padraig wondering how my disappearance had been received back home.

After a long wait we boarded a crowded train bound for Reading where we were to pick up the Port Clinton train. I was stuck by the appearance of the Pennsylvania railway carriage or car as the Americans call it, for unlike the small British carriage, the American car was a long cabin like affair with rows of wooden seats and doors located at both ends. Once we left the city and were travelling through the open countryside, we eagerly pointed out to each other any differences that struck us between this new country and our homeland. We settled into our journey and to pass the time Bel and Padraig told me stories of their childhood in Kilmacow County Kilkenny, reminiscing fondly about happy times in their family home, an old stone house with a corrugated iron roof across the street from St Senan's church. I in turn talked wistfully of my adventures with brothers John and Will, and time spent with old Jacob, leaving out any mention of the Waterloo medal and Mary and Albert.

We exited the wooden railway station at Port Clinton on a dreary foggy late March day, feeling the chill air and fine rain assail our faces. Bel was clutching a letter from her sister which provided directions to our new home. 'Come out of the station and head south until you reach Broad Street then turn right and soon after cross a river,' said Bel reading from the ever dampening letter.

'Sounds easy enough,' said Padraig, confidently leading the way, as he struggled with his luggage and some of Bel's, 'come on let's get going.'

We soon arrived at the corner of Broad Street and Centre Street and there in front of us stood a three story wooden building with the legend *B. O'Flahavan General*

Store and Boarding Rooms' emblazoned in bright yellow lettering over the doorway. Padraig and Bel immediately dashed to the store entrance shouting mischievously, 'Maureen O'Flahavan will you not come out and greet your brother and sister after their long journey.'

I could hear a delighted scream from inside, and then much laughing and excited conversation and even a little sobbing as I lingered outside on the boardwalk, not wanting to intrude on their family reunion. Presently with their inaugural greetings concluded Padraig came out and ushered me inside to meet his big sister. Maureen had a sisterly resemblance to Bel, she was about three inches taller, not quite so slender and her eyes were not so blue. Maureen greeted me warmly and then after closing her shop, shepherded us into her parlour and shouted for her children to come and meet their uncle and aunt. Needless to say, there was great excitement in the house that evening and much for the siblings to discuss for it had been over seven years since they had last sat down together. After a hearty supper I excused myself and leaving the gregarious family to their deliberations I made my way up to the attic room which I was sharing with Padraig.

Over the next few weeks Bel, Padraig and I settled into a comfortable existence in O'Flahavan's General Store and Boarding Rooms. Padraig and I took on much of the heavy work and the store deliveries. Bel mainly assisted Maureen in the tasks associated with the lodging rooms and in minding her nephews, and we all helped out in the store. Initially there was more than enough work to keep us all busy but after six weeks or so it was clear that

Maureen's business didn't need the four of us working full time to keep it running so I took on a job with a carpenter at the local sawmill and Padraig found work at the railway station freight yards. It was into this congenial situation that one fateful day in October James McKenna became entwined in our lives.

Étienne, before I explain the significance of this man McKenna, I will tell you a little about the Port Clinton locale as it will enhance your understanding of my tale. Port Clinton back in those days was a small town on the southern border of Pennsylvania's Schuylkill County. This was coal mining territory and men from all over the world brought their families here so that they might find a better life. Mining was a tough job, wages were low, working conditions were dangerous and safety measures inadequate causing hundreds of deaths and serious injuries each year. This was a rough part of the world in those times often attracting the worst in society, and over the years there had been frequent beatings, knifings, robberies, cases of arson and murders mostly connected with grievances about the mines and the poor working conditions which were ignored by the mine owners and the managers they employed. None the less many hard working families had settled in the surrounding towns and had brought their traditions both good and bad with them. It was into this milieu that McKenna emerged.

I was helping out in the shop on the day McKenna came in to ask about a room. McKenna, who had arrived in town by train earlier that day, was a slim but muscular man of medium height, with auburn hair, four or five days of stubble outshone by a bushy moustache and wearing round wire rimmed glasses over his hazel eyes. Smiling at Maureen he spoke with an Irish lilt, 'good afternoon Ma'am, have you a room for an honest working man who's far from home. The name's McKenna, James McKenna, and I'm looking for somewhere to stay for a while as I'll be working in the mines.'

Maureen, who seemed quite charmed by his friendly personality, confirmed there was a room available and explained the housekeeping rules which included payment in advance. McKenna finding this to his liking paid for his room and Maureen asked me to show him to the guesthouse accommodation. He told me he had previously worked in the Colorado mines and decided to come east to look for work. He seemed to be an amiable sort of fellow with a good sense of humour but even after this short acquaintance I got the feeling he was someone not to be crossed.

As it happened James McKenna proved to be an exemplary lodger. He was always polite, paid his bills early, and mostly got on well with our other boarding guests. While we never had any problems with Mr McKenna and enjoyed a most amiable relationship with him, the same could not be said for all the inhabitants of Port Clinton. There were many stories reaching us about his altercations with mine workers and officials in the town's more disreputable saloons and of his leanings towards a fraternity known as the Ancient Order of Hibernians. Jimmy McKenna had a sociable disposition and on a number of occasions Padraig and I were invited to join him on junkets to these saloons. He had an understandable penchant for establishments which were favourites with the Irish community, and we soon discovered he was a popular fellow around these drinking holes, often entertaining fellow customers by singing, spinning tall tales, and dancing Irish jigs. He had an amazing capacity for consuming whiskey and remaining sober while those trying to keep up with him became mortally drunk, a skill which he used to his advantage to even a score or prove a point in the numerous fist fights in which he engaged.

Padraig and I became quite friendly with McKenna, and he would sometimes try to persuade us to join him in the mines. Having worked in a colliery in England I somewhat warmed towards the idea, but Padraig was minded differently recounting stories he'd heard of the poor working conditions, explosions, flooded mines, and collapsing tunnels. He continued saying if all that wasn't bad enough, he'd been told that miners even had to buy their own explosives and tools for inflated prices at the mining company's store. I conceded that Padraig may well be right.

The anthracite coal mining industry in Pennsylvania at that time was a flourishing enterprise controlled by wealthy mine owners, but they put profit before improving working conditions and paying their workers a fair wage. Mine owners actively recruited immigrant workers offering much lower waged than they had paid American born miners who moved on to the more lucrative mines in the west. Many immigrant miners joined the ineffectual Workingmen's Benevolent Association, in the hope that by banding together they might achieve better conditions. Unfortunately, the mine owners were determined to disregard the union, causing much bitterness between the mine supervisors and the ordinary miners. This situation led to frequent strikes and acts of violence as miners sought revenge against their despised bosses. Realising that the Workingmen's Benevolent Association was incapable of improving their lot some Irish catholic miners, to resolve their grievances, turned to an organisation they had known in Ireland, the Molly Maguires.

In Pennsylvania the Molly Maguires strived to improve the pay and working conditions of miners. It was a sort of secret society which didn't have any political agenda and allegedly used intimidation, violence and even murder to resolve disputes they thought would not be tackled by what they believed was a legal system which discriminated against working class immigrants, and especially against immigrants who happened to be both Irish and catholic. In an attempt to enforce the rule of law the mine and railway owners established the Coal and Iron Police, but such was the solidarity of the mining community and the intimidation and violence meted out by the Molly Maguires that it was largely impotent in its attempts to bring trouble makers to justice .

The Molly Maguires was to have a big impact on our lives as its members intensified their activities in our area. One evening after our day's work we were sitting in Maureen's parlour when Maureen heard a noise outside in the yard. She went to see what the disturbance was and came back white faced clutching a note. 'Oh sweet

Jesus! Padraig what are we to do', she said passing the
crumpled note to her perturbed brother. Padraig read
the note then solemnly passed it on to me and Bel.

Mrs OFlahavon
it mite be wize if
you and youre family
is not at home
tonite if yous
wish to avoid danger

We has no gruge againts
yous
a frend

Padraig went into the yard to look out into the street
behind Maureen's premises. He ran back into the room
shouting, 'Maureen, Bel get the children and go out the
front through the shop, there's a fearsome looking mob

out there heading this way and I fear for our safety if we stay here.'

I looked through the window as the ringleaders entered our yard and gathered outside the back entrance to the lodging house. Then an enormous bald headed man who I didn't recognise shouted, 'Jackson you scum you'll get down here now if you know what's good for you.'

Jackson, who was one of our lodgers and a supervisor at the mine, clearly had no intention of meeting the mob and fired a pistol shot from an upstairs window striking the large man in the arm. This incensed the mob, and a number of shots were fired in retaliation. They burst through the lodging house door and ran up the stairs shouting obscenities, and then a couple more shots reverberated in the early evening twilight. Around this time Padraig, who had taken Maureen, Bel and the boys to the safety of a neighbour's house, returned just in time to witness flames beginning to surge from the upstairs window that was Jackson's room. The mob satisfied that its work was done ran off up the road towards the railway station. Padraig and I started running wildly towards the burning building, but the heat was too intense for us to enter, and we began to throw water on the flames. Presently some neighbours came to our aid but there was little we could do to save the wooden structure. The fire was spreading to the shop and before long all of O'Flahavan General Store and Boarding Rooms was ablaze.

There was little of O'Flahavan's still standing the following morning but by some good fortune, if you can call it that, the fire had caused little damage to the neighbouring buildings, and no one else other than poor Jackson had been harmed in the attack. Maureen, Bel and the two boys obtained temporary shelter with a neighbour while Padraig and I found accommodation with one of his colleagues from the railway yard. McKenna oddly had been absent when the assault occurred, for he was usually in his room at that time of day until supper. When we next saw him, he seemed relieved we had escaped the ordeal and said he would do what he could to see us right.

McKenna was as good as his word and a few days later told us he had heard there was a general store for sale in the neighbouring town of Pottsville, for half the price it would cost to rebuild the Port Clinton store. What's more it was a thriving business with Pottsville having a much larger population. He had even made arrangements for Maureen to meet with the current owners to fix up the sale. If all that wasn't impressive enough, he had also found jobs for Padraig and me at the nearby Indian Ridge Colliery. So, it seemed that in spite of Padraig's objections we were destined to be coal miners and we were soon to become residents of Pottsville in Pennsylvania's Schuylkill County.

Chapter 7

Six month later we were quite settled in Maureen's new general store in Pottsville. It was a pleasant enough town of approximately 12,000 souls. The store was paid for by insurance money Maureen had received from the Girard Fire Insurance Company from a policy taken out by her late husband shortly before he died and it was if I remember rightly, on the west side of Centre Street somewhere between Church Alley and I think Mahanantongo Street. The new store was at least a third larger than the Port Clinton premises and was a flourishing concern. Padraig and I had both taken jobs at the recently opened Indian Ridge Colliery, but our time underground didn't last long. We were both shocked at the dreadful working conditions borne by the men and children some as young as 5 years old. I was used with the poor conditions mine workers endured from my time in the colliery in England but conditions here were much worse and the pay did not compensate for that in any way. After three weeks Padraig had quit the mine and started a new job in the rail freight trade. I worked underground a week longer then moved to a job in the lumber yard which supplied pit props to the mines. We were both sympathetic to the demands of the miners in their disputes with their employers, but we did not condone the intimidation and violence that some of the agitators advocated.

James McKenna continued to visit us regularly having taken lodgings in nearby East Norwegian Street in the residence of Mrs O'Regan a middle aged widow woman with a side line in distilling and selling illicit whisky. So frequent were his social calls, that Bel expressed the view that she felt he was keeping a watchful eye over us, saying it seemed almost as though he felt responsible for our welfare, a view which Padraig dismissed as nonsense. McKenna was employed at the Indian Ridge Colliery and had become quite friendly with a man called Jennings who also lived at Mrs O'Regan's. Padraig had come across Jennings while he was working in the mine and had taken a dislike to him confiding in me that he believed Jennings was a bit of a ruffian who was frequently involved in trouble at work. Furthermore, Padraig believed that Jennings had introduced McKenna to Sheridan House, an infamous and popular saloon run by a garrulous Irishman known as 'Big Pat' Dormer who Padraig believed to be a senior man in the Molly Maguires. At Sheridan House McKenna continued his custom of entertaining fellow patrons by dancing Irish jigs, telling outrageous tales, and getting involved in the occasional punch-up. Sheridan House had a shady reputation in Pottsville for its dubious clientele were not averse to raucous behaviour and brawling. On one of his visits McKenna told us he had been arrested at the saloon by the Coal and Iron Police on a bogus complaint, questioned and beaten up then released without any charges being brought against him.

Over the next two years or so the peace of our community was beset by numerous strikes, several murders, frequent beatings, knifings, and episodes of sabotage and fire raising against the mine owners and their despised supervisors. These atrocities were mainly but not exclusively, carried out by the Molly Maguires. Perpetrators always seemed to escape justice as the Molly Maguires employed a practice of bringing in members from neighbouring towns to mete out their revenge so the culprits could not be identified by local residents. Moreover, the Mollies pursued such a robust practice of intimidation and vindictiveness that most public spirited citizens were too frightened to come forward as witnesses against them. This was the time of the Great Panic, one of the worst depressions in American history, which gave mine owners an excuse to introduce a new contract for their workers that lowered miners pay by between 10 and 20 per cent, resulting in what became known as the Long Strike. About seven months into the strike the state governor ordered troops into the county to impose order. The strike collapsed and the miners reluctantly returned to work with the imposition of reduced rates of pay.

The frequent strikes had their effect on the profitability of Maureen's business, and we were not surprised when she announced she was going to sell up and marry her long term suitor, Elijah Michael Collins, a physician from Port Clinton. They planned to move west, to the up and coming town of Tacoma in Washington State, where Elijah was to become a partner in a friend's medical practice. Maureen had known Elijah since she first arrived in Port Clinton, he had been the family's doctor, but there had been no romantic liaison until well after her husband Brendan had passed, in fact I believe their romance hadn't begun until shortly after Padraig, Bel and I arrived. Padraig had taken to the doctor straight away and was happy to see his sister marry a man who cared dearly for her and her two boys and one who had good prospects. The wedding some four weeks later was a small but grand affair in St Patrick's, Maureen's local church. Padraig had been delighted to be asked to give his sister away and was on his best behaviour throughout the service, but his resolve was tested to the limit at the celebrations afterwards when by the end of the evening he and I ended up roaring drunk.

Étienne my friend please bear with me, I can tell you are struggling to understand where my story is heading and wondering about the significance of my detailed reminiscences on the Molly Maguires. All will become clear presently, now if I may, I shall continue with my tale.

Maureen's imminent departure caused me to think about my prospects and what I hoped to achieve in my life. Since my arrival in America, I had been quite content living with Padraig and his family and hadn't contemplated changing my circumstances. Bel and I had become very close after our move to Pottsville. We had talked about spending our future together, although I had not been so bold as to propose to her, so it came as a shock when she said she was to follow her sister to Tacoma. Much to Bel's delight I too decided I would head west. When we told Padraig he immediately said he would come as well, for with his family gone there was no good reason to stay in this volatile town.

Maureen, her children, and her new husband left Pottsville about three weeks after their wedding. Bel offered to remain behind for another two weeks to tie up loose ends while the sale of the store was finalised.

Once the sale was completed the new owners asked her stay on at the store for another week so that she might instruct them in the finer points of running the business as they were new to the trade, but with a new family moving into the general store Padraig and I were obliged to move out, sharing a shabby room at Mrs O'Regan's across the corridor from McKenna's.

Bel, Padraig, and I had planned to travel west together to begin our new lives in Tacoma. We intended to travel as far as possible by train and then by stagecoach for the final part of the trip and were due to depart in a few days; however, the Norns had woven other plans for Padraig and I and we were obliged to stay put. A couple of nights before we were due to leave town McKenna persuaded us to meet him after work for a farewell drink. In spite of his reputation, he had been a good friend to us, and we gladly agreed to meet him in Lafferty's Tavern which was not far from St Patrick's church. We spent a pleasant few hours with McKenna who as usual was in good form, entertaining us with his tall stories and a couple of songs. We had work the next day and intended to take our leave of McKenna early that evening and get back to Mrs O'Regan's in time for supper, but with a bit of persuasion from McKenna and a couple of free whiskeys our intention melted like fat on a griddle. Hours later I managed to get Padraig out of the tavern, and we began the short walk to our lodgings.

We had not long left Lafferty's when we heard a commotion ahead of us. We spotted a man up a ladder apparently trying to extinguish a gas street light, then suddenly three men jumped out from behind a wall shouting something unintelligible and we heard two shots ring out. The man fell from the ladder onto the street and the three men making their escape came running in our direction. Padraig fearing we would be harmed, pushed me back forcefully against a wall to get me out of their path, as the men sprinted past us. We ran over to the fallen man and bending over him Padraig spoke, 'Jesus Mikey it's the police officer Benny Yost, I think they've killed him.'

Other people came out into the street to try to help. Yost was attacked just a few yards away from his own front door and his wife came hurrying out to his aid. Someone ran to fetch the doctor who lived at the end of the street, but there was nothing he could do for poor Yost was mortally wounded and he died in his weeping wife's arms.

Padraig had sobered up quickly and said to me, 'Michael we need to get away from here, and we need to go now. Did you recognise one of the murderers? I'm almost certain it was James Kerrigan, and I'm sure he saw us. Come on man let's get away home.'

Stunned by what I had witnessed I dumbly followed Padraig and we hurried off. Breathing heavily, we entered Mrs O'Regan's front door and went through to the parlour where we sat down and discussed what we had just witnessed. I went to make a pot of coffee and as I was about to pour it a familiar voice said, 'Mike me boy is there another cup in that pot?'

McKenna had entered the room looking as sober as a nun even though he had been drinking all evening. I got another cup and the three of us sat round the table in uneasy silence. McKenna sensing our agitation spoke up. 'Boys you're poor company this night for sure, you look like yer ma's poured your best whisky down the drain and switched it for cold tea, is there something that's bothering you? You're not having second thoughts about leaving poor ould Jimmy McKenna?'

I glanced at Padraig with a questioning look and sensed he felt we could trust McKenna. I related the story of the murder of Officer Yost and how we saw the three men run past us, almost laughing at the horror they had caused.

'Tis bad business boys that a man can be slain outside his own house, and no one will say a word against the murderers. So, you say there were three men run past you and two fired the shots? Did you recognise any of them?' asked McKenna.

'Yes, there were three men, but we knew only one of them, James Kerrigan,' said Padraig.

'You'd not want to cross Powder Keg Kerrigan boys, he's a dangerous man and one of the Mollies for sure, so it'll be for the best if you forget about what you saw. If anyone asks, you weren't there, you saw and heard nothing.'

Even though he advised us to forget about Yost's murder McKenna wanted to know every detail and he asked us to go over the story again. We felt better for talking to him and we assured him we would speak to no one about the murder. Around midnight we all went off to bed and for me an uneasy night's sleep followed, as I kept reliving the slaying of Benny Yost in my dreams. The next morning Padraig and I were up early finishing some long delayed packing in readiness for our trip to Tacoma. Padraig was cursing as he tried to close his bulging valise. I had finished packing and set out for the wash room but on reaching the door I noticed a slip of paper on the floor. Curious as to what might have been pushed under our door, I went to pick it up and on reading it a dire sense of panic ran through my body quicker than a lightning strike. Padraig noticing my countenance stopped his cursing and snatched the note from my hand.

'Jesus Mikey it's a coffin note from the Mollies, we're in big trouble if we say anything about last night. Powder Keg must have recognised us, and someone's brought this while we slept.'

I read the note again remembering that the Mollies sent coffin notes as a warning, it was not necessarily a death sentence, but somehow, I didn't feel any better. We concluded our morning ritual in uneasy silence and went down to breakfast in a sombre mood.

The other lodgers had almost finished breakfast when we entered the parlour; we poured some coffee but didn't feel much like eating and told Kate, Mrs O'Regan's helper, we'd just have some bread and butter and sat glumly nursing our drinks as the others left the room. About five minutes later McKenna came in and sat with us, presently Kate brought out McKenna's habitual sizeable, cooked breakfast, which he ate avidly. He spoke little until the last of the lodgers a guileful fellow by the name of Séamus Collins left the room. 'Boys,' he said when Kate was out of earshot; 'I can see you're still dwelling on last night's shenanigans. You've got to try to put it behind you and get on with your lives; what's done is done, it's no good dwelling on something you can't change.'

Padraig thanked him for his advice and resignedly said, 'Mike will you show him the note.'

McKenna read the note and handed it back to me. 'Lads,' McKenna said in a subdued tone, 'what are you going to do? It seems they know you were there and where you live.'

Padraig replied, 'Well Mr McKenna, I know you have some influence with the Mollies, I was wondering if you could let them know that me and Mikey saw nothing, and that even if we had we would keep quiet about it, not that we saw anything.'

McKenna seemed to think about this for some time and finally leaning towards us he said in a conspiratorial tone, 'I can do as you ask boys and it will all blow over this time, but there'll be other nights and other Yosts and other killings. Is that what you want me to do, or do you boys want to help bring all the killing and intimidation to an end? I want you to think very carefully before you answer for to say yes will surely put all our lives in mortal danger.'

McKenna seemed very sincere in his desire to move against the Mollies, I looked at Padraig and seeing him nod I said, 'yes we want to help but how do we know we can trust you McKenna?'

James McKenna said simply, 'boys you have my word,' then added 'lads I've heard the Pinkerton Detective Agency is about to bring charges against the Molly Maguires. They'll soon be arresting all the ringleaders and locking them away till their trial. I'm sure the Pinkerton's will have a great deal of evidence against the Mollies and your eye witness accounts of the murder of police officer Yost will be the icing on the cake for getting a conviction that will see an end to the Mollies activity in this county. Now don't be asking me how I know this, just believe that it is going to happen, and your witness could make all the difference. So, boys can I trust you, for if word of this got out it would likely be the death of me and you.'

We both replied we would tell no one. I was surprised to hear him talk about the Mollies in this way as we knew by his reputation that he was a trusted man in the local Molly Maguires hierarchy. I asked him why he had decided to turn against the Mollies. He responded saying, 'Mikey my boy, tis a long story and one that I'm not prepared to tell tonight, but believe this I am truly sickened by all the intimidation and violence I've seen, and it has to end.'

He paused for a moment as if thinking and then continued, 'I'll need some time to work out a plan to keep you boys safe and sound until the Pinkerton's do their work, so here's what you'll do. Go to work tomorrow as usual and then after work come straight back here to old mother O'Regan's and I'll speak with you after supper.'

We got up from the table to take our leave of McKenna shaking his hand as if to seal our conspiracy. Before he opened the door, McKenna warned us again not to speak about our conversation saying if we blabbed our lives would surely end with a bullet.

Chapter 8

After supper that evening on the pretext of having yet another farewell drink McKenna came to our room. He opened a bottle of Mrs O'Regan's finest home brew and poured three large drinks and taking a mouthful said, 'well boys it's all arranged, I 've got some fellows who will take you somewhere safe till the Mollies are arrested and put away, are you still sure you want to do this?'

Padraig and I looked at each other and nodded in agreement, 'yes we're certain,' I said, 'but we're supposed to be leaving Pottsville with Bel the day after tomorrow, we'll have to speak to her and tell her what's happened.'

McKenna replied, 'I'm sorry lads but if you want to come through this and live, I've got to insist that you make different plans.' McKenna then told us of the scheme he had arranged. 'Listen carefully lads for your very lives are on the line. In the morning leave here as normal as if you are off to work and take your usual route. As you're walking along Norwegian Street you will see a man with a cart looking like he has some trouble with a wheel. Ask him if he needs help to fix it and he will reply saying 'sure if you don't mind getting your hands dirty.' If he replies saying anything different just walk on by for it will mean he is being watched by the Mollies. If all is well when the waggon wheel is fixed, he'll offer you a lift to work as a thank you for your time. But he'll be taking you to a safe location. Have you got all that?', We both nodded in affirmation, then just to be certain we understood McKenna, then ordered us to repeat the plan until he was satisfied we understood.

'Tomorrow I'll start spreading the word that you boys have left town to join Maureen out west, so no one will be suspicious, and the Mollies'll think their coffin note's done the trick.'

McKenna offered to visit Bel that later that night to relate what had happened and make sure she caught the train as planned, but Padraig was troubled about abandoning his sister to the arduous journey west on her own without having an opportunity to explain.

'Mr McKenna I truly appreciate your assistance, but I'm unhappy at not seeing Bel myself for she would surely take the news better if it came from her brother and besides no one who knew our plans would think it was strange for us to go visit her the night before our journey.'

McKenna considering Padraig's entreaty replied, 'can you vouch for her to keep quiet?'

Padraig responded saying, 'Mr McKenna once she hears our lives are at stake, I am certain she'll be as silent as a tomb at midnight.'

'Padraig O'Brien you have a fine way with words, so you have, so I'm minded to agree to your behest.'

About fifteen minutes later Padraig and I sneaked out of Mrs O'Regan's backyard and headed for the general store. The store was in darkness and looked much as it always did except it now bore the legend 'Weber's General Store' in place of O'Flahavan's. We went round to the rear of the building so not to draw attention to ourselves and I knocked at the door trying to do so quietly but loud enough for the occupants to be roused. Presently Klaus Weber answered peering round the door which he had opened just wide enough to be able to see out. 'Aach it is you Herr Padraig und Herr Mike, please herein kommen,' he said in his strong German accent. 'It ist gut to zee you gentlemen, you have come to Bella visit ja?'

Klaus Weber told us Bel was in the store room where she was busy instructing Frau Weber in the intricacies of stock taking. We walked through to the storeroom where a self-effacing Frau Weber quickly excused herself saying she had to check up on her children. Bel smiled and asked if we'd come to make sure she was packed and ready for the train journey tomorrow. Padraig looking unusually serious said, 'Bella we have something important to tell you, but you mustn't say a word about it to anyone.'

The smile evaporated from her face as Padraig began to relate how we'd witnessed Yost's murder, our encounter with the Mollies and the subsequent coffin note. She listened quietly, visibly becoming more disturbed as I told her we had recounted our experience to McKenna, his offer of help and what that help entailed. Bel seemed shocked and angry in equal measure and said, 'but surely he's one of the Mollies. You stupid lads, what have you done, do you know what danger you could be in?'

Padraig responded saying, 'yes we thought so too but I sincerely believe in McKenna. I'm certain he will do all he can to ensure our safety till we have testified at the trial, for hasn't the man always looked out for us?'

Bel was far from happy with what we'd arranged with McKenna, but she reluctantly agreed to go along with the plan. 'It'll mean you travelling to Tacoma by yourself tomorrow,' I said.

Bel replied she was well aware of that and that she would get by, 'just keep yourselves safe and come to Tacoma as soon as you can. Now you'd better be getting back to old Mrs O'Regan's before you're missed.'

Bel accompanied us to the back door and hugged Padraig then as Padraig went outside, we embraced. Bel unfastened her silver and jade shamrock brooch and pressed it into my hand saying take this for luck and to remember me by and holding my hand tightly she bid me farewell saying, 'Mike stay safe. I love you and watch out for Padraig for I've a bad feeling about this.'

I assured her I would and that we'd both be with her soon. We hugged again and I kissed her goodnight.

The next day we saw McKenna at breakfast, he manipulated our conversation so it was mostly about our forthcoming trip to Tacoma, no doubt for the benefit of any Mollie sympathisers present amongst the other boarders taking breakfast. Presently we left the table and McKenna shook our hands and wished us good luck for our trip, in case he didn't see us again. McKenna's plan ran smoothly and a few minutes later we were helping a tall slim bearded man repair a loose wheel on his cart. With the wheel fixed the man asked where we were headed and offered us a lift to work. The man said nothing as we travelled, at first in the direction of the rail station and then south out of town. It was a bitterly cold March day, and the biting wind didn't encourage conversation, however once we had left Pottsville, he became a little more talkative, but remained vigilant constantly looking over his shoulder, in case we had been followed. By the time we were five miles or so along the road and heading west in open country he became more relaxed and told us he was Abe McClellan a Pinkerton detective, and he was escorting us to a remote farm house in the Black Creek valley where we would be staying until we were needed at the Mollies trial.

About two hours after leaving Pottsville, we arrived at the farmhouse in the midst of a driving blizzard. Apart from smoke billowing from a chimney the house looked deserted, one of the front windows was boarded over and it seemed like nature had started to reclaim the yard where a few young saplings had sprouted swaying drunkenly in the strong wind. McClellan steered the cart straight into the barn and then took us into the house which felt amazingly warm after our freezing journey. Sitting next to a log fire warming his hands was a man of medium stature, aged around 50, with grey eyes greying hair and a neatly trimmed beard, he greeted us and introducing himself as Detective John Webster, poured us a coffee from a pot warming on the stove and said, 'welcome to your new home boys I hope you'll be happy here.'

Abe McClellan who seemed to be in charge told Webster to go out to the barn and see to the horse, then he poured himself a coffee and divested himself of his hat and thick winter jacket. 'Well gentlemen you're here safe and sound, Webster and I will be taking care of you for the moment. There's not many rules but I've got to advise you not to go outside without asking us and stay away from the windows, other than that you've got the run of this place till the trial.'

The farm house had obviously been deserted for a while; there was a thick coating of dust on nearly all the fixtures and the board floors still bore the brush marks where someone had done a cursory sweep. In contrast the table, four chairs and kitchenware looked like it had been recently installed and a couple of newly glazed windows were hung with blankets as improvised curtains. Later Detective McClellan showed us upstairs to our room. The room was on the front of the house, the one with the boarded up window. It was as dusty as downstairs, and sparsely furnished with just an old washstand, a threadbare rug and some folded blankets, 'this is it gentlemen,' said McClellan, 'I'm sorry we didn't have time to get any beds set up, if it's any consolation me and Webster are in the same boat, but the good news is we're expecting some more home comforts in a few days. Webster's got some food on the stove if you fellows want to come down once you've settled in,' he said with a wide grin.

McClellan was as good as his word and three days later two waggons arrived laden with lumber, provisions and additional furniture, including beds and our valises from

Mrs O'Regan's, no doubt intercepted by McKenna. As the detectives were bringing the supplies into the house, I said to Webster that it didn't seem worth all the trouble they were going to seeing we wouldn't be there very long. He replied saying, 'son, I don't know who you've been talking to but setting up a trial like this takes a piece of time. You and your buddy are gonna be here at least till summer comes around.'

This revelation came as a bit of a shock to Padraig and me as we expected it would only be two or three weeks until the trial began not three months. I wrote to Bel to let her know about our situation and to tell her it could be many months before we were able to join her. McClellan said he would see the letter was mailed to Tacoma and would insert an address for any reply. The two Pinkerton men were quite companionable and did their best to make our enforced stay endurable. Webster had brought some books with him and in the evenings when we weren't playing cards, we would take turns reading episodes from his favourite James Fennimore Cooper titles, *The Spy* or *The Last of the Mohicans*, and towards the end of our internment he obtained a new book called *The Adventures of Tom Sawyer,* which greatly entertained us, and kindled my curiosity about Mississippi riverboats, and may have influenced my later travels.

I had never told Padraig the true reason why I had come to America. When asked I had always hinted there had been some trouble over a girl back home and left it at that but now with so much time on our hands and spending almost twenty four hours a day in each other's company I felt I needed to tell the whole story of Mary Scott's murder and my subsequent flight. Padraig listened to the story with intense concentration and when my narrative was done said, 'Mikey my boy, that's a fine tale you have there, what an almighty pickle to be in and what a bastard that Charlton fellow must be. It's clear to me that boy's done the deed and tried to pin it all on you and you've played right into his hands by running away. When this trial is over you should speak with McClellan and see if the Pinkerton's can help to clear your name.'

I was relieved and pleased Padraig had never once questioned my innocence and told him I would think about talking to McClellan. Week after week we endured a tedious existence, but at least we were safe. Most days we would go for a walk shepherded by one or other of the detectives and every couple of days we split timber for the stove. Surprisingly, Padraig coped with the ennui remarkably well especially after he determined he was an expert cook, and he began preparing most of our meals. Our boredom was relieved from time to time by the arrival of the supply waggon and after about six weeks at the farmhouse we received letters from Bel and Maureen. Occasionally Webster or McClellan would be relieved by the detective who brought the supply waggon and on his return after one such episode McClellan brought us up to date with details for the preparation for the trial and the arrests that had been made so far. To our great surprise McClellan disclosed that in exchange for leniency Powder Keg Kerrigan had agreed to testify against his erstwhile companions and as a consequence seventeen suspects had been arrested.

Padraig sounding greatly relieved exclaimed, 'that's good news to be sure, for with that boy's testimony you'll not be needing us?'

His relief was short lived as McClellan argued that our evidence in addition to Kerrigan's would only strengthen the case against the Mollies. A trial date was set for early May and even though life at the remote farmhouse had been wearisome at least we had been secure, but as the trial approached McClellan warned us that we would soon have to move closer to Pottsville to be more readily available when called as witnesses and that would certainly make our lives more perilous. About a week before the trial was due to commence Webster informed us, we would be moving the following day to a safe house about a mile north of Schuylkill Court House. Padraig was heartened at hearing this news and began looking forward to the conclusion of the whole sorry business and our journey to Tacoma. I was more circumspect and with the prospect of taking off and beginning a new life in the west drawing ever closer I began thinking of the last time I had to make an escape and the travails I endured on my retreat from England. I needn't have worried for the journey to the new house occurred without incident and this residence was certainly cleaner and more comfortably furnished than our dependable old farmhouse.

The day after our arrival McClellan told us the trial judge was to be Cyrus L. Pershing which meant little to us but apparently, he was infamous for his bias against immigrants and those belonging to labour organisations. So innocent or guilty the odds were stacked against anyone from that background coming up in front of Judge Pershing. After supper that evening and some talk about the forthcoming trial Padraig running his fingers through his unkempt hair and abundant beard declared, 'if I am to be a witness, I'd like to have a shop-bought haircut for I can't go in front of all those people looking like a blethering banshee just blown in from the bogs of Boora.'

We both looked to McClellan who ruminated on the request for a while before responding, 'well you have a point there O'Brien you do look a bit wild and your friend there isn't much better, I'll have a word with my boss tomorrow morning and see what we can do.'

The following afternoon detective Webster informed us the visit to the barbers had been approved and an escort was waiting for us outside. Padraig and I left the house and got into a covered waggon. There were two detectives on the waggon. We recognised the driver Detective Anderson, from our time at the farmhouse, the other man sitting next to him holding a shotgun was new to us. Anderson told us to climb into the back and keep our heads down and we set off for town. The waggon drew up outside the barber's shop, Anderson jumped down and entered the barber's and after checking the shop was empty signalled for us to come in, telling the other agent to stand guard outside. The barber seemed a little nervous but welcomed us cheerily enough asking who was to go first. Padraig insisted I have the first haircut so he could judge the skill of the barber before letting him loose on his mane. It was some time since I had a haircut and I decided to go for a shave and a short cut.

Presently my trim was completed, and Padraig took the chair. Padraig too declared he would like a shave, keeping his side whiskers and moustache, but decided against the short back and sides I had chosen and went for a longer style with a dapper central parting. The portly barber who was from Irish stock, had finished Padraig's shave and was chatting away about the finer points of horse breeding when two masked men rushed in through the back door and almost simultaneously the detective pushed me to the floor and three pistol shots rang out. A fourth shot came from Anderson as the two men ran out into the street. I felt a stinging pain. My face was wet, and I could taste blood when I licked my lips. I wiped it with my hand and saw blood from where a bullet had grazed my right cheek and nicked my earlobe. The barber who had been shot in the shoulder was lying groaning on the floor.

The detective from the waggon ran inside shouting, 'is everyone alright in here?'

Anderson looking round replied, 'I think so, the barber's wounded but no doubt he'll live.'

Padraig was sitting calmly in the barber's chair as if nothing had happened, Anderson went up to Padraig and shook him by the shoulder thinking he was in shock, and at that moment as he slumped forward I could see a bullet wound on his neck at the base of his skull oozing blood. My friend Padraig O'Brien son of Kilmacow, County Kilkenny was dead.

I spent a sleepless night tossing and turning and thinking about my friend and the senselessness of his death. I realised it was useless trying to sleep and decided I must write to Maureen and Bel. I spent hours with a pen in my hand staring at a blank sheet of paper thinking how I could explain the circumstances of Padraig's demise, but the words would not come, it was so hard to tell those women that their much loved brother was dead. It was a difficult task and with my tears flowing freely I eventually began to compose something that I felt was appropriate to Padraig's memory and the desperately sad situation. I spent the next few days closeted in my room hardly aware if it was day or night, unable to sleep for more than a few moments and not feeling like eating. I passed the seemingly endless hours consumed by thoughts of my friend Padraig, remembering times we shared and blaming myself for his death or feeling guilty about surviving and trying to work out what I could have done to save him. Webster came to check on me from time to time bringing me food and drinks and with little success attempted to rally me from my all-consuming despair. I remember telling Webster that I wasn't going to testify at the trial and to his credit he heard me out and didn't try to dissuade me. Eventually I decided that all I could do for my dear friend was to see that he got a decent funeral. Then as the days passed, I began to realise that I had to testify for not to do so would have meant Padraig had died for nothing, so venturing from my self-imposed solitude I sought out Webster and told him of my decision.

Étienne, I tell you that those sombre days were some of the saddest times of my life. Without warning my friend had been taken, and although I knew we were in danger, I had never expected ill fortune to befall us. We would tell our storey to the judge and then be off on our way to Tacoma with Pottsville and its violent events far behind us, but fate had weaved a different tapestry and I began to appreciate whether I testified or not I was now in mortal danger from unknown foes and must live my life forever looking over my shoulder until those who wished to harm me were successful or walked this earth no more.

Padraig's funeral was held in St Patrick's church, the mourners consisting of me and half a dozen Pinkerton men. As I left the church, I noticed a smartly dressed man who was sitting near the entrance, his hat pulled down low masking his face and his scarf pulled up covering his mouth, crossing himself as the coffin was carried out into the churchyard for the burial. The committal was soon over and the Pinkertons hastily ushered me to a waiting coach which took me back to the hideaway.

Chapter 9

The Pinkertons had no clue as to who had murdered Padraig. McClellan said they suspected his killers were friends of Hugh McGeehan and James Boyle the two men accused of Yost's murder. Padraig's death had not affected preparations for the trial and just two days after his funeral I was taken to Pottsville and entered Schuylkill County Courthouse on Second and Sanderson Street. I had never seen inside a court room before although my misadventures back in England could well have led me there some years earlier. The court room was full to capacity; I sat between McClellan and Webster and soon the jury trooped into their allotted places. It seemed the jury had been selected so that it contained no one who would be sympathetic to the defendants' circumstances. There were no members of labour organisations and as far as I could tell no jurors with Irish associations. The room became deathly quiet as Judge Cyrus L. Pershing entered and we all stood until he was seated. Judge Pershing was a slightly built but tall man who was clearly comfortable exercising his authority. I couldn't help thinking that his long neck, receding hair and stern face, studded with piercing eyes on which he wore small round wire framed glasses, gave him an eagle or vulture like appearance.

The trial commenced with opening statements from a prosecution lawyer, a thin weasel-faced man with a stooped back. I listened intently at first, but my mind kept straying to poor Padraig sitting lifeless in that barber's chair. Eventually the court adjourned for lunch and flanked by McClellan and Webster I was escorted into a small back room for safety. Lunch over, we went back into the courtroom and after a brief preamble a witness for the prosecution was called. A slim well-dressed man of medium height, with auburn hair, clean shaven with a neatly trimmed moustache entered the room flanked by two Pinkerton men. He stood in the witness box and was requested to take the oath. The man was asked, 'what is your full name?'

'My name is James McParlan. Just over three years ago I came to Schuylkill County under the name of James McKenna. I am a detective. I work for Pinkerton's Detective Agency and I was sent here by the chief Allan Pinkerton of Chicago. I came to find out about those who were connected with an organisation known as the Molly Maguires and gather evidence so that they might be brought to justice.'

There was a collective gasp in the court room from those with sympathies for the Molly Maguires at this dramatic revelation and I might add from myself. There could be little doubt that with McKenna/McParlan's testimony the outlook for the accused men was bleak. In front of the astonished gathering McParlan went on to recount how Franklin Benjamin Gowen, the president of the Philadelphia and Reading Railroad company, determined to break the rise of trade unions and destroy the Molly Maguires had turned to Allan Pinkerton's Detective Agency for help.

Like the others present I was staggered by McParlan's pronouncement and marvelled at the strength of character of the man who had kept up this deception for so long. McParlan's evidence continued for the rest of the afternoon. He revealed how he had adopted the persona of Jimmy McKenna and drifted through Schuylkill County's mining towns looking out for Irishmen who might lead him to the Molly Maguires. He told how he had little success at first, and recalled how soon after arriving in Pottsville, he became a frequent visitor to Sheridan House, a tavern run by an Irishman known as 'Big Pat' Dormer, hoping to gain access to the Molly Maguires. McParlan said he gradually became trusted by the tavern's regular customers and recounted how he deliberately got embroiled in a number of fist fights to earn a mean reputation among the rowdier patrons. To further enhance his reputation, he told them he was wanted for murder and counterfeiting in Buffalo, New York.

He went on to relate that soon after he had been arrested and beaten up by the Coal and Iron Police on made up charges, Pat Dormer had introduced him to Muff Lawler another high up Molly member, and sometime after that meeting Lawler had taken him to meet John Kehoe a more senior man in the Mollies who gave his approval for McParlan to join the organisation. McParlan went on to describe in detail his inauguration into the Mollies and how over the following two years or so he progressed up the ranks, in due course becoming secretary and ultimately bodymaster of the Pottsville lodge. McParlan informed the court that during this time his true identity was known only to Allan Pinkerton, Franklin Gowen and locally to Robert Linden, assistant superintendent of the Pinkerton's in Chicago, who had been installed as Captain Linden of the Coal and Iron Police.

I was not needed in court for the following few days while James McParlan gave the rest of his evidence and faced cross examination by the defence council, but I was given to understand that the defence attorney had tried to accuse McParlan of being guiltier than the defendants in that he had allowed murders and violence to happen. McParlan strongly denied this accusation saying on the contrary sometimes there was no time to warn intended victims and on occasion he had to let incidents go by so that larger atrocities might be prevented, but whenever possible he had always tried to warn victims and pass word on to Linden or attempted to hinder plots. McParlan said on the numerous instances he had been arrested and questioned he had given information to Captain Linden about the Mollies' crimes or planned activities and when he couldn't get to Linden personally, he sent letters to the head of the Pinkerton's at the Philadelphia office.

Eventually my day in court arrived and flanked by McClellan and Webster I took the stand and told how Padraig and I had witnessed the killing of Officer Benjamin Yost. The lawyer asked if the men I saw at the scene of the crime were present in the court, indicating McGeehan and Boyle, but as I had only caught a fleeting glimpse of their faces, I was not able to confirm without doubt that the two men I saw running past me that night were Hugh McGeehan and James Boyle. However, from the description I gave and McParlan and Kerrigan's statements the judge seemed determined to believe that they were responsible for the murder. After I had finished giving evidence, I was whisked away from Pottsville back to the safe house where I stayed for the next few days until the trial was concluded.

I wasn't present in court for the verdict, but Webster told me later that McParlan's witness combined with Powder Keg Kerrigan's testament made a powerful case against the men charged with various Molly Maguire related crimes. All the accused men James Carroll, Thomas Duffy, James Roarity, Hugh McGeehan, and James Boyle were sentenced to be hung. This was not the only Molly Maguire trial held around this time and in total another fourteen Molly Maguire men were sentenced to death and many more were imprisoned, and although the Molly Maguires as an organisation had been vanquished, there were still men at large who wanted retribution and I was their quarry.

Two days after the trial ended McClellan told me to pack my bags and be ready to leave the next morning. Naturally, I asked where I was going, and McClellan replied that someone wanted to see me in Philadelphia. I can't say that I wasn't pleased to be leaving the safe house, but I was apprehensive about who I might be going to see as McClellan wouldn't be pressed on the subject. Early the next morning before breakfast Webster arrived in a covered waggon and McClellan hurried me out of the house and off we went. McClellan wasn't particularly talkative, and it was Webster who told me we were headed for Pottsville railway station to board the first train to Philadelphia. To the relief of the two Pinkerton men, we arrived at Pottsville station without hindrance and were met by two more detectives who directed us to an empty waiting room where we remained until the train was almost ready to depart.

On-board the train McClellan, Webster and I travelled in the guard's car with the other two detectives standing guard at the entrance. Neither of the two men could be encouraged to talk much on the journey and I was relieved when we arrived at Philadelphia's New York Junction station. It was here I learned that Webster and McClellan were travelling back to the Pinkerton's Chicago office and after bidding them farewell I was hurried out of the station to a waiting Berlin carriage by the other two Pinkerton men. It was a sweltering summer afternoon and as we travelled through the busy city streets my senses were severely assaulted by the overpowering stench of horse excrement, which in those days was a common phenomenon at that time of year. The trip to Pinkerton's Philadelphia office at 46 South Third Street took about an hour and in spite of the stench it felt good to be free from my recent confinement. Presently we arrived at our destination and the detectives guided me into the four story brick building which housed the Pinkerton Detective Agency. A clerk at reception told the detectives to take me straight up to the next floor.

The Pinkerton men escorted me up the stairs and after knocking on a sturdy oak panelled door took me into a large office where I saw a man sitting silhouetted behind a gleaming mahogany desk. He jumped up quickly and then to my surprise as he moved away from the window, I realised it was James McKenna or McParlan to give him his proper name and he smiled broadly and shook my hand warmly saying, 'Mike my boy it's good to see you,' and then added in a quieter tone that he was so sorry about poor Padraig.

I didn't know whether I was angry or pleased to see him so mixed were my emotions. Did I partly blame him for Padraig's death or was it the fact that I didn't know if his friendship had been genuine? It is hard to say. We had a long conversation about the recent trial and McParlan's undercover activities. He made no apologies for having to deceive us, and once we decided to give evidence against the Mollies, I believe he did his best to keep us out of harm's way. McParlan asked what I intended to do now the trial was over to which I replied I still planned to go out to Tacoma.

'I thought you would, but before you go there are a few things you need to know.'

He went to the door and ushered in a medium built man with wavy grey hair and a short beard. 'This here is Jack Quinn, he's been watching over you from a distance since Padraig's murder, and I've had him digging around to try to discover who's responsible. Jack it's probably best if you tell Mike what you've found out.'

Quinn cleared his throat and said, 'well Mike I don't think I need to tell you you're still in some danger, we know the men who killed Padraig are looking for you. It seems they're cousins of James Boyle; they weren't exactly in the Mollies as far as we know but they subscribe to their methods. The thing is they seem set on revenge and they appear to be trailing you. The word is their names are Hugh and John Kerr, but no one's talking about them. They were in New York when Boyle was arrested then they moved out to Schuylkill. The problem we've got is we don't know what they look like.'

'These boys don't normally stray too far west so it's probably a good thing you're heading to Tacoma,' continued McParlan, 'Quinn's got some business to take care of out in St Louis, so I've arranged for him to travel there with you. After that I'm afraid you'll be on your own, but I've persuaded Mr Gowen, that he owes you a big favour for testifying and he's agreed to pay your train and stage fare out to Tacoma and give you a reward of $300 besides.'

Quinn and McParlan's comments did little to reassure me about my safety, I had considered that the men who killed Padraig might still come after me, but I'd hoped the Pinkertons would be able to capture them and bring them to justice. McParlan seeing I was uneasy continued saying, 'look Mike, we're not giving up looking for Padraig's killers or abandoning you, but we haven't got the men to spare to keep watching over you 24 hours a day. The deal from Gowen is the best you've got. If you get in any trouble out there telegraph me or Quinn here at the Philadelphia office and we'll get someone to you as quick as you can, but if I were you, I'd buy a pistol and learn to shoot.'

I gave him a less then reassuring smile and thanked him for his help, we shook hands again and McParlan said, 'Quinn'll take you over to your hotel and you'll both be on the train to St Louis the day after tomorrow. Good luck Mike and give my regards to Maureen and Bel when you see them.'

The Colonnade Hotel on the southwest corner of 15th and Chestnut Streets was a well-appointed brick building seven stories high which provided much more superior accommodation than I had previously experienced. As Quinn was about to take his leave, I decided to take McParlan's advice and asked him where I might buy a gun. Quinn offered to take me to a nearby gun seller the following morning and help me choose a suitable weapon. I was grateful for Quinn's assistance for up till that time I had never even held a gun.

As promised Quinn met me early the next day for our trip to the gun shop. It was only a short walk from the hotel to the Market Street premises of J C Grubb & Co gun sellers. I was glad of company, for without Quinn's advice I would have had no idea about what sort of gun to ask for or the quantity of ammunition to purchase. Inside the store there was quite an array of weapons of various sizes and shapes and an eager salesman greeted us both as if we were his best friends come for a visit. Quinn took the initiative and told the man we were looking for a simple handgun without expensive embellishments. The man produced a gleaming silver Smith & Wesson Model 3 Revolver with a mother of pearl grip and invited me to handle it to see how it felt. Next he tendered a Remington .31 calibre revolver which had a fine polished wooden handle. I remarked that both of these weapons seemed a little heavy and asked if he had anything a bit lighter.

Humming to himself, he rummaged around on a shelf behind him and turning back towards us said, 'I've got something here you might like, it just came in last week, it's a Remington-Smoot New Model No. 3 Revolver.'

I gingerly handled the proffered weapon and it certainly felt less cumbersome than the larger pistols still lying on the counter, but I felt I would like something a little more discrete and asked if he had anything slightly smaller. He smiled and went over to a display case and came back with another Derringer style pistol, a Remington-Smoot New Model No. 2 Revolver which he said had a 5 shot chamber. I took this to be a positive characteristic and cautiously picked up the pistol. It seemed to be a much better size and I felt it wouldn't be too conspicuous on my person. The salesman seemed gratified he had found a pistol that met my requirements and offered to sell me a smart leather holster to accompany the weapon. Before finalising the transaction, Quinn showed me how to load and fire the gun and suggested it would be prudent to purchase some cartridges and a few minutes later we left J C Grubb & Co with my newly acquired weaponry but $30 poorer.

Quinn met me in the lobby of the Colonnade the following day. We made our way out to a waiting carriage and set off for the railway station at a sedate pace. It was cooler today than of late and the odour of horse dung was less overpowering. The St Louis train departed on time and before long we were leaving Philadelphia behind, but a deep melancholy assailed me for I couldn't help thinking of my last train exodus from Philadelphia only a few years earlier when accompanied by Bel and Padraig, we were happily anticipating our new lives on our journey to Port Clinton.

Chapter 10

As we approached the Union Depot railroad terminal, I gleaned my first sight of St Louis from the train window. I was overcome with a mixture of astonishment and despondency at the vista before me. The city of St Louis was a vast sprawling accumulation of dwellings and industry sitting cheek by jowl spread out as far as the eye could see. Numerous ships steamed back and forth on the river, black smoke belching from their funnels, while on the shore the vast array of industrial workings dispersed their own disgusting smells and unwholesome vapours. Nearly every factory used coal to fire steam boilers which in turn added dust, smoke and all sorts of obnoxious substances to the air and water supply. Quinn, who had frequently visited the city, warned me that the various factories that slaughtered animals for meat consumption, prepared hides to be cured and tanned, and fat and bones to be rendered emitted particularly offensive miasmas and if the wind blew from a certain direction, you could taste and smell St Louis long before you reached it. Unfortunately, our arrival had coincided with one of those days.

Quinn took me to a boarding house on Walnut Street where we were to spend the night and then excused himself saying he had some business at the St Louis Pinkerton office and hurried off leaving me to explore the city on my own. I wandered around the neighbourhood arbitrarily taking left or right turns. St Louis like many other towns had a mix of well to do areas and poverty. Its grand buildings, like the houses I encountered in Lafayette Square, contrasted starkly with its more down-at-heel areas, but I was mostly struck by the mix of people from different nations all trying to make a living and mostly trying to get along. I felt I would have liked to have more time to get to know the place better but my future in Tacoma beckoned. Lost in thought I suddenly became aware of a tall, long haired bearded man trailing me at a distance.

At first, I was uncertain if I was being followed, but continuing to turn left or right at random he mirrored my movements for three or four blocks, then on turning a corner I saw another man emerge from a parallel street and he started to run towards me. The first man taking his lead from his companion also began to sprint in my direction. I took off as fast as I could go but I couldn't help noticing they were both holding pistols. I had no idea where I was going and looked for somewhere to hide. I noticed an open warehouse door about half way along the street and sprinted towards it scrambling inside, I took refuge behind some agricultural machinery. I heard the men's rapid footsteps as they approached my hideaway and one shouted, 'I think I saw him go into that Barnum and Brothers building.'

The two men entered and began searching for me. I was so unnerved I never thought about reaching for my gun and I edged my way gingerly towards a rear exit. One of my pursuers saw me and fired a shot which harmlessly glanced off one of the farm implements and I bolted out through the rear door. My lungs were aching with the effort of running but my sheer terror kept me going, my pursuers were tiring, and I was gaining ground on them. I had no idea where I was, but I needed to get off the street quickly so composing myself I entered the first shop I came to, Sumner's Sewing Machine and Piano Emporium. Walking quickly through the store I astounded the staff, and myself, by getting out my pistol and demanding to be shown the rear exit. A timid shopkeeper, who may not have been so timid had I not pointed my gun at him, indicated a passageway saying, 'the door is at the end sir, it's not locked.'

In spite of my urgency, I thanked him for his help and hurried out putting my gun away as I did so. I continued heading west and eventually I was relieved to find I was on North Eighth Street as I knew the way back to my lodgings from there. I hurried to the hotel, walked speedily through the lobby then ran up the stairs taking two at a time, entered my bedroom, locked the door and remained there anxiously listening for my pursuers for the rest of the afternoon. Later that evening when Quinn returned, I recounted my experiences. Quinn dutifully made some notes of my exploits and asked me to describe my two assailants in as much detail as I could remember. We went down to supper, but I had no appetite. Quinn had no such issues and helped himself to my meal as well as his own. He said he had some business at the Pinkertons Office early the following morning and would send a telegraph to McParlan to let him know it seemed the Kerr's were on my tail.

The next day Quinn suggested it might be for the best for me to accompany him to the Pinkerton office and stay there till he got a reply from Philadelphia. I hung around the office most of that morning observing the routine and drinking coffee. Presently Quinn emerged and taking me aside said McParlan had replied saying to get me on the next train to Kansas City so I could continue my journey to Denver and then pick up the westbound stage from there. I supposed he thought I'd given the Kerrs the slip and if I got to the train without incident, I would be fine.

Étienne I can tell you that was not the response I had been hoping for. I had expected Quinn, or another detective would get orders to get me safely to Tacoma, but I assumed a brave mien and accepted the situation and having already missed that day's Kansas train I spent another night in St Louis before going to the railway station the following day.

At the station Quinn left me to relieve himself and I waited anxiously for his return. There had been no sign of the Kerrs and all being fine I would soon be leaving them well behind. As I waited for Quinn a well-dressed man his hair cut high on the top of his head with the sides cut short and a neatly trimmed beard approached me and asked, in what I took to be a slightly southern states accent, if he might trouble me for a Lucifer for his cigar. I rummaged in my pocket and as I handed over the matches, I noticed he had quite forceful compelling eyes and it seemed a habit of blinking more than was usual. We spent a couple of minutes in amicable conversation. He asked where I was headed, and I told him I was on my way to Tacoma. Making small talk I asked about his journey and he replied he was riding the train on business. I asked if he was employed by the

Missouri Pacific Railway. He replied smiling, 'not exactly son but I do have a great interest in the railroad,' then he moved away further down the platform.

Quinn returned and not long after escorted me to the waiting locomotive, telling me to look out for myself and get in touch if I encountered any more trouble. I thought to myself this was sound advice, but I doubted if I hit trouble there would be time to get in touch with anyone let alone a Pinkerton detective hundreds of miles away.

On boarding I found a seat in the last car at the back of the train and on sitting down I noticed the stranger I had spoken with while waiting for Quinn, he acknowledged me with a nod, and I did likewise in return. He seemed to be watching for someone or something on the train for he appeared to scrutinise everyone who passed along the car. The train got up steam, there was a loud shout from the conductor telling all passengers to board followed by a whistle blast and then we were off, gradually gathering speed as we pulled out of Union Depot.

We must have travelled about 20 miles or so to Chesterfield the next station on the route. I was staring out of the window and to my horror I saw the Kerr brothers on the platform. I quickly slunk down in my seat worried that they might see me and when I looked round, they were getting on the train. They entered my car and sat down at the far end of the car from me. The train resumed and the brothers sat tight appearing not to be taking any heed of me and I began to think I hadn't been noticed and trying to keep things that way I pulled my hat down low, rested my hand on the side of my face and turned towards the window. Presently the conductor passed along the car. Soon after that the two men stood up and came and sat next to me. They didn't speak but looked at me with an unblinking malevolent gaze. I knew now that they had certainly recognised me and if I was in any doubt the one sitting next to me pushed his pistol, which was shielded from the view of the other passengers by his coat, into my ribs. The other brother smiling grimly whispered, 'get up real slowly, without any fuss and come with us.'

Having no choice, I complied and got up from my seat, slowly following one of the Kerrs to the rear door of the car while the other walked behind me with his pistol firmly pressed against my back. The leading Kerr opened the door and went out onto the viewing platform at the rear of the locomotive, his brother and me close behind. The door slammed shut. I jumped on hearing the bang. 'Feeling jittery son,' said the Kerr with the gun in my back, 'you've got good reason to, see me and my brother Hugh here don't take kindly to what happened to our cousin Jimmy, and we hold you kind of responsible. You and that scumbag O'Brien, but he's already paid his dues so now it's your turn to die like the dog you are.'

Hugh Kerr drew his colt 45 smiling in anticipation of avenging his cousin. I closed my eyes expecting a bullet any second. I heard a gun cock and braced myself, then a quiet voice said, 'I wouldn't do that boys if I were you. Now why don't you just throw down those pistols?'

Opening my eyes, I saw the stranger from the railway station with a gun pointed at each of the Kerrs. The brothers, looking anxiously at each other, then back to the stranger decided to comply, and tossed their guns from the train. 'That's more companionable,' said the stranger, still with a pistol aimed at each of them. 'Now young fella, get yourself over here.'

I quickly scrambled past the Kerrs and stood beside the stranger. 'These men been causing you some mischief?' I nodded in reply. 'You fellas have outstayed your welcome and I suggest you get off the train.'

John Kerr said pleadingly, 'you can't mean for us to jump off the train mister?'

'That's exactly what I mean, unless you'd prefer I shoot you first, go on jump.'

Seeing the stranger meant business the brothers looked at each other momentarily then jumped from the moving train, one from each side of the viewing platform.

I was shocked by what I had just witnessed but grateful for the man's assistance and thanked him for his timely intervention. 'Think nothing of it son,' he said, 'you did me a kindness earlier, I'm just repaying the compliment.'

I thanked him again, and then we went back in the carriage and returned to where I had been sitting. We chatted cordially for the next hour or so mainly about my trip to Tacoma and a little about his time in the Confederate army during the war. He told me his work was concerned with banks and lately the railroad and asked about the men who tried to kill me. I told him about Padraig and the Mollies and how I'd had help from the Pinkertons. He revealed that he'd had some bad experiences with Pinkerton men but didn't go into detail. The train had reached Franklin by this time and he said, 'It's been a pleasure meeting you Mike, but I've got to take my leave now.'

We shook hands and I said, 'I don't even know your name.'

He smiled and said with a wink, 'the name's James, Jesse James,' and with that he was gone.

Chapter 11

John Kerr came to with a mighty pounding in his skull
and aches all over his body. There was a deep gash in his
forehead, his left wrist was badly sprained, and his
trousers were holed at the knees, but that aside at least
he was alive. Where was Hugh? He got up gingerly, his
legs and back hurt like hell but he was able to walk. He
looked back along the track and saw his brother lying
unmoving a few yards away on the other side of the rails.
John shouted but got no reply as he limped urgently
towards his prostrate brother. Hugh was lying face
down. John feared he was dead, but as he got closer, he
could hear soft groaning. He reached his brother and
examined him carefully before attempting to turn him
over. When he touched him Hugh's moaning became
increasingly louder. John sat him up. Hugh didn't look
good, he had taken a blow to his face which had broken
his nose and removed two of his front teeth and it
looked like Hugh had a dislocated shoulder or broken
collar bone or maybe both. If it was the former John
knew how to fix it, for although he hadn't performed the
procedure himself, he had seen it done often enough.
Hugh's face and beard were covered in blood and like
John; his clothing had been torn when he hit the ground.

The Kerrs were alive, they weren't feeling great but at
least they had survived. They moved away from the
track and found some shelter in a small copse where
they were fairly well hidden. Hugh was regaining his
faculties quickly now, he coughed to clear his throat and

his ribs complained mightily. He ached all over, his knuckles were bruised and bleeding and it looked like he had a couple of broken fingers. He flexed his other hand, his gun hand, it was still intact, he could still shoot a pistol if he had to. Where were their guns? When they had rested an hour or so the two men walked back along the track, one on each side, looking for their discarded weapons. Hugh found his pistol first, he checked it and it was undamaged apart from a few scratches. Soon after John retrieved his revolver, the brothers felt better already.

'We had Wilson in our sights, if it hadn't been for that interfering stranger, we'd be on our way back to East by now, not stuck here in the middle of nowhere,' said Hugh. 'Do you think he was a Pinkerton man?'

John replied, 'I don't think so, not even a bastard Pinkerton would force a man to jump from a moving train.'

The brothers decided to head back down the track to Chesterfield, figuring it was closer than Franklin the next station heading west. They would get the next train from there to Kansas and resume their search for the man they knew as Mike Wilson. After all it wasn't as if they didn't know where he was heading, for didn't their buddy Séamus Collins wire them saying old Mrs O'Regan told him Wilson's girl was in Tacoma and he was taking the stagecoach there from Denver. If they didn't catch up with him before Denver all they had to do was meet up with brothers Tom and Andrew in Laramie City and follow the stage route and they'd find him sooner or later, probably sooner if they could get their hands on some good horses.

Chapter 12

I had remained on the Missouri Pacific Railway locomotive all the way to Kansas and after a welcome overnight stop, I boarded the Kansas Pacific train for Denver. It was a long way from St Louis to Denver, around 900 miles. The trains passed through many towns and stations on the journey which slightly relieved the tedium, none the less I was thankful when I eventually reached Denver's train depot on 16th and Wynkoop Street and I was able to leave the train for the last time. The railroad did run further west in those days, but my ticket was only valid as far as Denver and henceforth I was to travel by Wells Fargo stagecoach. I asked a Kansas Pacific worker if he could recommend a not too expensive hotel and was directed to Planter's House Hotel situated on a corner of Blake Street, which I was told offered comfortable beds and wholesome food for $1.50 a night. After spending so long sitting in the train I was enjoying a brisk walk through the streets of Denver on my way to the hotel. It was a ten minute walk to Planter's House, but I took a slight diversion into Larimer Street to visit the Western Union Telegraph Office to let the Pinkerton's and Bel know I had reached Denver. My message to the Pinkertons said I'd had another encounter with the Kerrs and to send any reply to Laramie. On my walk to the hotel I remember being impressed that all the buildings I passed were constructed of brick and most looked like they had been built fairly recently. The hotel proprietor told me later that there had been a huge fire in the city about 16 years earlier that had spread rapidly through the old timber structures, including his hotel, and since that time all new buildings were required by ordinance to be brick built.

I spent the following day exploring the streets of Denver. I kept mainly to the thoroughfares in the commercial district, maintaining a vigilant mien, so as not to be taken unawares should the Kerrs reappear. Noticing Jacob's outfitting store while strolling along 15th Street, I decided to enter with the intention of buying a new hat, having lost mine during my encounter with the Kerrs on the observation platform of the Kansas train. It was a large well stocked establishment, and an overzealous salesman assessed my hat size and soon produced an array of headwear for me to try. I was particularly taken by a natural coloured flat brimmed felt hat with a straight crown and rounded corners. The salesman informed me this was a waterproof Boss of the Plains hat and an excellent choice for a discerning gentleman. Anticipating a sale, he produced a mirror and proceeded to tell me how much the hat suited me, making me look every inch the westerner. Succumbing to his fawning I decided to take the hat. I paid him $12 and left the shop feeling well pleased with my purchase as I proudly strode along sporting my new Boss of the Plains.

Farther along 15th Street I came to the Wells Fargo Office. It was an attractive one story red brick building with long gothic style windows. I entered the building and stood in a short queue in front of the ticket desk. A harassed bespectacled clerk was having difficulty explaining to a belligerent middle aged lady the various connections she would need to make on her journey and why she could only take 25lbs of baggage. Waiting patiently for my turn, I decided to attach the silver and jade brooch Bel gave me to the band of my new hat. That task completed, I observed, on the wall behind the clerk, a poster portraying a code of etiquette for stagecoach passengers. As I perused the notice, I was particularly troubled to see the rider "*expect some discomfort and hardship.*"

RULES FOR PASSENGERS

- ❖ EACH PASSENGER IS ALLOWED 25LBS, OF BAGGAGE FREE.
- ❖ GOLD DUST, BULLION, COIN, BANK OR TREASURY NOTES CANNOT BE CARRIED UNDER THE DESIGNATION OF BAGGAGE.
- ❖ SWEARING IS NOT ALLOWED, NOR IS SLEEPING ON YOUR NEIGHBOUR'S SHOULDER.
- ❖ SPITTING ON THE LEEWARD SIDE OF THE COACH IS NOT RECOMMENDED.
- ❖ DRINKING SPIRITS IS ALLOWED, BUT PASSENGERS ARE EXPECTED TO SHARE.
- ❖ IF THE DRIVER ASKS PASSENGERS TO GET OUT AND WALK, DO SO, AND DON'T GRUMBLE.
- ❖ DON'T OIL YOUR HAIR, DUST WILL STICK TO IT.

EXPECT SOME DISCOMFORT, AND HARDSHIP

WELLS FARGO & COMPANY

Eventually the irate lady seemed to be placated and she left thanking the clerk profusely for his assistance. The next three customers were dispatched quite speedily, and I approached the clerk. As I extracted my ticket from my jacket inside pocket my hand caught on my gun and it landed on the clerk's desk with a mighty bang, startling the young man and knocking over his inkwell. I apologised and quickly re-pocketing my pistol said lamely it was fortunate it wasn't loaded and then I somewhat sheepishly enquired when the next Salt Lake City coach was due to depart. The clerk replied that tomorrow's stage was fully booked but he could reserve me a place for the following morning. I was happy to take up this offer and he informed me the stage would leave at 7.00a.m. from outside this very building. So, with my seat on the stagecoach confirmed I stepped outside determined to enjoy my final hours in Denver as an advance reward for enduring the 'discomfort and hardship' I was soon to experience. That evening I treated myself to a delicious, but not too expensive, meal of roast trout with mushrooms and vegetables at James Cella's restaurant on 15th Street, followed with a couple of bottles of Schueler & Coors Golden Lager Beer. Fortified by my imbibing of Schueler & Coors I decided to see the show at the Opera House which was almost next door to James Cella's. There I was distracted by Dion De Marbelle's theatrical troupe performing 'The Gold Seeker', a story about a man from Boston who went to the plains with a glorious dream of finding gold but instead endured suffering and heartbreak. On leaving the performance I resolved that the next night I would forego the pleasure of the Opera House and merely indulge myself with an agreeable meal and afterwards perhaps seek some gold myself in the form of Schueler & Coors Golden Lager Beer.

I awoke with a pounding headache, the cause of which was no doubt the result of too many bottles of Golden Lager Beer the night before. My pocket watch said it was almost five minutes before six o'clock, but a distant church clock was already chiming for the sixth time. After a quick wash to refresh myself, I dressed in my oldest clothes in readiness for my journey. I had ample time for a cup of coffee before leaving Planter's House and heading off to the Wells Fargo depot for the seven o'clock stagecoach. As I entered 15th Street, I could see in the distance the six-horse Concord stagecoach painted in the red and gold livery of the Wells Fargo Company. The driver or whip as he was more commonly called, was sitting on the high front seat with two outside travelling passengers perched behind him. Even though it was still about twenty minutes before seven it seemed the stage was almost ready for departure. The whip's colleague, known as the guard or more usually the shotgun, because they were issued with a short, double-barrelled shotgun, was busy helping the arriving passengers and bid me to board.

I clambered inside and looked round for a seat. The stage could accommodate nine passengers inside, with room for up to six more outside. The interior wasn't particularly spacious, with passengers sitting squashed three abreast in the back and middle rows, both facing forward, and at the front of the stage in a third row facing the rear. As I scrambled aboard, I had to clamber over some mail pouches that had been placed inside the carriage. The three seats in the back row were already occupied, and I made myself comfortable taking a forward facing seat in the middle row next to the window, placing my baggage on the seat next to me. In the front row across from me there were two fellow travellers, one was dressed in the dark blue tunic of a U.S. army lieutenant and the other sported a city suit of the kind a salesman or a banker might wear.

There wasn't very much leg room and even though the stage was not full, to achieve any comfort I had to sit with my knees sort of dovetailed with those of the two men facing me. To add to the general discomfort, even though it was early morning the temperature was already rising, and I prepared myself for an uncomfortable and potentially stifling journey. The shotgun guard climbed up onto the high seat next to the whip and without any fanfare the stage pulled away, slowly at first then gradually increasing speed to a steady trot as we travelled along 15th Street. I looked at my pocket watch it was ten minutes before seven o'clock.

Once we left Denver and were travelling through more open countryside it seemed that the heat became increasingly oppressive as the morning advanced and the copious dust clouds kicked up by the six horses became progressively more asphyxiating. Stage travel was indeed an experience. Concord coaches may have been designed to withstand rough roads, sharp bends and daunting terrain but alas the human body is not so robust. The almost constant jostling of the carriage as the horses and stagecoach bounded and rolled over the trail made it nearly impossible to sit in comfort for any length of time and trying to sleep proved to be a thankless task. My companions so far had little conversation, apart from the salesman, who every ten minutes or so, took a quick sip from a bottle he kept in his carpet bag, then smiling broadly each time told us it was medicine to counter the dust. However, to me it appeared to smell remarkably similar to whisky.

The stage was able to maintain a speed of around four miles an hour and could travel about 120 miles a day, but to maintain this regimen the horses needed to be changed regularly. To expedite this Wells Fargo maintained a series of swing stations located roughly every ten to fifteen miles along the route. These stations usually had at least two attendants or agents and generally comprised of a small wooden or sod built house with a large barn and corral which could accommodate up to six teams of horses.

We had travelled for ten miles or so when we reached the first swing station where we stopped briefly to change the horses. As we neared the station the whip or shotgun blew a horn which warned the station attendant of our approach. The station agent on hearing the horn would swiftly make ready a fresh team of horses so no time was wasted. As we halted at the station the station manager and his assistant were waiting with the new team of horses already harnessed. The two men appeared to be a mismatched pair, the manager being a middle-aged, short and portly fellow with long black thinning hair arranged carefully over his bald pate and his assistant a tall gangling sandy haired youth, however they worked efficiently together and in a matter of minutes the stage team were uncoupled, and the replacement horses were hitched in their place. The changeover was so quick, that there was barely time for us passengers to make use of the toilet facilities or to get some coffee, beef jerky and biscuits before we set off again.

Stopping at swing stations offered only a brief respite from the privation of the journey but every fifty miles or so we were treated to a stop of around 40 minutes at a more substantial home station. The first home station I encountered was at a place called Loveland, which was fairly typical of most of the home stations on my journey. Loveland was similar in design to the swing stations we had visited earlier but its dwellings were larger, and it had more outbuildings, including a bunkhouse for the use of passengers. Loveland was constructed from pine and most of the other stations we were to call at en route were built from pine or cedar and occasionally from stone but where these materials were not available sod constructions were the order of the day. The home station keeper would usually be aided by his family, if he had one, otherwise he would generally have two or three helpers one of whom would serve as the cook. At a home station as well as changing the horses there would sometimes be a change of driver, and occasionally a passenger would leave the coach or a new one join the travelling group. Of much more significance to us passengers, there was time for a meal. I found the type of food served at all the home stations to be remarkably similar, but none the less it was a welcome comfort, and I would happily feast on eggs and bacon, hot biscuits with dried apples or peaches and coffee for around $1. Only rarely would we sleep at a home station for a few hours overnight for when conditions were good the stage would trundle on twenty four hours a day.

After we left Loveland the three passengers who had previously occupied the back row had left the stage and my two companions and I settled down for the next step of our journey. Stretching our legs and having a bite to eat seemed to improve the disposition of my fellow travellers and we occasionally engaged in discussion as the stage rumbled on. It was the salesman, who perhaps encouraged by his consumption of 'medicine', initiated most of our early exchanges. He introduced himself as Zachariah Babington from St. Louis, a purveyor of agricultural supplies, travelling to Laramie. At first the conversation merely covered banalities but it helped to pass the time. In response to his questioning, I told Babington I was originally from England and was travelling on to Tacoma to be reunited with my fiancé and her family and was fairly evasive when he pressed me further.

Having little success eliciting my life story Babington then turned his attention to the Lieutenant. It transpired that Lieutenant Harold Garthwaite Brownbridge, a native of Quincy in Norfolk County Massachusetts, was not long out of West Point where he had graduated 34 out of 87 in his class. Lieutenant Brownbridge was travelling to his new posting at Fort Laramie where he was to report to the commanding officer Major Edwin Franklin Townsend, of the Ninth United States Infantry.

Babington seemed fascinated by all things military and after interrogating Brownbridge about his time at West Point he then proceeded to bloviate at great length about the current Lakota Sioux uprising and how given their advantage of belonging to a superior civilisation it should be easy for the military to subdue Sitting Bull's undisciplined and uncivilised natives. This was a fairly one sided conversation, as the Lieutenant merely nodded and occasionally looked uncomfortable listening to the man's ramblings which became more incoherent and irrational as his sipping of his "medicine" became more frequent. I was unable to join in this exchange as to my embarrassment I had not been aware of the Indian unrest, being completely absorbed in my own affairs these past few months. The Lieutenant seemed fairly nonchalant about the situation and remarked that General Terry and Colonel Custer would soon track down the natives and bring them into line.

In an attempt to make up for my ignorance I asked Brownbridge how the uprising had begun. The Lieutenant replied 'Well I don't rightly know all the details but whatever the rights and wrongs of the situation there's been unrest in the Black Hills for a while now. The government claims the Lakotas had attacked settlers and miners who'd moved into their territory and then President Grant's administration attempted to buy the Black Hills region from the Indians. Naturally, the natives refused to sell, and then they were ordered to report to reservations by the end of

January this year. If you recall there was some pretty bad weather out there this winter, so even if the Lakota and Cheyenne wanted to comply it was almost impossible for most of them to make it to the reservations in time, so when they didn't come in the government told the military to take action against them. Last I heard General Crook's forces had found them along the Rosebud and after camping overnight at a bend in the river they were attacked by Sitting Bull's warriors. By all accounts the scrap wasn't going too well for Crook, when luckily he was reinforced by Captain Mills. The Lakota withdrew and soon disappeared into the wilderness, and as far as I know Terry and Custer are still out there tracking them down.'

'So, would you say we are in great danger of being attacked,' asked Babington anxiously.

'I'd say the chances are fairly slim, I reckon old Sitting Bull and his pal Crazy Horse are a good few hundred miles from here,' he replied smiling at Babington. 'I expect Colonel Custer and his 7th Cavalry will have caught up with Sitting Bull by now and the Lakota will have been well and truly subdued.'

The Lieutenant's reassurances seemingly did little to mollify Babington who was clearly becoming increasingly anxious about our journey and it appeared from his intermittent ramblings that he suspected there were hostile Lakotas Sioux or Cheyenne warriors hiding behind every tree and rocky outcrop, just waiting for an opportunity to jump out and ambush passing travellers. After this exchange the conversation died down for a while and I noticed Babington's frequent consumption of 'medicine' had warranted the opening of a second bottle.

Our journey continued peacefully with nothing else of note occurring until we stopped at the Moffat Ranch a swing station about 15 miles or so from Livermore. The Moffatt place was nothing out of the ordinary, it being pretty typical of the stagecoach swing stations we called at. The log built ranch house had been put up by Alistair Moffat a few years earlier in a sheltered spot on a low-lying rocky hillside, dotted with ponderosa pine trees. A nearby natural spring provided an essential water supply and from it water tumbled down the slope to a lively creek running past the left side of the house. Some of the more substantial ponderosa pines had been felled and used to build a large barn and in front of that was a corral for the horses. The family had a small beef herd and a few dairy cows. Alistair Moffat the station keeper and his two sons supplemented their income by hunting and selling the furs and meat in the local towns and villages. Mrs Moffat did the cooking for the stage passengers and other passing travellers and it was here at Mrs Moffat's table I met Luc Beauséjour.

My first impression of Luc was less than favourable. He was sitting at Mrs Moffat's table head in hands clearly the worse for an excess of alcohol. He was perhaps a year or two older than me, wearing a light grey wide-brimmed low-crowned felt hat pushed well back on his head, a filthy single breasted buckskin coat, with a fringe running across the shoulders and continuing along the sleeves, over an equally grimy red and black hickory-checked shirt and sturdy dark canvas pants, he looked like he had just emerged from the coal mines. Luc was about six feet tall with fair shoulder length hair, steely blue eyes, a faint scar across his forehead, a short stubbly beard which did little to hide a massive purple bruise on his face. He looked up as we entered the room and attempted a smile by way of an acknowledgement.

Mrs Moffat on seeing Babington, the Lieutenant and I enter called to Luc to make room for us so she might serve us with some coffee and biscuits. The stranger stood up and moved to sit at the end of the table and introduced himself saying, 'good day gentlemen, excuse my appearance I was thrown by my horse into a brook a few miles back and although I am much recovered thanks to Alistair Moffat's rye I am still feeling considerably the worse for wear. Unfortunately the same can't be said for my poor horse who broke his leg in the fall and has gone to paradise.'

Babington anxiously uttered his commiserations and positioned himself as far away from Luc as possible nervously glancing up at him from time to time as he sipped his coffee. The Lieutenant was not so reticent asking the newcomer where he was from and where he was going in rapid succession.

'Well I guess as we're to be travelling companions I may as well introduce myself to you gentlemen. I am Luc Beauséjour recently from New Orleans and heading to Fort Bridger where I hope to find employment.'

We briefly introduced ourselves and proceeded to hastily take our refreshments armed with the certain knowledge that as soon as the driver was ready to resume the journey the stage would not delay its departure for us. There were now four of us travelling in the interior of the stage, the Lieutenant and Babington in their customary places and myself and Luc Beauséjour on the opposing seat. Luc had placed his saddle bag on the seat between us and busied himself cleaning his Smith & Wesson revolver.

Beauséjour was quite a loquacious character and I quickly found myself warming to his sanguine personality and ready sense of humour. He told us he had been working for his brother on a Mississippi riverboat but hadn't greatly enjoyed the experience and had left with a mind to see the west. Luc said he was the son of a lawyer who had died when he was ten and as his mother had passed away when he was almost two, he and his elder brother were raised by their grandfather in Sainte-Rose near Montreal. He inquired about our experiences out in the west, and it transpired only Babington, who had once visited Boulder Colorado, had been much father west than our present position. The Lieutenant admitting that all his training and soldiering had been back east. Babington who had difficulty pronouncing Luc's last name, joined the conversation, asking him about the origin of his moniker. Luc revealed he was of French descent, his great grandparents having come to Canada from a place called Équemauville, near the French port of Honfleur.

Chapter 13

Tom and Andrew Kerr weren't best pleased at being drawn into Hugh's vendetta, but they knew better than to challenge their elder brother. They had travelled out west after hearing stories about the gold strikes in the Black Hills, with the intention of heading for Deadwood and getting rich, but now the brothers were stuck in Laramie and seething at having to kick their heels at Mrs Staples lodging house waiting for Hugh and John to arrive while other prospectors were purloining their imagined riches. Hugh had told them not to draw attention to themselves, but such was their irascible disposition that they didn't have to go looking for trouble, it usually found them. They had already had a few clashes with the locals and Andrew was nursing a black eye from a saloon confrontation the previous night and itching to get even, but Laramie City marshal John Colford had other ideas for Andrew, and he had dispatched a couple of deputies to Mrs Staples' place to take him into custody.

John and Hugh Kerr left the Union Pacific train in Laramie City feeling sweltered, stiff and drained after their journey from Denver. As they exited the railroad station the strong dry July wind driving into their faces did little to relieve their discomfort but at least they were bolstered by the knowledge that they were hot on the trail of their quarry. Hugh had made enquires at the Wells Fargo office in Denver and the clerk informed him that a man meeting Wilson's description was travelling to Salt Lake City and his stagecoach was due to arrive in Laramie in two days' time. The brothers had hastened to the rail depot and taken the first train to Laramie, Wilson may have evaded them on that train a while back but when the stage arrived tomorrow, he wouldn't escape their retribution a second time. They were meeting their younger brothers Tom and Andrew in Laramie and the four Kerr boys would show little mercy to that snitch Wilson when they caught up with him.

Hugh stuck a Lucifer match on the heel of his boot and watching the white phosphorus flare, lit his cigar, while John waylaid a jittery porter to get directions to Mrs Staples' boarding rooms where Tom and Andrew were lodging. John might be the oldest brother but Hugh being the most resourceful, conniving and meanest was acknowledged by all the siblings as their leader. Before the familial reunion Hugh wanted to find out when the Denver stage might arrive, so the two men set off to find the stage depot. An elderly bespectacled clerk proved eager to assist them and proclaimed that the stage usually arrived between 3 and 6 o'clock in the afternoon and that because of the 4th July centennial celebrations it wouldn't depart again till 5 o'clock on the morning of the 5th. Without thanking the clerk, the brothers left the depot and headed for a welcome reunion with Tom and Andrew. It had been a while since they had all been together and they had some catching up and some drinking up to do before they resumed their mission of meting out their form of justice to young Wilson.

Hugh and John arrived at Mrs Staples' establishment just in time to see a handcuffed Andrew being frogmarched out of the front door by two lawmen. Their brother Tom was running alongside them shouting and cursing and loudly proclaiming Andrew's innocence. The taller of the two lawmen sternly told Tom to desist or he too would be arrested but Tom wasn't at the head of the queue when brains were served up and he continued his vociferous protestations as the deputies marched Andrew to their jail wagon. With Andrew firmly incarcerated the deputies again ordered Tom to be on his way but Tom still furious at Andrews' seizure was in no mood to be placated and jumped up on the back of the wagon and wouldn't get down despite the deputies' threats. The shorter deputy losing his patience jumped down from the wagon and drawing his gun levelled it at Tom shouting 'son we've given you enough warnings, now slowly get off there and lie face down on the ground with your hands where I can see them.'

Tom on hearing the pistol cock, lost his bluster and reluctantly complied as the other deputy took his gun and knife, handcuffed him and bundled him into the black jail wagon with his brother. Hugh, hiding his annoyance at his brothers' behaviour, went up to the deputies now sitting on the box seat and ignoring his kinsmen asked what was going to happen to the two men.

'Well, I guess that'll depend on the judge. Why what's it to you?' said the tall lawman.

Hugh replied, 'well I had kinda hired those boys to do some work for me, so I was wondering if they'd still be around after the July 4ᵗʰ.'

'Like I said that'll depend on the judge,' continued the deputy, 'one of these fellas caused quite a bit of damage at Pringle's bar last night and the other's made a nuisance of himself just now. If you're troubled, you can attend their trials at the court house tomorrow afternoon.'

Hugh thanked the lawman for his time and barely able to contain his frustration ambled off to join John. John had learned from bitter experience not to question his brother when he was riled and waited patiently until Hugh was ready to reveal his thoughts. Presently he declared in an irascible tone, 'tomorrow I'll go to the court house and find out what's gonna happen to those lowlifes we have the misfortune to call brothers. Meanwhile I want you to go to the livery and get us four horses, and after you're done go to the stage depot and watch for Wilson's stage and when it gets in follow him and see where he goes. We'll meet up later at the boarding house, keep out of trouble and don't let him see you.'

The next morning John woke up late with a pounding headache, the result of too much whiskey the previous evening. Hugh showing no sympathy for his brother's condition, cruelly pulled the covers from John's bed while insisting he get up and they go down to sample Mrs Staples' cooked breakfast. John, who had fallen into bed still fully dressed, reluctantly got up and clumsily pulled on his boots as Hugh heartily reminded him of his tasks for the day. Hugh revelled in his brother's obvious discomfort as he wolfed down his breakfast while John, his head supported by one hand, pushed his food around his plate and intermittently sipped his coffee. Breakfast over, to John's dismay, Hugh insisted that they take a brisk stroll around Laramie to familiarise themselves with the neighbourhood.

There was an air of excitement in the streets that morning and it seemed almost everywhere they went people were busily preparing for the centennial celebrations the following day. Red, white and blue bunting and Star-Spangled Banner flags were erupting on nearly every building and somewhere in the distance a band was rehearsing for the 4th of July parade. It was a hot and windy day but somehow the strong breeze did little to mollify John's hangover and he struggled to match Hugh's lively pace. Hugh stopped outside a barbers' shop and telling John to wait, went inside to smarten himself up for his visit to the court house. Twenty minutes later he emerged clean shaven and with his lanky hair trimmed. Next, they entered a nearby store where Hugh bought himself a new hat, handing his old one down to his brother as he habitually did with much of his cast off garments. The discarded hat was far from new, but it was in a much better condition than John's ancient dust and sweat stained felt derby. They stopped at a quiet restaurant for a coffee and afterwards Hugh handed his brother $550 to purchase horses and saddles from Collins Livery which Hugh said was on 2nd Street. John couldn't help smiling when he grasped the folded notes, but Hugh warned him to seek a good deal and buy only sound horses, and to encourage John to bargain for a keen price told him he could keep half of any money left over. The brothers separated and Hugh made for East Grand Avenue and Laramie's court house.

There were a few people milling around outside the court house by the time Hugh arrived. He wasn't much given to appreciating aesthetics but even he was impressed by the smart two story detached building with large, sculpted church like arched windows and neat stone steps leading up to the main entrance. The doors had just opened as he reached the steps, and he followed the other interested parties into the building, taking a seat to the rear of the court room.

There were three or four men tried before Tom Kerr was brought into the room. The tall deputy described Tom's behaviour on the day his brother was arrested. M.C. Brown the defence attorney endeavoured to make out there were mitigating circumstances, but the Judge quickly decided Tom was guilty and sentenced him to four days in the Wyoming Territorial Prison. A case of theft followed by a drunk and disorderly charge came next and then Andrew Kerr's case came before the Judge. Andrew was accused of assault and causing damage to property at Pringle's Bar. Defence attorney Brown argued that Andrew had acted in self-defence and that in protecting himself it was necessary to inflict damage to furniture and fittings in the bar.

Andrew caught sight of Hugh sitting at the rear of the room and couldn't mistake the fleeting disparaging look his brother gave him. Finally, after a couple of witnesses from Pringles were examined and counter examined the

Judge called a twenty minute adjournment. During the break Hugh took the opportunity to step outside and smoke a cigar before returning to his seat. The Judge entered and resumed proceedings by finding Andrew not guilty of assault, but guilty of causing damage to property fining him $10 and sentenced him to three weeks incarceration in the Wyoming Territorial Penitentiary.

John Kerr had been busy purchasing horses, saddles and harnesses. He was pleased with the deal he had made with Mr Collins, for not only had he bought the animals and equipment he had also negotiated feed and stabling and all for $460, leaving himself a tidy sum of $45. Feeling well satisfied and imagining receiving some begrudging praise from Hugh he set off for the stage depot. He still had at least two hours before the earliest possible arrival of the stage, so he decided to stop off for one or two drinks on the way, but one or two became five or six by the time he left the bar, so thirst quenched but mind slightly addled, he set off again for the stage depot at the Kuster Hotel in Ivinson Street. John was in high spirits, Hugh usually took care of their money and doled it out grudgingly, but he had made a good deal at the livery and for once he had money in his pocket. Fortified by the alcohol he had the urge to spend some of it and when he came to Della's bordello on South 4th Street that urge was assuaged.

Sometime later John left Della's establishment no longer feeling the day was going well, not only had be spent his share of the money but somehow Hugh's portion was no longer in his possession. He had just decided he'd tell

Hugh the horses cost the full $550 and forgo any brotherly praise, when a church clock began to chime five. Fearing he might have missed the arrival of the stage John ran the rest of the way to the stage depot. There was no sign of the stage and fleetingly John thought that was good news, and then he had an uneasy foreboding that the stage might have already arrived while he was engaged at Della's. With a sinking feeling he entered the depot office and asked the clerk when today's stage from Denver was due. The clerk gave him a quizzical look over his thick glasses and said 'mister you're too late it arrived about 40 minutes ago. The next stage out of here is 5 a.m. on July 5th, if you're interested.'

Feeling far from interested John asked the clerk where the passengers went as he was supposed to be meeting a friend. The clerk replied, 'I've no idea son, I guess those that live near here will have gone home and the others will probably be holed up in a lodging house.'

John described Wilson and asked the clerk if he had seen him. The clerk couldn't recall anyone filling that description but suggested a couple of greenbacks might improve his memory. John had thought of another way of refreshing the clerk's recollection and was about to grab the unsuspecting man by his shirt when he remembered Hugh's instructions to stay out of trouble. Reluctantly he resisted the impulse to beat the information from the clerk, hastily left the building and began walking to Mrs Staples', mentally rehearsing the story he would tell Hugh. He was no longer looking forward to being reunited with his brother.

Chapter 14

Tom and Andrew Kerr were feeling far from happy, the fact that they were about to be incarcerated was a concern, but a greater concern was facing the wrath of big brother Hugh when they were released. They had spent most of the day penned up in the court house holding cell, first awaiting trial and then waiting for the jail waggon to take them on the short journey west of Laramie along Snowy Range Road to Wyoming Territorial Penitentiary. Still the brothers had got some advantage from their situation. Before going in front of the judge they had passed the time playing cards with a couple of other miscreants and had won a few dollars but better than that they had cultivated the acquaintance of Dusty McGregor. Dusty was a local ne'er-do-well who had frequently been in and out of the pen since it opened back in '72. He boasted that for $25 he could arrange their escape and that in all probability they'd be free as the birds this time tomorrow.

Around 5.00pm the court business was concluded, and deputies escorted Dusty, Andrew and Tom and two other prisoners to the jail waggon. Once the handcuffed prisoners were safely locked inside, the guard and driver climbed up on the box seat and the waggon trundled off on the short drive to the Territorial prison. The journey was uneventful, but it gave the Kerrs the opportunity to find out about their new abode. Dusty related some of his previous experiences in the prison and the brothers quietly asked about escape. Dusty told them that escape was a fairly regular occurrence on the account of understaffing and poor security, and he reckoned as many as one out of every four prisoners who skedaddled got away scot-free. He told them he'd never bothered to escape himself as he'd never been sentenced to more than a few weeks jail but just knowing that he could get out anytime he wanted gave him some kind of comfort. The brothers asked Dusty how he could arrange to get them out, but he refused to tell them in the jail waggon saying if they wanted his help they'd have to pay him now while they still had their cash. The brothers were reluctant to part with their money without some idea of how they would escape, but they were even more reluctant to prolong their stay in the pen, so Tom begrudgingly handed over the money. Dusty furtively glancing round to see if anyone was looking swiftly grasped the notes and hastily stuffed them down inside his boot, telling the brothers to look out for him later on in the prison dining room.

Wyoming Territorial Penitentiary stood in open countryside about a mile and a half west of Laramie city. The main buildings had walls at least two feet thick and were constructed from rough greyish-beige sandstone, with contrasting brown sandstone corner stones and window arches and the facility was surrounded on three sides by a twelve feet high wooden stockade. The jail waggon entered through a sturdy gateway and drew to a halt in front of the principal building. Two guards emerged and assisted by the deputies decanted their prisoners from the iron barred carriage. The captives were quickly shepherded towards the building, giving them little time to appreciate the aesthetics of their new surroundings. They entered the prison through heavy iron doors and were directed to the processing room. Here the men were lined up; their clothes and possessions were taken from them to be replaced by black and white striped prison uniforms, and then they received their bedding. Once the convicts had changed into prison garb a stocky rodent eyed guard explained that the prison followed the Auburn Prison System. Recognising Dusty as a prison regular the guard ordered him to explain the rules. Dusty scratched his head and began a monotone recital, 'convicts are to be silent at all times unless asked to speak, convicts must wear black and white striped uniforms, convicts are to be known by a number instead of their names, convicts will walk about the prison in lock step when instructed, convicts must keep their cell in perfect order.' The guard flashed a rat-toothed smile and said, 'not bad McGregor but you forgot, work for convicts is mandatory.' He went on to elucidate the meaning of lock step, 'when walking to cells, the dining hall and work places prisoners will walk in single file with their arms locked under the arms of the man in front.' Observing rodent had finished, his colleague issued the men with their prison numbers. Andrew was 182, Tom 185 and Dusty was to be known as 197. Next the men were given a haircut before being conducted to their cells to make up their beds.

The prisoners lined up and in lock step formation were taken from the processing room along a corridor passing the wardens office and then going on through another heavy iron door they entered the cell block. Inside the vast space were three tiers of cells on one side, and on the other wall were tall dormer windows allowing light in to the interior. The cellblock had a stone paved floor and whitewashed walls. In cold weather fireplaces at either end of the wing provided heating. Tom and Andrew were given a cell on the ground floor tier and Dusty and another prisoner were deposited in the cell next door. The pokey cell had a trellised iron door and was furnished with two wooden stools, a spittoon, a chamber pot and a wooden bunk bed. The brothers quickly made up their beds and waited for the guard to inspect them. As it was now late in the day they were not expected to work and soon prisoners who had been labouring were ushered back to their cells. Presently the guards appeared and tier by tier the convicts were lock stepped to the dining hall.

The dining hall was a long austere room with the ubiquitous whitewashed walls and iron barred dormer windows. Long wooden tables with benches furnished the room and the men sat in silence as they waited for the kitchen helpers to serve their food. Once the prisoners were seated only one guard supervised meal time, but others remained in hailing distance nearby. Tom and Andrew elbowed another prisoner out of the way to claim a place next to Dusty, the man's instinct was to protest but one look at the intimidating Kerr boys changed his mind and he grudgingly gave way. The brothers sat, ate their food and waited for an opportunity to converse with Dusty. As they sat in silence a kerfuffle between two prisoners and a kitchen helper erupted at the far end of the room, with the guard's attention diverted Dusty not looking at him, spoke quietly to Andrew. 'Listen young fella, this here is a key that will get you out of your cell and through that iron door at the end of the cell block,' he said, surreptitiously pressing a key into Andrews' hand underneath the table. 'Go after two o'clock tonight, there's usually no guard around then and remember to lock your cell and the block door after you. Then head for the prison kitchen, next room down the corridor from here.'

He looked around to make sure they were still unobserved and continued with his instructions for their exit, once stopping talking abruptly as another guard entered the room from the corridor and went to the assistance of his colleague. Order was soon restored, and the offenders were marched off to solitary confinement and soon after the convicts were escorted back to their cells for the night.

For Tom and Andrew, the evening passed slowly. Andrew tried to sleep while Tom passed the time chewing tobacco and aiming for the spittoon. They had no way of knowing when two o'clock came but they had to be long gone by waking up time at 5.30am if they wanted to make good their escape. Presently they heard Dusty whispering hoarsely from the next cell, 'hey boys it's time you were away. Remember to lock the doors after you and leave that key in the flour sack like I told you, so we can use it another time.'

Andrew retrieved the key from the spittoon, wiping it dry on Tom's shirt sleave, and gingerly unlocking the cell door they cautiously stepped from their cell and approached the cellblock door. Carefully unlocking and slightly opening it without a sound, Andrew peered into the main corridor. There were no guards in sight, and they were about to head off to the kitchen when Dusty in a gruff loud whisper reminded them to lock the doors. They stealthily moved down the corridor past the processing room and dining hall and reached the kitchen door which was unlocked. There had been some lighting in the corridor, but the kitchen was in darkness. Once his eyes adjusted to the gloom Andrew could make out a small barred window with storage shelves to its right. The crescent moon momentarily free of clouds cast a little more light in the room just in time to stop Tom walking into a barrel standing next to a central table. On the table was an open flour sack and Andrew thrust the key deep into the white powder and headed for the shelves on the far wall. It was just as Dusty described it. They slid some storage boxes along the bottom shelf, to reveal a grill cover on the wall. Carefully Andrew prised the grill loose and Tom squeezed into a dark passage. He was stockier than Andrew but managed to scrape his way down the narrow shaft into the cellar below.

Andrew, going through the gap feet first, pulled the heavy wooden boxes back across the opening and with a bit of difficulty managed to manoeuvre the grill back into place. The cellar was pitch black. Andrew struck a Lucifer, and a stairway was revealed. The brothers warily climbed this stairway and reached the wooden door that opened onto the woodwork room. As expected, the woodwork room was deserted. Andrew cautiously opened the door that led to the prison courtyard and looked to see if their route was clear. He quickly pulled the door shut, there was someone moving slowly along the walkway on top of the wooden perimeter fence.

The two men waited in the dim woodwork room for about thirty minutes until Andrew hazarded another look. This time the raised boardwalk was clear, and the brothers ran furtively from the doorway to the welcoming shadows of the boundary fence. They stood pressed against the palisade for a few minutes to make sure no guards were about then looked for somewhere to climb. The perimeter fence was around twelve feet high and topped by a raised walkway with a number of watchtowers situated at intervals along its length. Andrew was the more athletic of the two men and he determined that Tom should climb up on his shoulders and pull himself up on to the walkway and then drop down over the fence. Tom did as he was bid and was able to hoist himself up onto the walkway with a little effort, the only mishap being a painful kick to Andrew's nose as he did so. With Tom successfully over the barrier and out of the compound, Andrew stepped back and took a run at the forbidding obstacle; he managed to catch hold of the walkway and pulled himself up on to the platform using his elbows to gain purchase until he could swing his leg over and drag his dangling body up on to the exposed walkway. Freedom was only a few steps away, and with a last look round he stood up, hastily crossed the walkway and dropped down over the perimeter fence to join his waiting brother.

Tom was crouched down with his back pressed rigid against the fence rubbing his wrist which was skinned and bleeding from contact with the rough wood when he slid over the fence, otherwise the two men were unharmed. Andrew grinned at his brother, his tobacco stained teeth glinting in the moonlight, and indicating some bushes about two hundred yards away he set off running. The ground outside the penitentiary was quite flat and almost completely devoid of covering vegetation to mask the flight of the fugitives. Fortunately for the Kerrs the crescent moon was about to be veiled by thickening cloud. Andrew and Tom sat concealed by some sagebushes deciding what to do next. They determined they needed to get to Laramie and find Hugh and John who should be at Mrs Staples'. Hugh would be sure to come up with a plan once they found him.

They could see the Laramie River in the distance as they hurried to cross the open ground that lay between them and the Snowy Range Road. They followed the deserted road for a few yards then leaving the road ran on towards the watercourse and the welcome shelter of its tree lined banks. Taking a while to get their bearings, Andrew noticed some feint lights in the distance that he reckoned were coming from Laramie. Keeping close to the river, which for a while flowed almost parallel to Snowy Range Road, the two men slinked ever closer to the settlement. Eventually they re-joined the road where a bridge crossed the river and unnoticed the fugitives reached the outskirts of the town. By this time, the sky was showing the first signs of the approaching dawn with the early July sunrise being around 5.30. Suddenly the men stopped dead in their tracks, they could hear the sound of approaching hoof beats. Andrew grabbed Tom by the sleeve and pulled him off the track down into some scrubby grasses and sagebrush at the side of the road. Fortunately for the brothers it was merely a farmer's cart and in the early morning gloom there was just sufficient vegetation to hide them but in daylight they would have been easily spotted by anyone casually glancing their way.

Andrew was becoming increasingly concerned that if anyone saw them they would be quite conspicuous dressed in their prison uniforms and he ordered his brother to look out for anything they could use to cover their convict suits. The cart was the first of many heading into Laramie for the centennial celebrations that day, and the brothers were forced to crawl further back from the road to avoid detection. Deciding the best course of action was to keep away from the main thoroughfare the siblings set off across open country in the direction of Laramie, crawling, walking or adopting a low crouching run depending on the available cover.

As the sun rose the brothers heard the report of a cannon followed by small arms fire announcing the start of the July 4th revelries. Hidden by some scrawny sagebrush they were reconnoitring a barn and hoped the noise didn't bring out the owners. They waited ten minutes, and all remained still, so while Tom kept watch, Andrew cautiously entered the outbuilding. He was looking for something they might use to disguise their prison clothes. He didn't see anything suitable at first but as he was about to leave, he noticed an old horse blanket hanging in a stall near the door, he eagerly grabbed it and using a fortuitous scythe made a hasty cut to fashion the blanket in to a rough poncho, then picking up a length of rope he ran back to join Tom. Donning the poncho Andrew explained his plan to his bemused brother.

They continued towards Laramie keeping away from the road and passers-by as much as possible but as they got closer to town they couldn't hope to avoid being observed. The poncho pretty much hid Andrew's prison uniform but Tom was still quite conspicuous. Using the rope, Andrew loosely tied Tom's hands in front of him and then looped the rope round his brother's neck like a halter. If challenged Andrew would say he had captured an escaped prisoner and was taking him to the marshal in Laramie. Maybe it wasn't a good plan, but it was the only one they had to see them through the increasing number of people travelling to the Independence Day centennial. As they proceeded Andrew had to explain himself a couple of times, but the ruse seemed to work and they got into Laramie without incident. Andrew had another idea. He had noticed people milling around in various costumes and he surmised that they could walk freely through the crowds in their prison attire as long as they kept close to others who were in fancy dress and hope people would assume they were part of the parade. So, casting off the makeshift poncho and rope the brothers joined the July 4th parade and boldly marched through Laramie until they got close enough to bolt into Mrs Staples' lodging house.

Hugh Kerr had been furious the previous evening when John related his tale about missing the arrival of the stage, and today he was still mad at his repentant brother. Wilson was in town somewhere and John had squandered their best chance of tracking him down. Over breakfast Hugh decided on a new stratagem. They knew Wilson was close by and it was likely he'd be out watching the parade so they'd go out looking for him and if they found him they could wait for an opportunity to shoot him or if that wasn't feasible, capture him and take him somewhere to finish him off. Having explained the situation to his brother, Hugh's mood was improving as he stepped through Mrs Staples' front door into the street, but it soon changed when he saw Andrew and Tom running towards him. Hugh greeted Andrew with a vicious punch full on his nose. Reeling from the blow Andrew began to grapple with his elder brother but John stepped in separating the two men saying, 'this isn't the time to settle your differences boys, let's go inside without creating a fuss.'

The four men hurried up the stairway to their room. Hugh was still angry but Andrew, wiping the blood from his face with his sleeve, tried to defuse the situation saying, 'I guess I deserved that welcome big brother.'

Hugh's anger was soon put to one side as he adapted to the changed situation. It was clear they couldn't go looking for Wilson; the prison would have noticed his brothers were missing by now and the hue and cry would be under way. It couldn't be long before the law turned up at Mrs Staples'. Tom and Andrew changed out of their prison clothes and waited for Hugh to speak. 'Now listen good boys, this is what we'll do. John you go off to Collins' Livery and get the horses ready and take Andrew with you. Tom you pack up our stuff and those damn jail suits too. I'll go and pay Mrs Staples for the board and feed her some tale so she ain't curious, and we'll meet up at the Livery and hightail it out of here.'

Tom looking perplexed interjected, 'and what about Wilson?'

'I haven't forgotten him Tom,' Hugh said menacingly, 'we're gonna ride out ahead of that stage and scout out a likely place and then we'll deal with him once and for all.'

Chapter 15

The stage had made good time and around 4.00pm we arrived in Laramie stopping outside the stage depot at the Kuster Hotel in Ivinson Street. The shotgun told us the stage would be travelling no farther that day and wouldn't be setting off again till after tomorrow's centennial celebrations and to ask the stage depot clerk about overnight accommodation. Lieutenant Brownbridge was setting off almost immediately on the 110 miles or so journey to his new posting at Fort Laramie, so Babington, Luc and I headed into the depot office. We approached a grizzled haired clerk who sat slumped behind a highly polished wooden desk. Seeing us approach he sat up and pushed his thick lensed glasses firmly up on his bulbous nose and remarked, 'You gents just off the stage from Denver? You'll be looking for somewhere to stay?' And not waiting for us to respond continued, 'the company's booked a couple of rooms for travellers, I got a room for two at New York House in Front Street and there's two single rooms across the street at Western House.'

Babington interjected saying he'd take a Western House room and hurried out of the door without so much as a thank you or goodbye, which meant Luc and I were to be roommates at the hotel in Front Street.

At sunrise, the sound of canon fire announced the commencement of the Centennial and early morning revellers joined in with small arms fire to usher in celebrations for the big day. The noise summarily woke me and seeing Luc, who was already dressed, standing at the window, I leapt up from my bed and joined him to observe for myself the commotion in the street below. We saw early risers emerge from their homes eager to share in the festivities and these revellers were soon augmented by an ever increasing enthusiastic influx of celebrants from elsewhere in the city and its rural hinterland, all bent on enjoying the July 4th proceedings to the full. I witnessed people dressed in variety of costumes, no doubt in readiness for the parade later that morning.

I was keen to get out and join the throng, so I dressed quickly and forgoing breakfast dragged a reluctant Luc out of our lodgings into the frenetic hubbub. We walked amongst the revellers exhilarated by the electric atmosphere. The streets were noisy and bustling, with everyone in high spirits and if it were possible there appeared to be even more flags and bunting than the day before. I had participated in July 4th celebrations back in Schuylkill County but somehow this one felt unique. We savoured this cheerful hullabaloo for a while and presently I heard the sound of a band wafting towards us indicating the parade had commenced somewhere in the distance.

The procession had started near the rolling mill and before long the vanguard of the parade appeared. At the forefront was a band led by a drum major whose selection of music added greatly to the ambience of the occasion. The costumes of the participants marching behind the band were particularly striking, their exotic outfits depicting various historic themes and faraway lands, including groups dressed in the militia uniforms of 1776, native Indians, Ethiopians and other Orientals in fine apparel, buccaneers looking particularly menacing brandishing cutlasses and even a couple of furtive looking fellows in drab stripy convict uniforms. Then behind them marched the mayor and prominent citizens followed by the band of the US Second Cavalry who played some rousing tunes.

After the music ceased a preacher recited a short prayer then a solemn dignitary narrated the Declaration. There was some more music followed by a military man who addressed the assembly extolling the virtues of the United States and its special place amongst the nations of the world. By now the scorching sun was blazing down in a cerulean sky but the assembly continued to give their unwavering devotion as he went on to pay tribute to Jacques LaRamie, the French-Canadian trapper whose name was given to the city, and then to the early pioneers and settlers who did so much to develop it. Finally he gave praise to the boys in blue who he said kept the frontier safe and were as necessary to the development of the west as those hardy first pioneers had been. After this patriotic homily the ceremony took on a lighter tone as a lady recited a centennial poem and the band played some gentle airs.

I had enjoyed the proceedings and even Luc, who had been reluctant to join in, perhaps because he was a French-Canadian by birth, appeared to have a smile on his face. It was now nearly noon and the president of the event closed the morning's formal activities by reminding everyone that there would be foot races and games commencing at one o'clock and the day would conclude with a grand ball given by the Wanless Hose Company followed by a grand firework display.

Over a congenial lunch, I persuaded Luc that we should go and watch the foot races later that afternoon, so around two o'clock we made our way along to the sports field where an enthusiastic crowd had gathered for the days' events. There was much side gambling on rival local favourites and Luc unable to resist the temptation, ran his eye over the hopeful challengers and fortuitously made a few dollars from his wagers. Towards the end of the races we participated in two events, finishing well down the pack in both. I managed to finish in front of Luc twice, but I suspected he wasn't trying too hard. Later we watched a baseball game and afterwards listened to a concert for a while. Foregoing the Wanless Hose Company's grand ball, we ended the evening in one of Laramie's many saloons before staggering outside much later to join the crowd to view the firework display.

Étienne you will not be surprised to learn that as a result of our early awakening, our busy day, late night fireworks watching, and yes you are right, abetted by our imbibing of alcohol, we overslept the following morning and by the time we reached the depot at the Kuster Hotel the stage was already gathering speed at the far end of Ivinson Street. So, it was not until the next day that Luc and I resumed our journey. We were the only passengers and we sprawled over the interior seats in a futile attempt to make ourselves more comfortable while we attempted to recover from the excesses of the previous night.

It was another baking hot day. The merciless heat and copious dust thrown up by the coach and horses as we travelled through the flat treeless countryside colluded to make our lives even more disagreeable. Towards the end of the day we crossed the Medicine Bow River and arrived at the Elk Mountain swing station. We were thankful for a longer stopover, the prospect of a hearty meal and the opportunity it provided to stretch our legs. Two new travelling companions joined us at Elk Mountain, a lady school teacher and her young son. They had celebrated the centennial with her parents who ran the Medicine Bow post office and were returning home to Rawlins. We travelled throughout the night and arrived at Rawlins before noon the following day.

At the Rawlins home station an animated discussion was in full swing when we entered the building. A stage had not long arrived from the north bringing shocking news of Custer and his Seventh Cavalry. Luc asked what the fuss was about and one of the station hands thrust a newspaper at him saying 'Custer and the Indians.'

Luc read the headlines from the paper, 'Terrible fight, Lieutenant Colonel Custer killed, Seventh Cavalry cut to pieces, 300 dead'.

Lieutenant Brownbridge was right, Custer had indeed located Sitting Bull, but events hadn't progressed the way the Lieutenant envisaged. I looked at Luc's grim face, as he paraphrased the rest of the account, 'W. H. Norton the Helena Daily Herald's chief correspondent writes, Muggins Taylor, General Gibbons' scout brought dispatches from the Little Horn River. On the morning of 25 June, Custer's scouts came across Sitting Bull's camp of about two thousand lodges on the banks of the Little Horn. It seems Custer intended to move the Seventh Cavalry to a position to attack the camp at dawn the next day, but some warriors caught sight of a few soldiers and Custer anticipating they would hurry to notify Sitting Bull, decided to strike immediately. He attacked with five companies, but the Lakota and Cheyenne warriors returned superior fire and Custer his two brothers, a nephew and a brother-in-law were all killed, not one of his men escaped. The dead are estimated at more than three hundred.'

Fortunately, we weren't in any immediate danger from the Sioux, the scene of the battle being over 300 miles from Rawlings and our route would take us even farther away but nevertheless the news was disquieting and we were still in a pensive mood when we returned to the stage. The next leg of our journey was as uneventful as the flat featureless landscape we travelled through, however we made good time and arrived at Washakie home station ahead of schedule. Washakie station was solidly built from locally quarried red sandstone and in front of it stood a corral and hay storage shed. Here a fresh whip and shotgun took over and all too soon we were travelling again. I can't remember now all the names of the other stations we passed through along the way, but I do well remember my time at Green River.

It was about 8.30 in the evening when we reached Green River home station. It was one of those rare occurrences when we were to make an overnight stopover. The sun wouldn't set for another half hour, so after the oppressive confinement of yet another day in the increasingly claustrophobic concord I decided to take a stroll down to the river to get some exercise and perhaps to catch a cooling breeze. I walked stiffly at first, becoming looser in my gait as I advanced. I observed the aptly named Castle Rock soaring above the township and wondered about the adventurer who named it and mused that it probably occurred long before the early pioneers arrived and erected their first adobe dwellings. Lost in thought I found myself on the banks of the swift flowing greenish waterway that gave its name to the town. As I stood contemplating the scenery my Boss of the Plains was knocked from my head and suddenly my world went dark. A sack was thrust over my head and powerful hands twisted something tightly round my neck. I kicked out hopefully at my attacker, twisting and squirming I thought I would break free as his grip wavered, but then I felt a sharp blow to my skull.

I woke with a throbbing head and the taste of blood in my mouth. My head was still covered by a sack. I tried to sit up but found my hands were bound and a gag had been tied over my mouth. I had no comprehension as to how long I had been unconscious, but I was certain it wasn't long. My captor pulled me to my feet and ordering me not to make a fuss, roughly shoved me along, keeping a gun pressed firmly in my back as we walked. A couple of times we stopped abruptly and once he pulled me down into the underbrush , always keeping his gun firmly pressed against my body. After a few minutes we stopped. I heard the sound of a door swinging on its hinges then he pushed me forward kicking me violently. I stumbled falling heavily on my face, then without warning the man grabbed my legs and tightly bound my ankles, chuckling to himself as he did so. 'Well, that's you all nicely packaged up' he said. 'Don't go getting too comfortable Wilson, you'll not be here that long, my brother Hugh is eager for a final reunion.'

I heard the door close and the sound of the man walking away. I waited a few minutes then squirming on my back along the floor I reached a wall and using my head and feet I managed to achieve a sitting position. I was alone for the moment, but I guessed it wouldn't be long before my abductor returned, reasoning that whatever might be my fate my tormentor would seek to execute it under cover of darkness. I now had no doubt that my captor was one of the Kerr boys. A sense of terror and desperation churned through me, but I realised I had to fight this despair if I were to survive. I tried to remove the sack by rubbing the back of my head against the wall. Fortunately, on my fourth or fifth attempt it snagged on a splinter protruding from the log wall and I gently eased my head from the sack. There wasn't much light, but I was able to discern I had been dumped in a barn. I tried to remove the gag rubbing my face against my shoulder and twisting my neck violently but couldn't free myself. Then I concentrated on my hands which were tied in front of me. I tried to force my hands apart and fortunately felt a little slackness in the rope binding my right hand. I braced my left arm and pulled as hard as I could with my right hand and felt the rope move ever so slightly down my wrist, but I couldn't pull it down over the heal of my hand and thumb. I sat for a moment then I bent my knees and pulling my bound hands up against my left knee managed to force the course hempen rope over my right hand, almost dislocating my thumb in the process. I quickly untied the rope from my left hand then freed myself from the gag and studiously set to work loosening the rope binding my ankles.

I hurried over to the door and as I expected it had been barred on the outside. I pushed hard against it, but the door wouldn't budge, and I realised I would have to look for another exit. I quickly explored the rapidly darkening building hoping to find a gap in the wall or a crack in the roof I could use to make my escape, but to no avail. I walked back to the door to have another attempt at forcing it open when I heard the sound of the bar being lifted. I looked around for something I could use as a weapon. It was quite dark now, but I managed to locate a pitchfork. As the door opened, I charged at the unsuspecting shape silhouetted in the entrance, intending to skewer him with the pitchfork, and hoping I'd do enough damage to prevent him shooting me in the back as I ran like hell to the home station. The silhouetted figure was Luc Beauséjour. My mind was racing, could he be working for the Kerrs? Just in time I altered my trajectory, and the pitchfork stuck the doorpost. 'Mike that's a fine way to greet your redeemer,' he chortled handing me my crumpled Boss of the Plains.

As we walked towards the home station Luc explained that he'd been on his way to join me earlier when he noticed a man approach me at the riverbank, then seeing our scuffle decided to follow us to the barn. He'd listened outside and was about to come in when he heard the man leaving so he'd taken cover and waited a while until he was sure he was out of sight. I realised I owed Luc some sort of explanation but for the moment we hurried back to the home station with his questions still unanswered. Once we were back at the home station, I had a quick wash at the standpipe to refresh myself while Luc stood over me. Luc cast me a concerned glance which I interpreted as him asking 'Mike what the hell's going on?'

We walked across to the corral and leaned against the fence gazing at the horses. I began my tale recounting how I had met Padraig and Bel and detailing my time at Port Clinton. We moved inside and sat at a table and I continued my story describing how I met McKenna/McParlan, my life in Pottsville and how Padraig and I witnessed the slaying of Benny Yost, our subsequent warning from the Molly Maguires, my dealings with the Pinkerton's, Padraig's murder and the Molly's trial. I concluded with my present journey and my encounters with the Kerr brothers. By the time I had finished and answered all of Luc's questions it was getting close to dawn. The whip and shotgun were outside preparing the concord and horses for leaving. Still in conversation we ate a speedy breakfast which we were just finishing when the shotgun announced the stage was ready to depart and we were back on the road again.

Chapter 16

By the time we arrived at Fort Bridger I had come up with an embryonic plan to shake off the Kerr brothers. It was over 1000 miles to Tacoma and it seemed as if the Kerrs were well aware that was my destination. Luc had explicitly pointed out that if I remained with the stage it was only a matter of time before they caught up with me again and my luck couldn't last indefinitely. So, in my naivety I decided to abandon the stagecoach at Fort Bridger and strike out overland for Seattle or Port Townsend, reasoning I'd be far safer away from the predictability of the stagecoach route, but at that time my logic paid little heed to the possible new dangers I might face crossing the wilderness.

Fort Bridger standing on the Black Fork tributary of the Green River was nowhere near as grand a place as Laramie. It had been set up as a trading post around thirty five years earlier by a fellow named Jim Bridger and his partner Louis Vasquez. In those early days it had succoured mountain men and Indians, and later received westward bound emigrants, Mormon pioneers and the United States Army. It was on the old Pony Express and Overland Stage routes and from Fort Bridger the Oregon Trail headed north, and the Mormon Trail continued another hundred or so miles west to Salt Lake City. It was a busy junction with travellers continually coming and going, so it seemed to me to be as good a place as any to put my plan into action.

As we were approaching Fort Bridger I told Luc I was going to be leaving the stage to strike out on my own towards Tacoma by less travelled routes. To my great surprise he offered to accompany me. His boast that he had some experience of living off the land in the wilderness and that the Beauséjours were naturally skilled trackers and passable hunters made it impossible for me to refuse his offer. It was early evening when the stage arrived in Fort Bridger. We had decided not to linger there for long, but it was too late in the day to procure the necessary supplies for our journey, so taking our baggage from the concord we sought accommodation for the night.

That evening I composed a short letter to Bel letting her know I was well and still bound for Tacoma albeit by a different and potentially much longer route. I didn't want to alarm her about my encounters with the Kerrs so I merely said it was possible they were following the stagecoach so I was striking out overland with a companion to thwart any attempt they might make to track me down. I finished by telling her not to worry if she didn't hear from me for a while.

The following day having pooled our ready money we went in search of the necessities for our adventure. I was quickly impressed by Luc's expertise; he seemed to know what supplies we would need and was successful in driving down the price when he felt storekeepers were overcharging.

Étienne dear friend I will not weary you with the details of our inventory, suffice to say it consisted of the variety of items one might suspect are necessary for two gentlemen from the East going off to the wilderness on a hunting trip, which was the story we told anyone who enquired about our business. Having persuaded me I should purchase a Winchester Model 1873 .38-40 repeater rifle, we made our final acquisition of two sturdy horses and prepared to leave town around noon. As I stood contemplating my pony, I was forced to admit to Luc I had little experience of riding. He assured me I would soon get the hang of it, so I clambered gingerly onto my poor mount. I decided to wait for another occasion to tell him I had never before used a rifle.

It was another searing July afternoon as we rode, or rather Luc rode and I clung on frantically to my horse, following a trail heading roughly north towards Eagle Rock some 200 or more miles distant. After a couple of miles Luc stopped and suggested we rest the horses for a while. I suspected the horses didn't need a break but rather that Luc seeing my lack of horsemanship thought I could do with some respite. Luc suggested we should get off the trail, but travel parallel to it, to make ourselves harder to find if the Kerrs somehow managed to discover where we were heading, and he ventured with a grin, 'two gentlemen out hunting would have more chance of coming across some unsuspecting quarry away from the trail than if we stuck to it.'

All too soon we were travelling again. Getting back on my horse filled me with foreboding, but somehow once I remounted the horse proved to be more understanding of my intentions than previously and we journeyed for another four hours across the parched flat landscape stopping only once, before Luc announced we should find a spot to make camp for the night.

There had been little to shoot at by way of game, in fact we hadn't even been tempted to use our rifles, so our supper consisted of salt beef and beans washed down with strong coffee. We were up the next morning around 5am and after a breakfast of pancakes and coffee we set off. We had brought some oats for the horses but our supply was quickly exhausted so we had to allow time for the horses to graze and to find supplies of fresh water, so we were lucky if we travelled 12 miles a day. This was to become our routine for the next couple of weeks and it was with some anticipation that we reached the settlement of Eagle Rock at the beginning of August.

Eagle Rock stood on the main route north at a crossing point on the Snake River. Its timber frame toll bridge had been constructed about ten years earlier, and since then quite an assortment of properties had sprung up nearby. Aside from an array of houses and barns, there was a bank, a blacksmith shop and livery stable, an eating house, a post office, a stage station and a store. Luc took the horses off to the livery stable while I got us accommodation at a log cabin operated by the Anderson brothers, the closest the town came to having a hotel in those days. Luc was eager to continue our journey the next day, but I explained I was getting low on money, having spent much of the funds I'd brought from Philadelphia, and while I had some savings, I'd transferred them to a bank in Tacoma. We'd had a lot of expenditure to get this far but we were going to need additional money to replenish our provisions. I suggested we try and get jobs and stay in town or camp nearby until we had enough money for supplies. At first Luc was reluctant but he soon changed his mind when he discovered he only had $10, so later that day Luc got a job at the livery stables and I found labouring work with a local farmer. We stayed there for three weeks, all the while keeping a look out for the Kerrs.

On leaving Eagle Rock we more or less followed the trail northwards for two days, always keeping the Snake River to our right, before arriving at a place called Market Lake. It was a very small place, but it managed to support a post office, a stage station, a saloon and a store and it was in John Adam's store that fate introduced me to the outwardly obsequious Ezekiel Ramsey. Luc was checking on the horses while I ventured into John Adam's General Store to replenish our supply of coffee and beans. Next to me purchasing similar items stood a man of about 50 years old; he must have been just over five feet tall, with a bit of a belly on an otherwise slender frame. He had tight curly greying ginger hair, aside from his balding crown, and the sort of weatherworn face that invites you to trust its owner.

'Heading out on a trip young fella?', he asked in a fatherly manner. I was usually reluctant to talk to strangers about my business but there was something about this man's disposition that made me open up to his enquiries, and before too long I had divulged that Luc and I were heading up north by way of Salmon and looking to do a bit of hunting on the journey.

'Well, there's a fine coincidence, I've got some business up that way myself. I'd be more than happy to tag along with you and your partner if you need a trail guide and you don't mind some company. I've travelled that way many's the time so you could say I almost know every tree and sagebrush along the way by name.'

Étienne, in those days I wasn't as assertive as you find me now and I was soon persuaded by his eloquence and kindly disposition that his services as a guide would be indispensable, and I found myself unable to refuse his offer to travel with us. We shook hands as if sealing a deal and on paying for my purchases I took him over to the livery stable to meet Luc.

Luc was just leaving the Livery as we approached, he looked at me questioningly observing my acquaintance, but before I could say anything my new companion rushed up to Luc and shaking him warmly by the hand said, 'You must be Luc, mighty pleasured to meet you, the name's Ezekiel Ramsey but you fellas can call me Zeke.' Eyeing Luc he continued, 'this fine fella's just hired me to show you the way to Salmon.'

Luc looking at me with a bemused countenance replied, 'well I don't rightly know if we can afford a guide Mr Ramsey.'

Zeke interrupted saying, 'Luc, Luc, hold on there I'm not expecting you fellas to pay me, well apart from maybe a bottle of whisky' he said with an anticipative smile, 'and sharing a campfire and a hot meal now and again? I'm going your way so I'm happy to show you the trail, it can be mighty bewildering if you stray out there.'

Luc quizzically glanced at me and said, 'well Mr Ramsey, Zeke, I guess that makes us travelling companions.'

Zeke seemed delighted by the agreement and we arranged to meet at the livery stable after breakfast the next day. Once we were alone, as I expected Luc challenged me as to why I'd enlisted Zeke. I replied imitating Luc's faint Canada-French accent, 'you're the one who said well Mr Ramsey, I guess that makes us travelling companions. You could've said no.'

Luc rejoindered. 'Yes, but so could you.'

'But Luc, did you see his face? He was delighted to have us for companions. How could anyone have the heart to say no to a man that happy? I guess he's just a lonely old trapper looking for some company. And besides, we don't know the way, and while I'm not belittling your hunting prowess, it would be good to get some fresh meat now and again and if he knows the wilderness as well as he claims to, he'll know where the game is.'

Early the next morning, we set off towards the town of Salmon with our new guide. Zeke turned out to be good company, entertaining us with stories of his time as a trapper and the adventures and scrapes he got into. He was also a mine of information on the flora and fauna we encountered along the way and we soon got used to his easy manner. He told us it would take between ten and fourteen days to get to Salmon and from there he would take us on to Coeur d'Alene by way of Missoula, arriving at Coeur d'Alene towards the middle of October from where we could strike out west for Tacoma.

We soon came to take Zeke's companionship for granted. Most mornings when we woke Zeke already had the campfire blazing and was busy preparing hot coffee and breakfast. If he wasn't around, he would soon turn up bringing back some game birds or a snowshoe hair he'd shot for our supper. At first, we would share the evening cooking, but Zeke happily took over this chore too, not finding our culinary skills to his liking. As the journey progressed Zeke sometimes took us hunting with him. Luc proved to be an able marksman and was usually able to add a blue grouse or suchlike to our food stock, but my rifle skills were so woeful that I never came close to bagging any quarry.

The weather remained hot and sunny and towards the end of our first week Zeke suggested we take a couple of days out to go hunting. Luc was keen for a diversion from our routine and I reluctantly agreed to the excursion. As we travelled towards what Zeke called Diamond Mountain Luc merrily recalled some of his hunting experiences as a youth with his brother and grandad back in Canada. We travelled for a couple of hours without seeing much in the way of game and Zeke suggested he and Luc go off and find something for our supper, while I set up camp for the night and maybe take the opportunity to get some shooting practice. It didn't take long to set up camp, and then I took Zeke's advice and fired off a few rounds at a distant target. My aim hadn't improved much since my last attempt. I got bored with my ineptitude and lay down to bask in the warming late afternoon sun and soon fell asleep. A few hours later my triumphant companions returned with a couple of jackrabbits and a sage grouse.

The next day we set off early still heading in the direction of the snow-capped Diamond Mountain. Before long Zeke signalled for us to be quiet and get down from our mounts. Telling Luc and me to mind the horses he slinked off soundlessly on the trail of some prey he had spotted in the distance. Luc and I could see nothing. We watched Zeke stealthily moving into a position where he could gain a good vantage point but not spook the animal. He disappeared from our view then a few minutes later I spotted him taking aim with his rifle. Suddenly Zeke fired and we saw an animal momentarily leap then fall. Zeke shouted for us to bring the horses and when we reached him, he was already butchering a medium sized white-tailed deer.

After the success of Zeke's deer hunt, we headed back to the trail and again settled into our regular routine. The rest of our journey passed without incident and we arrived in Salmon sixteen days after leaving Market Lake. The town of Salmon was a small place, there being around eighty or so houses and an assortment of warehouses, but it was large enough to support a hotel and saloon and a few other businesses. We decided to make an overnight stop in Salmon. Zeke, who claimed he knew the place well said we could leave our horses at John Snook's livery stable where they would be well looked after and we would be equally well catered for at the International Hotel on the corner of Main and St Charles Streets, next door to McDonalds saloon where he intended to spend the evening. We left Zeke at the livery and soon found the hotel in a narrow street lined with fine-looking, tall cottonwood trees.

The International Hotel, owned by Mr. and Mrs. Edwards, was a two story wooded frame structure with the lobby, dining room, kitchen and owner's accommodation downstairs. To save money we decided to share a room and not long after our arrival Mrs Edwards was instructing a maid to fetch hot water for our baths. Later feeling much refreshed after a good long soak I met up with Luc in the lobby and we went next door to McDonalds for a drink. Zeke was sitting at a table playing cards with some newly made acquaintances and he hailed us over to join him. His new friends weren't keen for us to join the game but were happy enough for us to buy them a drink, so after a short while we made our excuses and left them and returned to the International for a meal.

Early the following morning we set out to find Shoup's general mercantile store to stock up on our provisions as Zeke had suggested when we first arrived in town. He had insisted we needed quite a lot of basic foodstuffs for the next stage of our trip telling us it was always useful to have things to trade if we came across any Indians. He recommended we should buy some extra ammunition too as it was a least a month's travelling time to Coeur d'Alene and there weren't that many places to stock up on our journey. Zeke persuaded us we needed a mule to carry our supplies and told us he knew a fella who had one for sale at a reasonable price. He added, with a twinkle in his eye, that we should think of it as an investment because we'd be able to sell it after we'd completed our journey.

After purchasing the supplies, we headed off to John Snook's livery to find Zeke and our new mule. We didn't need to walk that far though because we saw him sitting on the boardwalk outside the Post Office, clearly the worse for his drinking session the previous night. He smiled and waved when he saw us and tried to get up, and promptly rolled over. Not daunted by his failure he attempted to stand again only to achieve the same result. It was soon obvious that Zeke Ramsey was in no state to travel. We picked him up and with his arms over our shoulders we managed to get him along the street back to McDonalds. The bartender didn't seem too pleased to see him complaining that Zeke had been responsible for bit of a ruckus, and he owed $10 for his share of the damage. We apologised on behalf of Zeke, who smiled obliviously at the bartender, and paid for the damage giving him a bit extra to bring us some coffee, pancakes and bacon. Zeke ate his breakfast and asked for another and more coffee, but when it was time to leave, he still had trouble standing never mind walking, so we steered him back to the International and took a room for another night.

The next day Zeke was up at 5am bright-eyed and bushytailed, seemingly completely recovered from his libations and eager to get back on the trail. We collected the horses and mule from the livery and made a quick detour to where Zeke had been staying to collect his bedroll, pay for the mule and set off towards the mountains and Nez Perce country. From Salmon onwards our route became more scenic as the once distant mountains came steadily closer. Zeke told us they were the Salmon River Mountains, their peaks partially covered in snow even though it was mid-September.

We soon settled into our previous routine and as the weather was still excellent made good progress. We followed the trail up to North Fork crossing the river there, and after about a week into our journey Zeke suggested we make a diversion to a good hunting spot he knew to add some fresh meat to our diet even though we still had a good quantity of the supplies we'd purchased in Salmon. Luc and I were ready for a break from our routine and welcomed the opportunity for a bit of adventure, so we readily agreed and the three of us headed off towards the Bitterroot Mountains on a little used track. Zeke said it would take us three or four days to reach his hunting spot and then maybe a couple of days more depending on the success of our hunt. As we reached higher ground forests of ponderosa pine, Douglas fir and lodgepole pine began to cover much of the land, with spruce and fir adorning the higher slopes, but occasionally this pristine forest vista was interrupted by grassy meadows and steep sun-washed, treeless slopes.

Zeke became more animated as we rode deeper into the wilderness, speculating that at any time there would be signs of good hunting. We travelled into the mountains for three days before Zeke announced we had reached his chosen hunting grounds. He told us when he first hunted in these parts the area was teeming with elk, deer, beaver, otters, big horn sheep, mountain goat, antelope, moose and all manner of game birds and that they were scarcer now but there were still plenty to be found if you knew where to look. There were also bears, wolves, mountain lions, bob cats and coyotes to watch out for.

The first day's hunting was remarkably unsuccessful with only a couple of birds for the supper pot to show for it. Zeke was up early the next morning tending the campfire and starting breakfast as was his habit, but he seemed quieter than usual and after breakfast busied himself rearranging the supplies. It was another warm day and by around 8am we were following the trail of an elk or deer. We were on foot having left the horses a mile or so from our campsite. We tracked our quarry for well over an hour before crossing a stream then after working our way up and down both banks Zeke said, 'sorry boys but it looks like I've lost her.'

We set off again back towards the horses then Zeke took us out of the trees up on to a grassy slope and finding a vantage point motioned for us to lie flat. We were now on the lookout for mountain goats or big horn sheep. I was drifting off to sleep when Luc shook my arm and pointed into the distance. Zeke and Luc had their rifles trained on a flock of big horns. Zeke whispered, 'Luc don't shoot until I say so, I've got the ram on the right.'

We watched silently as the flock came closer, they were well in range now but then something spooked them, and they scattered. Zeke and then Luc fired. Zeke's ram fell but Luc's shot missed. 'Well one will have to do for today young fella,' Zeke said as he walked towards his kill.

Luc and I went to fetch the horses so we could carry the carcass back to camp. Needless to say, we ate well that evening, and there was plenty of meat left over to see us through a few more meals.

Chapter 17

The next morning, I awoke expecting to see Zeke tending the camp fire and starting breakfast as was his habit, but today there was no sign of Zeke, and the fire was out. Something didn't feel right, and I hurriedly woke Luc who sleepily suggested Zeke had probably gone off in search of some game and had taken longer than usual to return. When I looked around, I realised that it was not only Zeke that was unaccounted for, our horses and mule had gone along with our rifles, spare clothes and most of our supplies. Luc quickly stirred and ran down the trail shouting after him, but Zeke was long gone. 'That duplicitous, double-dealing, two faced, scheming bastard' were some of the words Luc used to vent his anger.

I rummaged through what little was left of our supplies. Including some big horn meat, Zeke had left us with barely a week's rations; he had taken all the rifles and ammunition, our mule and horses, even my Boss of the Plains was gone. I was shocked that I could be so deceived by the man and even now in my maturity I still look back incredulously at my youthful gullibility in thinking he was a lonely old trapper who merely sought out some company. To this day, I still feel let down, betrayed and angry.

Although Zeke had made off with our rifles, he had left us our knives and pistols, a little ammunition, and most of our money and we still had our now useless saddles which we used as pillows. He hadn't chanced taking these as we had been sleeping with them close by, and no doubt he hadn't wanted to take the risk of disturbing us. As I said we had about a week's food supplies but Luc was sure if we were careful, we could eke this out for about three weeks and even longer if we managed to hunt some animals. So, while we weren't imminently going to go hungry, we were to all intents and purposes lost in the mountains and faced the daunting problem of finding our way to Coeur d'Alene.

While we hadn't been aware of it at the time, our detour into the mountains was clearly Zeke's plan to disorientate us and to abet his getaway. Now with Zeke gone we decided to push on to Coeur d'Alene rather than head back to North Fork. I reckoned we still needed to go North West and so leaving behind our saddles and anything else that would be no use to us, Luc and I set off in what we hoped was a north westerly direction. The terrain was quite difficult in places, and I lost count of the number of streams, valleys and slopes we had to cross, some forested and a few sun baked and almost treeless.

After three weeks our supplies had dwindled desperately low but we, or rather Luc, had a little success hunting, having shot a jackrabbit and a few days later downing a mallard. Around four weeks after Zeke deceived us, we were following a river looking for a crossing point when we heard a flock of Canada geese up ahead. Realising that this might be a rare chance to augment our meagre supplies we went chasing after them, pistols at the ready in case there was an opportunity to shoot. As we hurried along, I stumbled on a rock or a plant root and plummeted head over heels down the mountainside. As I rolled over and over trying to protect myself from rocks and other obstacles, I thought I heard a couple of shots and a faint whoop of joy just before I came to an abrupt halt and lost consciousness.

I came round to find Luc leaning over me. 'So, you've decided to wake up then, we've lost the best part of a day due to your idleness.'

I realised he was trying to mask his concern with bravado and responded in kind saying, I was sorry I'd overslept.

'When I noticed you were gone, I came back along the trail and found you out cold sprawled around a tree trunk, a few feet from the river. I tried to get you into a more comfortable position and you woke briefly, cursed, groaned like the devil and passed out again. So, how're you doin' really?'

I tried to sit up and felt pain shooting down my shoulder and through my arm, my ribs were aching, my knee hurt, and the back of my head was smarting where I'd bumped it during my fall. 'Not too good Luc,' I replied, 'but maybe after a night's sleep I'll be fine to travel in the morning.'

He passed me a canteen of water and I took a welcome swig. Luc suddenly jumped up shouting, 'damn the goose has fallen on the fire,' and he rushed over to the cooking fire to rescue the bird.

A little while later he brought me a couple of slices of warm goose breast and after our frugal repast Luc banked up the campfire and we settled down for the night. I didn't sleep well, mostly because of the discomfort from my injuries, but also because it was now late October and nights up in the mountains had turned noticeably colder.

The following morning Luc roused me from my slumber with the last of our coffee. I drank slowly relishing the warmth of each sip. Luc was waiting patiently to see if I was fit enough to travel. The ache in my arm and head had subsided so I attempted to stand but as I did so I felt a searing pain in my left knee which became worse when I tried to bear any weight on it. I tried a step, but the agony was too much, and I slumped to the ground. Luc looked at me with concern and came over and examined my leg. 'Well Mike there's no sign of a break, but your knee's quite swollen.'

'I must have twisted it in the fall,' I said dolefully, 'I don't think I'll be able to walk far anytime soon. You should leave me here and try and find your way out of the mountains.'

However, Luc would hear none of it and insisted we should stay together. As we weren't going to be moving on for a few days we needed to find a better campsite. Our present location, which was on uneven ground and quite exposed, was chosen because of my accident not because of its situation. Fortunately, Luc found a more sheltered place not too far distant and with his help and using a crutch Luc fashioned, I was able hobble there hopping on my good leg. While I was incapacitated, not wanting to waste the opportunity, Luc decided he would go foraging for food. He generally set off at day break each day leaving me to look after the campsite, always reminding me to keep my pistol ready in case of trouble. Four or five hours later he would return, often empty handed. Occasionally he brought back some late season berries or nuts, and once he returned with a scrawny rabbit, but generally he didn't get close enough to shoot at anything with any hope of success.

We remained at this site for nearly a week before we attempted to resume our journey. Our progress was painfully slow. I was able to walk aided by my crutch, but after a mile or so my armpit became desperately uncomfortable with the friction from the crutch , my good leg ached with the added strain, and I needed to rest. I was capable of travelling only three or four miles a day before I became too exhausted to continue, but I felt my knee was getting stronger. While I was resting Luc would forage for food, and we got by on any wild game, mushrooms or autumn berries he was fortunate enough to find. He was using my pistol for hunting now, his having run out of bullets. Luc only shot at unsuspecting quarry if he felt he had a reasonable chance of success as ammunition for my Remington-Smoot was low, so most days we went hungry.

It was now early November, the temperature had fallen, the days were much shorter, and we were growing weaker and gradually starving to death. We stopped speculating whether we would get out of the mountains before the winter snows set in and began to wonder if we would get out of the mountains alive. November wasn't a good time to be up in the Bitterroots especially without provisions or winter clothing. The sky was often overcast and even when the sun did break through temperatures rarely seemed to rise above freezing. We had no idea where we were or how far we might be from civilisation. Smiling grimly, Luc assured me that while we might go hungry, we wouldn't starve, for he reckoned he would be able to make some traps and fashion a fishing spear so we would still be able to hunt once our ammunition was exhausted.

We had discussed setting up a winter encampment before the harsh weather set in, and while we still had strength enough to construct it. We were following a river upstream scouting for a potential campsite when Luc who was leading the way, suddenly cried out, 'Oh my Lord I don't believe it, Mike get over here.'

I hobbled up to him as quickly as I could manage and there in front of Luc was a large chinook salmon. It was dead, but not long dead, and curiously although it was about fourteen feet inland from the riverside there were no marks on it to suggest that it had been caught by a predatory animal or bird. 'Well, here's a stroke of luck for once. It's almost like it had been put here for us to find,' beamed Luc.

'I remarked excitedly, 'it's large enough to feed us for at least three days.'

Luc picked up the fish and we continued on our quest reinvigorated by this unexpected prize. The astonishing bounty didn't end with the salmon, two days later we woke to find a brace of teal set out near our campfire.

Clearly someone was looking out for us. It was unnerving thinking that we had a mysterious benefactor who at any moment could be watching us. Luc was more disturbed by this than me and called out in vain for our donor to show himself. We started taking turns keeping watch when we slept but still didn't see anyone. Two days later on our journey we came upon a mallard which had clearly been left for us to find. It seemed that whoever was supplying us with game had no wish to harm us, but why wouldn't he make himself known to us?

We rose next morning to find a light dusting of snow covering the ground for the first time that winter. The day was overcast with a chill biting wind gnawing at us as we breakfasted on the remains of the mallard. As we prepared to leave camp, I noticed a silhouetted figure in the distance, he seemed to be signalling for us to follow him. I pointed him out to Luc, we quickly decided to take a chance and do just that. We trailed him all day, but we never got any closer to him, if we stopped walking, he stopped until we started walking again.

The next morning, the mysterious stranger was waiting for us again and we tailed him until mid-afternoon when he went out of sight on a bend in the river. We rounded the bend cautiously and were astonished to see at the head of the valley a rough-hewn log cabin, with smoke rising from a chimney, standing close to a makeshift log built barn. Walking towards us were two men one of whom was our saviour. Luc spoke quietly saying, 'they don't seem to have weapons Mike but be alert just in case of trouble.'

I heard him cock my pistol as we walked to meet the two strangers. As we came closer I could see that the taller of the two men was wearing an otter fur hat with a fur coat, unfastened, and buckskin shirt and leather trousers. He was aged about 40, of medium build, slim but muscular, with long dark hair and a beard covering the lower part of his weather-beaten face. The young man walking alongside him was about 17 years old and was dressed in the garb of a Native American.

'I don't get too many visitors out here,' the older man said, 'especially without horses, but if you mean no harm and you're willing to pitch in you're welcome to stay for a while.'

He laughed and said something to the boy in a language I didn't understand. The boy responded and they both laughed again. We've got some stuff that I guess belongs to you back in the cabin, young himíin 'ilp'ílp here found it and brought it back here, so I sent him out to look for the owner. He tracked you down about two weeks ago and he's been keeping an eye on you ever since. Looking at me he continued, 'I don't suppose you realised it, but you fellas have mostly been going round in circles.'

We followed them into the cabin. The older man put some more wood on the fire and as it blazed, removed his hat and coat and sitting on the only chair in the room, said ' I trust you fellas don't mind resting on those pelts', indicating a pile of furs in the corner.

We sat enjoying the warmth, and related how we had been deceived, robbed and abandoned by Zeke. They listened to our story attentively without interrupting.

'Well, I never met the scoundrel, but I guess he wasn't all bad, most of these rascals would have just shot you or slit your throats as you slept. I reckon you boys were lucky. I suppose you'll want to rest here a while. Truth is whether you want to stay or not, you won't get far in any case. The weather's turning for the worse and this is no place to be travelling in the winter.'

He stood up and stirred a cooking pot next to the fire. 'I'm sure you boys would appreciate a hot meal. The name's Samuel van de Beek, folks usually call me Sam or Dutch and the young fella is himíin 'ilp'ílp.'

We introduced ourselves and assured Sam a hot meal would be very welcome. A few minutes later himíin 'ilp'ílp filled some bowls and the four of us dined on steaming hot elk stew; it was the best meal I have ever tasted. Luc was the first to break the solemnity of the meal, addressing himíin 'ilp'ílp. Stumbling over pronouncing his name he said, 'himíin 'ilp'ílp, I guess we've got you to thank for the food you left for us, we would have been in a pretty bad way without your help.'

Luc asked Sam to translate for him but there was no need as we were both surprised to hear himíin 'ilp'ílp acknowledge Luc's thanks in fairly good English. It was still light when we finished eating and Sam and himíin 'ilp'ílp went out to get some wood and feed their horses. We offered to help with the wood but Sam recognising our feeble condition said we should rest by the fire. As they went out himíin 'ilp'ílp went to a corner of the room and removing a fur uncovered our abandoned saddles saying, 'I find and bring these here for you.'

Not long passed before the two men returned with armfuls of timber for the fire. Sam gave us some skins for bedding, and we made ourselves comfortable. We chatted a bit about our journey west and Sam entertained us with some stories about his trapping and some of the scrapes he'd had with bears in his early days. himíin 'ilp'ílp told us he had been visiting Sam for four or five years when his people the Nimipu (or the Nez Perce as the Europeans call them) were in the area. Sam had always been on friendly terms with the Nez Perce and had helped himíin 'ilp'ílp improve his English. He informed us his name meant Red Wolf and if it was easier for us he wouldn't be offended if we called him that. And so we passed the first night of many in the comfort of Samuel van de Beek's cabin in the mountains.

The next morning when I woke only Luc and I were in the cabin. I got up opened the door and saw two horses tied to a rail in front of the barn. Red Wolf and Sam were both preparing to leave. It was a freezing cold morning and Sam's snorting horse launched a plume of hot mist into the air. Red Wolf mounted and shouting something I didn't understand rode off slowly up the mountainside. There was a covering of snow on the pine trees and it floated to the ground as Red Wolf brushed past the lower branches. Sam spoke, 'I didn't want to wake you boys, I'm off to check on my traps, I'll be back before dark, help yourself to coffee and food if you want it, himíin 'ilp'ílp won't be back today he's gone off to the Nez Perce winter camp. If you're feeling up to it you could bring some more logs into the cabin, there's a big pile next to the barn that need chopping.'

Not waiting for a reply, he picked up his Hawken muzzle-loading rifle and rode off. We ate the remains of the previous night's elk stew for breakfast and went out to chop wood, although truth be told Luc did most of the work as my knee still troubled me. We didn't have winter clothes, so we were glad of any activity to keep us warm. Just before dark Sam returned, he had trapped a beaver and a marten, which he'd already skinned, bringing them into the cabin to dry out. He plonked the beaver's tail on the floor in front of me saying, 'boys, here's our supper.'

I thought he meant for me to cook it and began to explain I didn't know how to prepare it, when Sam laughing picked it up, saying, 'watch and learn boys.'

Étienne if you've never tasted roast beaver tail, I can heartily recommend it, it made a fine meal for us that evening. During supper, our conversation was stilted and intermittent, though by no means aloof or unfriendly, Sam wasn't an easy man to talk to until you got to know him. He often seemed to be far away, deep in his own thoughts, staring blankly into the distance and unaware of the present, then with a start he would suddenly return to the moment looking mildly perturbed. After supper in one of his more talkative phases Sam revealed he hadn't always lived in the cabin, 'for the first three or four years out here I lived with the Nez Perce in a tepee, made from buffalo hides stitched with sinews and wrapped around a frame of poles. It kept me warm in winter and cool in summer. Each year when I had the notion, I built a bit more of this cabin. I'm not so sure it's as good for keeping out the cold, that's why I covered the walls and roof with hides.'

After this revelation, the conversation petered out again and Sam busied himself mending a trap whilst he smoked his pipe.

By mid-December, my knee had recovered but it was too late in the season to contemplate resuming our journey even if we had the means to do so. Sam appeared in no hurry for us to leave, and even furnished us with skins and furs to fashion winter clothes. With Sam's help we were soon kitted out in beaver fur mittens, otter fur hats with ear flaps, leather trousers, leather moccasins and bighorn sheep coats. Sam had given up setting his traps for the winter, but there was still plenty to keep him busy, preparing skins, repairing saddles and traps, mending clothes and when the weather was suitable venturing out to seek fresh game.

Luc and I took charge of bringing supplies of timber into the cabin for cooking and heating, taking care of horses and getting fresh water from the nearby river. This wasn't such a simple task as it sounds, for as winter increased its grip, getting water changed from merely filling a bucket at the river side to using an axe to chop through the ever thickening ice to get to the water below, or sometimes when conditions were bad bringing large chunks of river ice into the cabin to thaw. As our relationship with Sam became more relaxed and we discovered he had a good sense of humour. We spent the long evenings sitting before the fire listening to his tales of trapping and time spent with the Nez Perce, but he never told us anything about his life before he came to the Bitterroot.

The days leading up to Christmas were bitterly cold. Across the valley a stream that had formerly cascaded vivaciously down the steep mountainside was now a solid sheet of ice, glistening fitfully in the occasional winter sun. Inside the cabin we made preparations for Christmas. Sam told us that he always kept Christmas even though it had been many years since he had had company on the day itself. I imagined Christmas would be similar to any other day out here in the wilderness, but I was surprised at how Sam and Luc in particular, threw themselves into preparing for the festivity. Luc decorated the cabin with spruce and larch branches and Sam surprised us all by making a special cake using some dried fruits.

On Christmas Eve the snow fell relentlessly all day, threatening to engulf the front of the barn, and we had to go out on acouple of occasions to clear the snow away from the door. In the evening the blizzard relented, and when the horses were fed and our chores were done, we settled down to a meal of left over mountain goat stew and wheat flour cakes that Sam had made for dessert. We spent an amicable evening storytelling, joking, card playing, and arm wrestling which Sam easily won. Christmas day was clear and cloudy with the temperature staying well below freezing. We all stirred early, greeting each other with a cheery 'merry Christmas'. Then as was our habit Luc and I went out to fetch logs and water and Sam tended the horses before we sat down to breakfast accompanied by coffee and a shot of rum which Sam said he kept for special occasions.

After breakfast Sam put on his black bear fur coat saying he had to go out for a while. He returned about ten minutes later with a huge haunch of mule deer under his arm. 'Merry Christmas boys hope you like venison. Can't let Christmas pass without a celebration meal.'

He deposited it on the table with a loud thud; it was quite frozen but would soon thaw in the heat of the cabin. Sam who wasn't an outwardly religious sort then said a short prayer of thanks as Luc and I stood with our heads bowed in fellowship. After the moment of solemnity Sam suggested we should have a shooting contest while we waited for the meat to thaw. Donning our winter garb, the three of us stepped outside into the translucent winter sunshine. We each took three shots at a distant target. I missed three times while Sam and Luc both scored three out of three. We moved on to a target about twenty paces further away. Luc and Sam fired again, both having three successful shots. To find the dead shot marksman of the Bitterroots , I made a target with snow on a dead tree trunk roughly twelve paces further away. Both men hit the target three times, but Sam was adjudged the winner as his shots were grouped closer together. 'Now Mike,' Luc suggested, 'let's have a competition where you have a chance of winning, a foot race.'

We decided on the finishing point, a distant whitebark pine, discarded our coats and the race started when Sam shouted 'go.' The start was incredibly competitive with Sam and Luc doing their best to obstruct and trip each other, I ran gingerly over the frozen ground wary in case I damaged my recently recovered knee. I won easily with Sam and Luc more concerned with trying to stop each other than beating me. We then engaged in a snow ball throwing contest first for distance which I won, and then for accuracy in which Sam emerged the victor, and that was the conclusion of what we later called the Bitterroot winter games.

Back in the cabin Sam prepared the haunch for cooking, seasoning it with some dried herbs and smothering it in sheep's fat before taking it to the fire to cook. He also prepared a boiled flour pudding for dessert. While the food was cooking Sam produced a well-worn copy of Charles Dickens' Great Expectations and confirming we could read suggested we each take turns reciting chapters from the story. So, we passed the afternoon in happy companionship not only reading from the book but questioning and debating about the story as it progressed. Eventually Sam announced that the haunch was ready, and we began the day's feasting. It was a fine feast and when we were sated, we settled by the fire and resumed the story of Pip and Jaggers until it was time to once more check on the horses.

When we returned Sam opened the bottle of rum and poured us each half a cupful. Relaxed by the feast and warmth and maybe uninhibited due to the rum, Sam asked how we came to be out in the Bitterroot. Luc responded first. He went on to relate how he and his brother were raised by his grandfather after their father's death. His brother being some eleven years older left the family home near Montreal and made enough money in the goldfields of Williams Creek to buy a Mississippi riverboat. 'After school my grandfather got me a job with the local newspaper and after a couple of years, I decided I wanted some adventure, so I ran away to New Orleans to join my brother, but things didn't work out so I decided to take a look out west, and I guess in a few years I'll probably go back and settle in Sainte-Rose. It's quite a simple uncomplicated story unlike Mike here.'

Sam looked at me expectantly and I hesitated about where to begin and how much to reveal. So I started from when Padraig, Bel and I were living in Port Clinton, and went on to explain about our run in with the Molly Maguires following the murder of Ben Yost, our subsequent dealings with James McParlan and the Pinkertons, Padraig's murder and my flight to the west to join Bel and escape the Kerrs. It was quite a lengthy monologue and feeling parched when I had finished, I took a gulp of rum. Sam had listened attentively and seemed somewhat touched by the horror and injustice of my story and remarked, 'It seems wherever you go there's folks who want to cause trouble and it always seems to end in people suffering and getting hurt or worse. I guess that's why I came out here after the war.'

He sat silently for a moment in contemplation and then in a quiet far away tone opened his narrative.

'It was back in '61, the Confederate forces had just attacked Fort Sumter, and people back home in Indianapolis were all fired up against the South. Me and my brothers, Tomas and Pieter, fervently followed the newspaper reports of those early days of the war, and I guess we got caught up in all the flag-waving hysteria, and at the end of July we all joined up with the 19th Indiana Volunteer Infantry Regiment under Captain William W. Dudley. Our first major fight was about a year later when we moved into Gainesville. I remember it was a fine evening. We were all in good spirits, looking forward to making camp and a warm supper, when all of a sudden, we were taken by surprise and attacked from the rear by the Confederate Cavalry, and a hail of canon fire from a battery on the wooded ridges to the north.'

'Boys, that artillery had the range so accurately that the shells were exploding directly over our heads. For what seemed like an age but was probably less than a minute we stopped, not knowing what to do, then we had the order to high tail it towards some woods. Pieter, Tomas, me and another fella stuck close together. Shrapnel was flying everywhere. We dashed for the cover of the woods and just as we got there, that's when poor Tomas was hit. He was shot through the windpipe. I was standing next to him when he fell but there was nothing Pieter or I could do to save him. He lived for a few minutes and then he died in my arms.'

Clearly upset by recalling this event Sam paused and rubbed his eyes and took a deep drink of his rum. He picked up his tale telling us how the 19th Indiana fought in the Second Battle of Bull Run, where they were part of the rear guard covering the retreat of General Pope's Union Army. They went on to fight in the Maryland Campaign, where they attacked Turner's Gap in the Battle of South Mountain and took on General Robert E. Lee's Army of Northern Virginia at Antietam Creek. 'Man, that battle was the bloodiest I ever fought in. I saw rifles shot to pieces in the hands of soldiers, canteens and haversacks were almost jumping as they were showered with bullets. Men were dropping all around me. Pieter and me stayed close throughout the battle, watching out for each other. All around us dead and wounded were dropping by the score. At times seeing the soldiers drop was like watching a fellow scything a cornfield.'

With tears welling up in the corner of his eyes Sam continued, 'I looked back to shout to Pieter to stay close and as I turned my head, I saw a bullet hit him full in the face blowing off his cap, taking the top of his skull with it.'

Sam was quiet for a few moments then sniffing loudly and rubbing his hands across his face he resumed, 'I don't know how it was possible for anyone to survive that onslaught, yet I got through it without a scratch. I reckon the Union lost around two thousand men including my brother at Antietam and the Confederate around five hundred less, with thousands on both sides maimed and wounded but I don't think either side could say they'd won. We'd stopped Lee pushing through into Maryland but there was still plenty fighting to come.'

'The rest of my war's too long a story for a Christmas day tale boys, but the kernel of it is in July '63 I was at Gettysburg where the 19th forced part of Archer's Confederate brigade off McPherson's Ridge, before withdrawing to nearby Culp's Hill, where we dug in and luckily saw little action for the rest of the battle. Later that year we were part of the Bristoe and Mine Run Campaigns. The 19th joined with the 20th Indiana

Infantry in '64 and I was with them at the Siege of Petersburg and right through the rest of the war to the battle of Hatcher's Run in '65 where I got wounded in the buttock on the second day, and by the time I was fit again the war was over and my soldiering days were done, and I was discharged from the military'

'After the war I went back home to Indiana but it wasn't the same place I'd left. My ma had died back in '59 and pa in 53, and with my brothers gone it just seemed kind of empty. I tried to settle down and returned to my old job as a tailor, but somehow I couldn't fit back into that life, and I couldn't get all the war, bloodshed and suffering out of my head. Then one day I came across a book by a fella named Henry David Thoreau, called *'Walden or, Life in the Woods,'* and it set me thinking about my life and what I needed to do. I still remember his words, *"I went to the woods because I wished to live deliberately, to front only the essential facts of life, and see if I could not learn what it had to teach, and not, when I came to die, discover that I had not lived,"* and these words kind of helped me make some sense of my turmoil. I packed up my belongings, sold or gave away what I didn't need or couldn't carry and headed west and finished up here. Well, there you have it boys that's why I'm out here in the wilderness, trying to live a simple life and escape the horrors of my war.'

Chapter 18

The Kerr brothers had spent a wearisome autumn. They had been on the move for weeks chasing after traces of Mike Wilson. They were cantankerous, saddle weary, and hungry most of the time. Hugh had become meaner than ever, if that was possible, since John had let Wilson escape from the barn at Green River. They'd arrived at Fort Bridger too late to catch up with Wilson's stage and rode on to the Evanston home station getting there ahead of it, but when the stage arrived there was no sign of Wilson or his new pal. They'd questioned the shotgun, but he and the whip had picked up the stage at Fort Bridger and hadn't seen anyone resembling Wilson. So the Kerrs trekked back to Fort Bridger and started asking folks if anyone had seen their friend Mike Wilson who was supposed to meet them there. No one at the stage depot remembered him so they visited the saloons, eating places and stores to question the proprietors and their staff. Eventually John had a stroke of luck when a storekeeper remembered selling a Winchester Model 1873 to a man that fitted Wilson's description right down to the Boss of the Plains hat. He rushed to find brother Hugh to tell him hoping it would make him a bit less riled with him for losing Wilson at Green River. Unfortunately for John, Hugh already knew having just visited the livery where a stable hand remembered Wilson and his friend buying some horses. He recalled they said they were going on a hunting trip and had probably headed out town towards Saddle Mountain.

So that same day the Kerrs set off in the direction of Saddle Mountain but found no sign of Wilson during the three weeks it took them to get there. They spent another couple of weeks searching the area and then feeling irate and dispirited they decided to head back towards Fort Bridger. On the way they passed through a neighbourhood on the Snake River called Eagle Rock but there the brothers couldn't find anybody who could remember seeing Wilson. They spent a couple of wasted weeks camped just outside of town watching in case Wilson showed up, then Hugh decided they should move on along the trail and go up to a place called Market Lake. They arrived at nightfall a couple of days later.

Market Lake was a small town, but large enough to merit a post office, a stage depot, a saloon and a general store. It was in John Adams' general store that the Kerr's got lucky; the storekeeper remembered serving 'a young fella with an English accent wearing a Boss of the Plains hat. He was talking to an unsavoury looking man who dressed like a trapper. He'd be about 45 to 50 years old, just over five feet tall, lean but with a bit of a belly. Oh, and he had a weather-beaten face with tight curly ginger hair, going grey, but balding on top.'

A rare smile broke on Hugh Kerr's face as the storekeeper continued, 'and I overheard the younger man say he and his partner were heading to Coeur d'Alene by way of Salmon. The old trapper offered to guide them there.'

Furnished with that knowledge the Kerrs arrived in Salmon just a few days before Christmas.

Ezekiel Ramsey had money in his pockets, a lot more than he was used to. He'd made quite a bundle selling Winchester rifles, ammunition, horses and other possessions he'd taken from those boys he'd abandoned in the mountains. Zeke didn't worry about them, he didn't have a conscience and anyway if he did think about them, he reckoned they were probably dead, no doubt starved or frozen and eaten by wolves or other scavengers. Still, he didn't need to worry, he'd got a warm place to stay at the livery, a load of provisions, money to spend and there was alcohol to be drunk, but Zeke hadn't reckoned on the Kerr brothers.

Salmon was a small place, but it was large enough to support a hotel and saloon and a few other businesses, and just now the Kerrs were enjoying a rare night of warmth and comfort at the International Hotel on the corner of Main and St Charles Streets, next door to McDonald's saloon. Zeke made his way along a narrow tree lined street, the tall cottonwood trees frosted with snow moved gently in the light breeze. Zeke shivered in the chill night air and adjusted his Boss of the Plains hat before stepping into the warmth of McDonald's saloon. Since arriving in town he spent a few good nights here, playing cards, winning some money and drinking some whisky. He went to the bar and ordered a drink then found a table and waited to see who might make an easy victim.

 Zeke was a good card player, but he was an even better cheat, and the playing and cheating was easier if the other fellas had plenty of drink. He soon spotted a couple of likely targets and waiting till their glasses were empty, he went over to their table brandishing his whisky bottle. 'You fellas want some company?'

Without waiting for a reply, he sat down and started filling their glasses to the brim. He introduced himself and began his usual stories about his life as a trapper and the scrapes he been in, which were tried and tested for gaining the confidence of strangers. The two men listened politely making encouraging noises at the right times and quite happily accepted regular refills without much urging from Zeke. Zeke was careful to make sure he didn't drink too much, often feigning taking a drink, and also faking becoming inebriated; he needed to keep his wits about him till later. When the bottle was nearly empty, he ordered another and asked the two men if they'd fancy a game of cards. As was his usual ploy he lost the first few hands, deliberately playing badly so they'd assume he was too drunk to think straight, then when their guard was down the serious playing and cheating began. As the night wore on, the little money the two men possessed was now placed in front of Zeke. The card game was over, but there was still half a bottle of whisky to finish and now Zeke was able to drink. Zeke who was always happy to do most of the talking, carried on with his outlandish stories as the whisky bottle emptied.

Sitting at a table on the other side of the saloon Hugh and John Kerr were definitely not drunk unlike their card playing brothers. Hugh had been studying his brothers' confrère and was convinced the man with Tom and Andrew was the trapper the storekeeper in Market Lake had described. John was certain when he saw the

Boss of the Plains hat he wore with the silver and jade shamrock pin on the band. The two men went over to join their brothers sitting either side of Zeke. Zeke seemed unnerved by their arrival and made to stand up, but Hugh and Andrew pinned his forearms to the table. Hugh spoke in a quiet but malevolent tone, 'I think you know a friend of ours, goes by the name of Mike Wilson.'

Zeke blanched and denied he knew the name. John continued,' I heard you were taking him and his partner to Coeur d'Alene.' Zeke squirmed but couldn't rise and shook his head in denial. 'So why did he give you his hat?'

Zeke declared he didn't know Wilson, asserting he'd found the hat on the trail. Hugh smiled, 'I don't believe you. John what d'you think?'

'Well, I'd say he's lying.'

'Let's take a walk outside and talk this through.' Hugh continued taking a gentler tone, 'I don't think you understand Zeke. All I want to know is where Wilson is, you tell me and you'll come to no harm. Look I'll make it easier for you. You seem to have a lot of money, you've got Wilson's hat. Wilson seems to be missing. So Zeke did you kill him in the mountains and take his things?'

Zeke could now feel Hugh's gun pushing against his ribs. Sobering up in an instant Zeke decided to tell his version of the truth.

'You got to believe me I didn't kill them. Yes, I took them up into the Bitterroots to get them lost and then early one morning I left them, but they were alive. I took all the horses so they couldn't follow me and their rifles and skedaddled, but I left them with plenty of food and their pistols. They'll be fine, there are mountain men and Indians out there; they're probably with them now. Look if you give me some paper, I can draw you a map of where I left them, it's only two days ride from the trail.'

So getting a pen and paper from the bartender, Zeke drew a map. The Kerrs had no way of knowing if it was genuine but they reckoned Zeke was too scared to cross them. John Kerr let go of Zeke's arm. Zeke realising his ordeal was over got up and hurriedly walked to the door.

'So how much did you boys loose,' Hugh asked turning to his brothers.'

'All we had,' replied Andrew.'

'You realise he was cheating,' Hugh continued, 'he was even cheating when you won just so you wouldn't get suspicious.'

Zeke hurried home to John Snook's livery stable where he was sleeping, frequently looking over his shoulder to make sure he wasn't being followed. He turned off Main Street into the dark alley that led to Snook's livery. Zeke didn't hear Andrew Kerr sneak up behind him and he didn't see the heavy log Andrew smashed down on his skull, but he certainly felt it. He tumbled to the ground moaning quietly. Andrew worked quickly rifling through the man's pockets taking back the money he and his brother had lost and another $25 besides. He noticed the silver and jade brooch on Zeke's hat, and pocketed it, he could sell it later. No one saw him, it was late, a bitterly cold evening and the snow was falling. He walked away satisfied, he'd got their money back and taught Zeke a lesson.

John Snook's stableman found Zeke the next day, lying in the alley, dead, frozen stiff and half buried in a snow drift. Folks reckoned he'd been drunk, slipped or fallen, banged his head and the weather had done the rest. Andrew Kerr didn't feel he needed to put them straight.

Hugh Kerr didn't let things like Christmas stand in the way of his plans. On the morning Zeke's body was discovered he and his brothers took the trail northwards. They spent a snowy Christmas day at a stagecoach swing station and two days later when the weather improved set off again. The respite was brief; they got almost as far as Corvallis before the worst of the winter weather called a halt on their movement. Large white snowflakes tumbled slowly, swaying erratically in the gentle breeze as they fell to earth and covered the already white landscape. As the wind increased so did the intensity of the snowfall, before long it was hard to see farther than a yard ahead. As visibility deteriorated the horses were reluctant to move forward and the brothers were obliged to dismount to guide them. Progress was painfully slow, in places the snow was thigh deep and as the blizzard raged they quickly become disorientated so Hugh decided they should seek what shelter was to hand and wait out the storm.

The unrelenting blizzard lasted four days. They sheltered as best they could in the under tall snow covered pine trees, occasionally being able to start a fire and when they couldn't they kept close to their horses for warmth. The delay was unfortunate, but Hugh was unperturbed, they'd continue on to Corvallis as soon as the winter relented. He lay shivering under his bed roll anticipating the moment of Wilson's demise; his would be a death worth waiting for. Wilson was heading to Coeur d'Alene so Hugh would go there too.

Chapter 19

It had been a hard winter. Sometimes three of four days or more would pass before the weather relented enough to allow us to go outside but we had been warm, comfortable, and well fed. I had learned a lot while holed up in Sam van de Beek's cabin. To pass the time Sam had taught us a few phrases of the Nez Perce language but Luc and I found many of the words difficult to pronounce. I fared much better when Luc offered to teach me French for which I found I had a natural flare and I quickly became quite fluent. I had learned how to repair traps, make clothing from furs, sinews and skins and could I make a passible set of snowshoes. Sam taught us how to prepare and tan hides with a glutinous emulsion he concocted from the brains of animals, a task I didn't greatly enjoy, and how to cache food and hides in the ground to prevent spoilage. By the end of the winter I was well on the way to becoming a trapper but one thing that hadn't improved was my skill as a marksman.

As the long winter's grip weakened and the weather steadily improved Sam began trapping again. He told us late winter and early spring were the best times for trapping, as the animals still had their thick winter pelts which being of better quality fetched more money. We sometimes accompanied him when he visited his traps and with Sam's approval even set a few of our own. Unlike some mountain men Sam wasn't trapping to get rich, he did it to maintain his independent lifestyle in the wilderness, so when he felt he had enough skins to see him through another year he would then only trap for food. As spring inexorably scurried towards summer, our thoughts turned to resuming our journey. Luc and I discussed our dilemma, we had no horses, no supplies and truth be told had no idea where we were or how to get to Coeur d'Alene. We hesitated to ask Sam for even more help as he had already given us so much, but we had no desire to stay in the mountains indefinitely.

We debated over a few days how to broach the subject of our departure without resolution, however one morning Sam unexpectedly settled our predicament. We'd just finished breakfast and Luc and I were getting ready to go and check on our only remaining trap when Sam remarked that Red Wolf would be arriving someday soon to help him take his furs to a buyer in Stuart, which was about ten days ride away. 'I reckon you fellas will want to be on your way then too,' he added.

Luc asked him if Stuart was on the way to Coeur d'Alene.

Sam replied, 'no, Coeur d'Alene's at least three weeks away traveling north but unless you've got a special reason to go there heading through Stuart's a much quicker route west to Tacoma.'

'No,' I said, 'we've got no reason to go to Coeur d'Alene it was just another name on our route before we ended up lost in the mountains, so it seems like we're all going to Stuart.'

During the following few days before Red Wolf returned, we helped Sam make ready his cache of furs for the journey. Just as Sam predicted Red Wolf arrived late one evening bringing with him with a couple of extra horses and the morning after the four of us left Sam's cabin and rode off towards Stuart.

Travelling through the mountains proved demanding at times but was otherwise uneventful and we reached Stuart, at the confluence of the Southfork and Middlefork of the Clearwater River, six days later. Sam was keen to sell his furs as soon as possible and leaving Luc and me outside town to set up camp, went with Red Wolf to find his buyer. They returned a few hours later. Sam had been paid more than he had expected for the pelts, and he had already purchased a load of supplies to see him through till his next trip to Stuart. He gave Luc and me some money which he said was from the sale of the pelts we had trapped, but I believe he gave us more than they were really worth. He informed us he was going back to the mountains the next morning and Red Wolf had agreed to take us on as far as Fort Lapwai where we would be able to pick up a stage going west. Sam wasn't one for goodbyes; he had already departed when we rose the next morning.

After breakfast Red Wolf, Luc and I set off towards Fort Lapwai where Red Wolf was expecting to join up with his uncle. On our journey Red Wolf voiced his concerns that there could soon be conflict between his people and settlers. He related that several Nez Perce had been murdered by settlers who had moved into their ancestral lands, causing animosity between his people and the interlopers, which had lately worsened as the authorities had done nothing to find or punish the culprits. He explained that the Nez Perce had always tried to get on with the settlers and to safeguard their land had over the years agreed various treaties with the government. Over ten years earlier some of the Nez Perce bands had consented to move to territory near Lapwai but other leaders hadn't agreed because the land offered didn't include their ancestral Wallowa valley and these bands had remained on their homelands, but about five years ago the authorities said they could stay in the Wallowa Valley. However, the government had another change of mind and was now insisting his people move to the Lapwai reservation. His uncle Joseph, who was one of the Nez Perce leaders, was travelling to Fort Lapwai to meet with General Howard where he hoped to broker an agreement that they be allowed to remain.

Red Wolf wasn't hopeful that even if an accord could be reached it would be the end of the matter, for there was a history of treaties being agreed between his leaders and the government only for the Nez Perce to later be coerced into conceding more of their land to the encroaching settlers as treaties were ignored or broken.

We reached Fort Lapwai after a week of travelling and took our leave of the remarkable Red Wolf who went off to find his uncle's camp. Within an hour of our arrival, we had boarded a stagecoach and were on our way to Lewiston where we were told we could join a stage bound for Tacoma. It was not as grand a coach as the Wells Fargo concord and only had a team of four horses rather than six, but the whip informed us that all being well, we should arrive in Lewiston the next day.

Lewiston proved to be an energetic town of wooden buildings and dirt streets nestling at the confluence of the Snake and Clearwater Rivers. The stage halted outside the Hotel De France which also happened to house the stage office. Luc and I entered the establishment and enquired about the stage to Tacoma. An ancient clerk, stooped but wiry, with long white hair and an eyeglass over his right eye, told us we would have to travel on to Waitsburg where we could pick up a Tacoma bound stage. To get there we would have to buy tickets for Dunwell's Waitsburg express stage which departed from Lewiston every Monday at 5am. Today was Wednesday. We duly purchased our tickets and then took rooms at Hotel De France for four nights for $6 each with breakfast and evening meals included. During our sojourn in Lewiston we spent our time idling around the town, taking lunch at Miss Frankie Jacob's Clarendon Restaurant, which was next door to Moxley's drug store, and then later in the afternoon, after a walk around the town or down to the river, we would invariably end up in Dan McElwe's saloon for a pre-dinner drink , taking our evening meal back at Hotel De France, which boasted a genuine Parisian chef. Étienne you may think we were being extravagant but after months of near incarceration in Sam's log cabin we were merely enjoying our freedom again and besides we had the money Sam gave us for our pelts.

At 5 a.m. on Wednesday morning Dunwell's Waitsburg express stage departed from the Hotel De France with

Luc and me and three other passengers on board. We passed the time by chatting, dozing and reading a copy of the previous day's Lewiston Teller which was proffered by one of our fellow travellers. Later that afternoon we arrived in Waitsburg stopping outside the Hanaford hotel. As we alighted, the shotgun announced that the Walla Walla to Tacoma stagecoach would be departing from the hotel at 5am prompt the next day. Étienne I shall not weary you with a description of the rest of my journey for nothing of note occurred, suffice to say that we passed through Walla Walla, Ellensburgh, Whittier and a great number of home and swing stations scattered in between, arriving in Tacoma at nightfall five days later.

Luc and I spent our first night in Tacoma at Blackwell's hotel located on Commencement Bay. I was excited at the thought of seeing Bel and a little nervous too, but the hour was late and while I had her address, I didn't know how to find her in this strange town, and besides it somehow felt inappropriate to suddenly turn up on her doorstep late at night without warning. Furthermore, I first needed to smarten up my appearance, my hair and beard were long and unkempt, and I still wore the crude fur, buckskin and leather clothes I had fashioned at Sam's cabin. I resolved to improve my shabby look before my reunion with Bel and her family.

I rose early the next day and after a well needed wash and a substantial breakfast, I headed out to find a barber's shop. As I sat in the barbers' chair and watched my untamed beard tumble to the floor piece by piece, my mind drifted back to that tragic day just over a year earlier when Padraig was murdered. In my anxiety I almost jumped out of the chair but stopped myself and settled back as the barber started to trim my wild mane. Twenty minutes later, satisfied with my haircut and shave, my next task was to get some new clothes. I soon found an outfitters store and purchased boots, woollen socks, dark blue trousers and a plain grey shirt. I was now ready to call on Bel.

Chapter 20

Hugh Kerr cursed the winter weather, he cursed his brothers because of their incompetence, he cursed the doctor in Corvallis for not being able to save his brother Andrew, but most of all he cursed Michael Wilson for he was the reason he and his brothers had been caught out for over a week in a cruel unrelenting blizzard. He would have his revenge. It had been the third day of the storm when Andrew complained of numbness in his toes, by the time they reached Corvallis ten days later it was already too late. Frostbite had led to gangrene. The doctor had amputated Andrews left foot and his right leg below the knee, but the gangrene had advanced too far and Andrew succumbed. It was another two weeks before the ground was pliable enough to bury him. John and Tom squabbled over Andrews meagre possessions, Tom claimed what little money his brother possessed, his leather belt, knife and pistol, while John commandeered Andrew's pocket watch and the silver and jade shamrock brooch on his hat band. Hugh sold Andrews horse and saddle to pay the doctor and the undertaker.

After Andrew's death, Tom and John had little appetite for continuing their brother's pursuit of Wilson, and quietly plotted to leave Hugh when an opportunity arose, but for the moment they decided to stay with him and travel on to Coeur d'Alene. Their journey took just over three weeks, it was now early March and the weather had started to improve, unfortunately the same couldn't be said of Hugh's mood. He had grown more bitter and surly since Andrew's demise and placed the blame for all the ills in his world on Mike Wilson.

Coeur d'Alene was a silver mining town situated on the north shore of Lake Coeur d'Alene, and Tom and John were quick to take any opportunity to part unsuspecting miners from their newly acquired wealth, while they waited for Mike Wilson to turn up. Hugh questioned everyone he met seeking news of Wilson, but by mid-April he hadn't shown up and there were no reports of anyone remotely resembling him being found dead in the mountains. John and Tom were convinced that Wilson must have died after being abandoned by Zeke Ramsey and tried to persuade Hugh to give up his pursuit and head back east, but Hugh was steadfast in his conviction that Wilson lived. Eventually the decision was made for them when Hugh read a newspaper report revealing that their cousin James Boyle and his fellow Molly Maguires would be executed before the end of June. The Kerrs left Coeur d'Alene the same day heading for an unwanted family reunion in Pottsville prison yard.

Hugh and his brothers reached Pottsville three days before the execution and headed for the house of their cousin Toiréasa Boyle. For Hugh this was an especially poignant time. In spite of an age difference of nearly ten years he felt closer to Jimmy Boyle than to his own brothers. As a youth his family had lived near the Boyles and Hugh had taken a great interest in his young cousin's welfare, looking out for him as he grew up and helping him through any problems, their relationship was more like uncle and favourite nephew rather than cousins. The immediacy of Jimmy's execution brought memories flooding back. Hugh couldn't believe his cousin was guilty of murder, it was that Pinkerton detective and Wilson's fault and one day Wilson would pay his dues and then maybe he would go after McParlan.

The day before the execution, Pottsville residents woke to a cold and blustery dawn with distant murky cumulonimbus clouds threatening rain, and Hugh thought aptly portending an impending tragedy. Hugh had been up early, helping to receive the superfluity of well-wishers calling at the Boyle household offering their support and help. Unable to take much more of their sympathy and small talk, he went for a walk through the town. There was an influx of visitors milling around and a palpable air of expectation. Farther along Norwegian Street he observed a newspaper reporter from New York, eagerly scribbling down the views of a group of people of Irish extraction on the forthcoming execution. Hugh found himself concurring with their belief that the trial had been unfair, the jury biased and the executions a vindictive move against Irish workers by greedy mine owners and their hired hands the hated Pinkertons. He listened but didn't contribute, he sensed the reporter didn't much care about the men awaiting execution, to him it was just another story. Hugh wanted to punch the man, but today wasn't the time. He walked on engulfed with despair and anguish, hands thrust deep in his pockets and his head bowed low.

The authorities were clearly expecting trouble for later that afternoon a neighbour came pounding on Toiréasa's door. Tom Kerr let him in and removing his hat, the breathless man blurted out, 'they've called out the militia, the Gowen Guards and the Pottsville Light Infantry are in town.'

Hugh quizzed the neighbour further, but he had no other intelligence except to say, 'There's been no trouble as far as I can tell, the town's pretty quiet, but word has it they're expecting a bunch of Mollies to riot.'

Toiréasa offered the man a cup of tea, there was to be no drinking of spirits in the Boyle household that day. The neighbour didn't stay long, he was eager to impart his news to others in the vicinity.

Pottsville's Sheriff Werner had instructed that relatives could visit the condemned men that afternoon, so Hugh, Toiréasa and her sister Rose ventured out to visit Jimmy in prison. The town was quiet. They walked slowly sometimes talking softly, often concentrating on their own thoughts. What do you say to a man who's going to be executed the next day? Their route to prison took them along Market Street past Roland Kline the undertaker's premises. Hugh glanced in Kline's window as they passed and saw six coffins on display. There was nothing unusual about that after all Kline was an undertaker, but each coffin bore an individual label and it wasn't a price ticket, it was the name and height of the six men sentenced to hang the next day and poor Jimmy's coffin was the third from the left. Hugh tried to shield the women from the spectacle, but they saw it and recoiled in horror sobbing loudly, there was nothing Hugh could do to comfort them.

It was 4 p.m. the time decreed by Sheriff Werner for all prison visitors to leave. The visit had been distressing for both Jimmy and his visitors, no one knew what to say, and at times their conversation had been stilted. Hugh told Jimmy about hunting down Wilson and how they lost Andrew. Jimmy was clearly dismayed to hear of his cousin's untimely fate, and then he smiled grimly and remarked, 'at least there'll be one friendly face to welcome me through those pearly gates tomorrow.'

Toiréasa was tearful, Rose was distraught, and Hugh was angry, but Jimmy seemed calmly resigned to his fate. They said their farewells and Toiréasa and Rose kissed then hugged their brother, Hugh shook Jimmy's hand. Jimmy remained stoic holding back his emotions. As Hugh reached the doorway Jimmy said, Hugh, don't waste your life being bitter, I don't blame Wilson, can't you find it in your heart to let the man be.' Hugh didn't reply.

Before they left the prison visitors were advised they would have a final chance to say good bye the following morning between 6 and 8 a.m. There would be a mass said for the prisoners at 7a.m. and 7.30 a.m. and the executions would take place between 10 a.m. and 3 p.m. The visitors subdued by these announcements were then escorted from the prison. Toiréasa, Rose and Hugh were in a sombre mood as they walked home. Pottsville was calm and the streets were eerily quiet apart from the patrolling Pottsville Light Infantry, members of the Coal and Iron Police, Gowen's Guards and a bevy of Pinkerton detectives, but the anticipated disorder did not happen.

June 21, execution day was showery, cool and windy. Toiréasa accompanied by her sister Rose had set off early to visit James and to celebrate mass in the prison where they were joined by the families of Hugh McGeehan and Thomas Munley two of the other condemned men . Boyle, McGeehan and Munley received Holy Communion and their last rites. Around 9.30 those invited to witness the execution were ushered to the eastern side of the prison yard where they were met by the harrowing sight of the wooden gallows. At around 10.50 a.m. the door to the prison yard opened and Sheriff Werner appeared followed by various other officials, behind them came Reverends Welsh and Beresford the condemned men's spiritual advisors briskly shadowed by James Boyle and Hugh McGeehan . McGeehan and Boyle looking smart in what seemed to be new dark blue or black suits, climbed smartly up the stairway on to the gallows platform as the two clergymen dressed in their black robes and white surplices prayed earnestly. McGeehan had red and white roses in his buttonhole and Boyle carried a large dark red rose which he continuously held to his nose as if to find some solace in its scent, as the priests completed the mortuary readings. Suddenly there was a loud shout from outside the prison and the sound of a distant shot being fired. As the Court House clock tolled the first stroke of eleven, James briefly looked up, then looked down again, as if contemplating on the crucifix he held in front of him. The condemned men kissed their crucifixes as they were taken from them, and the prison officials shook their hands. James Boyle then faced McGeehan and shook his hand, saying, 'goodbye old fellow, we'll die like men.' Hugh McGeehan silently nodded his head in reply.

Hugh McGeehan addressed the crowd seeking forgiveness from anyone he may have wronged and asked God for forgiveness and concluded by beseeching Christians to pray to God to forgive his sins. James Boyle spoke to the gathering saying 'Gentlemen that is about what I have to say. I forgive those that put me here and I hope they will forgive me.'

Hugh Kerr listened to James' magnanimous words but unlike his younger cousin he wouldn't forgive. The men's statements concluded, the guards then bound their ankles and thighs with heavy leather straps and handcuffed their hands behind their backs. As James was tethered he noticed McGeehan watching him and quietly said, 'I hope we will meet in a better world.'

McGeehan merely uttered a quiet, 'yes.'

Soon afterwards as the noose was placed around his neck McGeehan looked upwards at the overcast sky as if offering an inaudible prayer.

At ten minutes past eleven the men's heads were covered with white hoods and the priests moved away from their charges. The crowd was silent expecting more prayers, but suddenly there was a loud click followed by the sound of the trap doors opening. Toiréasa and Rose gasped and hugged each other. Hugh watched grim faced with the trace of a tear in his eye as the ropes tightened. For James Boyle death came quickly but Hugh McGeehan was not so fortunate, he suffered and struggled on the rope for four minutes until life flowed from him, the priests kneeling and praying all the while. It was a horrifying sight, Toiréasa and Rose sobbing profusely turned their heads away, Hugh did not, he was more determined than ever to seek retribution on those he held responsible for his cousin's death. Twenty minutes after the trap doors were released the two men's bodies were carried away and the gallows were made ready for the next execution.

James Boyle's wake was a time of tears and sorrow, remembrances and laughter, toasts and drinking. Hugh's brothers told stories of times they'd shared with Jimmy. Some people found comfort in remembering his life, but for Hugh memories only conjured up pain and anger. The funeral was held the next day. James Boyle was laid to rest next to Hugh McGeehan in St. Joseph's church yard in Summit Hill. After the ceremony Hugh Kerr rounded up his brothers, they had paid their respects, it was now time to move on.

Chapter 21

Mrs Blackwell, the wife of the proprietor of Blackwell's
Hotel, told me how to find Dr Harold. C. Bostwick's
residence, it being the dwelling of Elijah Collins' medical
partner and the only address I had for Bel. I found his
house easily enough and knocked at the door with some
trepidation. I heard footsteps, the sound of a bolt being
drawn back, the door opened slowly, and I was
welcomed by a middle aged maid asking if she could
help. I explained I had come from the east to call on
Miss Isabella O'Brien Sister in Law of Dr Collins. The
maid smiled, bid me enter and showed me into a
reception room where she asked me to wait. I anxiously
entered the grandly furnished room and perched
nervously on a leather upholstered chair. Presently an
elegantly dressed lady in her late twenties or early thirties
entered the room. I jumped up suddenly and introduced
myself again. 'Ah the mysterious Mr Wilson,' she said.
'We meet at last. I am Emma, Dr Bostwick's wife, and a
good friend of Bel's. She has told me much about you,
but I fear she has not heard from you for some time.'

I explained some of the circumstances of my delayed
arrival and asked if I could see Bel.

'I am sure that would indeed be possible Mr Wilson,
unfortunately she no longer lives here. Dr Collins and
family only resided here for a few weeks when they first
arrived in Tacoma, until their house was ready.'

Sensing my anxiety, she smiled at me compassionately and told me how to find Bel's residence. Emma reached out to side table and rang a bell, and presently her maid appeared. 'Agnes, would you fetch your coat and then kindly show this gentleman the way to Dr Collins' house.'

Five minutes later I was standing on the corner of Seventh Street where it joined with Pacific, where Agnes pointed out with some pride, a drug store her employer had opened a couple of years previously. She told me he had been a surgeon in the war before coming west and opening the first medical practice in Tacoma, and the drug store was just one of a number of enterprises in which he was involved. Moments later Agnes stopped outside the door of a modest sized wooden built house and promptly knocked on the door. 'This is Dr Collins' house sir,' she announced.

The door was opened by a servant boy with a mop of dark hair and equally dark eyes who gawked blankly at me. In his wake walking briskly towards the door a young Chinese maid appeared enquiring who was calling. In the lobby behind her was Bel; she instantly recognised me and ran into my arms. We embraced passionately. Too soon, she pulled herself free from me and holding back tears said, 'Oh Michael where have you been, you didn't write, we feared you were dead.' Bel noticed Agnes for the first time and looked quizzically at me. I quickly explained I had expected to find her living at Dr Bostwick's house and Mrs Bostwick had sent Agnes to show me the way. Bel thanked Agnes and charged her to return to her mistress. Bel led me to the sitting room, excitedly announcing 'Maureen, its Michael he's come back to us at last.'

Her two boys Nail and Padraig looked up and recognising their uncle Mikey came bounding over to me as if I'd never left them. Maureen promptly sent the boys away and after obligatory pleasantries, insisted I tell my story. It transpired that after they received my first letter advising them of Padraig's death none of my other letters arrived and they had assumed I was either dead or had deserted them. Not long after I had finished my narrative, Elijah returned home from morning surgery and I was obliged to recount my tale again, only this time I had a generous glass of whiskey to aid me.

I remained at the Collins' house for much of that day further relating my experiences and catching up on events since they moved to Tacoma, but unfortunately had little time alone with Bel before it was time for my departure. I promised to return to dine with them the following evening and they insisted I bring Luc, who they were curious to meet following my glowing references about him and the friendship he had shown me. I returned to Blackwell's hotel quite overwhelmed by my reunion with Bel and my return to society. Luc, who had passed his day seeking work, was eager to hear of my encounter and readily agreed to accept the supper invitation.

So, Étienne my life changed once again and here in Tacoma, Sam's log cabin, the Kerrs and Pennsylvania's Schuylkill County seemed a lifetime away. Luc and I soon found employment and we continued to live at Blackwell's hotel. I visited Bel often over the next two weeks and became acquainted with some of her friends and neighbours. It seemed to me as if our romance was undiminished by our long separation. However, one Sunday afternoon about three weeks after my arrival I had taken young Nail and Padraig out fishing while Maureen and Bel were entertaining friends and neighbours. We had a pleasant afternoon and the boys who had enjoyed themselves immensely were making fun of the fact that everyone had caught a fish except me. As we approached their home some of Maureen's guests were leaving which prompted Padraig to point out Charles Evans whom I knew to be a neighbour and a lawyer's son. 'See that man uncle Mikey,' Padraig whispered, 'that's the man Aunt Bel is going to marry.'

In that moment what had been a happy carefree afternoon became one of anguish and despair. I took the boys to their front door and instead of going inside with them I stormed off on my own in the direction of Commencement Bay. I must have walked the streets and alleyways of Tacoma for at least three hours preoccupied by young Padraig's revelation, before I eventually went back to Blackwell's hotel. I chanced upon Luc in the lobby and tried to pass him by without speaking but he would not be deflected and insisted on taking me for a drink. We entered a dimly lit saloon and sat in an uneasy silence for a while nursing our drinks, before Luc questioned the reason for my uncharacteristic melancholy. I was reluctant to talk, but with Luc's persistence I explained about Padraig's announcement. 'Mike are you sure that's what he said? You know what those boys are like. He's either trying to tease you or he's making something that was quite innocent into something else. I've seen you and Bel together and it didn't look to me like she had eyes for another.'

I agreed that I wasn't conscious of Bel acting any differently towards me since my arrival than she did back in Pottsville, but at the same time I speculated if I could be sure, seeing we'd been separated over a year, and she'd had ample time to find a new beau in Tacoma. Luc answered saying, 'that could well be the case, but if she had it certainly wouldn't be young Charlie Evans. Mike, if you've any concerns the best thing to do is speak to Bel, instead of moping around torturing yourself by musing endlessly on the situation.' He smiled playfully and concluded bluntly saying, 'frankly Mike the sooner you get this sorted out the better, for you're mighty poor company at the moment.'

It was a few days later when I next called on Bel. I had deliberated on how to best broach the subject but on seeing her, my well-rehearsed plan evaporated, and I simply told her what young Padraig had said. She smiled and looked embarrassed. I feared the worst, but she said, 'that foolish boy he's been teasing me with that for months. Charles is nothing to me, he's just the brother of my friend Lizzie. Lizzie's mother is a good friend of Maureen's, and she often invites the family round and Charles comes too. Lizzie once confided that Charlie had a crush on me and the boys overheard that's all, and since then it's been a sort of joke with them.' Bel reached out and took my hand saying, 'Charlie's a nice enough boy, but he's just a young lad, barely turned nineteen, oh Mike can't you see it's you I love.'

Needless to say, relief washed over me like a waterfall tumbling down a mountainside and then my new found tranquillity was shattered when Bel promptly chided me for ever doubting her. Étienne I won't delve into the intimacies of our ensuing conversations, but the consequence of our discourse was that Bel and I set a date to be married.

Some two months later towards the end of September, Luc and I were sitting in Saint Peter's Church on North Starr Street. Luc was doing his best to keep me calm but I sensed his tolerance was tested to the limit when I asked him for the seventh or eighth time if he was certain he had the ring. He attempted to distract me by relating entertaining anecdotes, but that didn't work. I was feeling nervous and had just asked him again if he thought Bel would turn up. 'Look Mike you've nothing to worry about, she'll be here, brides are supposed to be late.'

He attempted to divert me again by launching into another story. 'A fellow outside told me a curious thing about this church. Seems when they first got the bell, they'd nowhere to put for the church had no belfry. They puzzled about what to do, then a bright fellow had the notion to cut the top off a nearby tree, and a bunch of sailors set up some rigging and hoisted the bell up on top of the trunk.'

I was about to respond that I couldn't give a damn about the bell and the belfry when that self-same church bell began peeling to proclaim the approaching marriage of Michael Wilson and Isabella O'Brien. Then the church music signalled the arrival of the bride. I'm sure most grooms say their bride looked beautiful on their wedding day, but Bel looked particularly stunning as she was escorted down the aisle by Elijah Collins, flanked by her resplendent bridesmaids Lizzie Evans and Laura Clancy.

Three weeks after our wedding Luc left us to travel to San Francisco, while Bel and I made plans for a new life in Canada. Even though there had been no sign of the Kerrs, I was still anxious that they might turn up and find us, especially as the Tacoma Herald had published details of our wedding. Bel suggested I should share my worries with Elijah. I had reservations about seeking his assistance for although my relationship with him was cordial, I had always regarded him as a bit of a cold fish. Happily, I was to be proven wrong as in my time of need he turned out to be a true friend. Elijah agreed that it might be safer for us to move away and told me he had an acquaintance, a Mr Dunsmuir, who happened to own the Wellington Colliery at Nanaimo about 200 miles away, and he was certain if he vouched for me Mr Dunsmuir would see that I got a job there.

Elijah was as good as his word and at the beginning of November everything was organised, for not only had Elijah secured me a job, but Mr Dunsmuir's agent had also organised our accommodation. By some happy coincidence it transpired that the husband of Bel's bridesmaid Laura Clancy, was the captain of a steamship and he arranged our passage to Seattle then on to Nanaimo for which Elijah paid. By mid- November that year we were settled in our new house in Wellington, some six miles from Nanaimo. Our home, in a row of houses owned by the mining company, was a modest two roomed wooden building with a rent of $6 a month and close to the pithead. I was now once again known as Michael Wilkinson. I had started work underground at South Wellington Colliery and Bel and I were very happy.

Throughout all my travails my family back in England had never been far from my thoughts and now we were settled I found time to write to my brother John. It was many months before I received his reply.

Sleekburn
Bedlington
Northumberland
30 April 1881

Dear brother

I was both shocked and delighted to receive your letter. It took a long while to reach me as I am no longer working as a clerk in Sir James Alexander's business. You appear to have had quite an adventurous time since we parted. I trust the incidents you related about those dreadful Molly Maguires and the Kerr brothers are now behind you. I was pleased to hear of your marriage, and I hope all is well with you and your dear wife.

Much has happened here since your departure, and I am at a loss as to where to start. Firstly, our dear parents are still in good health. They had feared the worst, so were overjoyed to hear you lived still, and listened avidly while I read them your letter. They talk of you often and send their love and hope you will return home to them one day.

Speaking of returning, you will be pleased to hear there is no longer any impediment to you coming home. About two years after your departure, Alfred made away with himself. He left a note expressing his remorse for the murder of poor Mary and exonerating you of any blame.

We are living at Sleekburn now. Father is a master shifter at the pit and Sarah has four daughters. We rarely see William. He was a policeman for a while but had to quit under dubious circumstances and now he seems to be flitting from job to job and mixing with a variety of unsavoury characters.

I am doing well for myself. I am employed as a head clerk and emigration agent, but I now combine that employment by working for myself as an auctioneer. It is doubly profitable as I make money from both the sellers and the buyers, and as an agent helping people move abroad, I have a ready supply of sellers seeking to raise money from their possessions before they emigrate.

I am looking to set myself up in business as an auctioneer, printer, newsagent and stationer in Ashington in the near future. It is an up and *coming place due to the expansion of the coal mine, and I expect to develop a very profitable business as there is a large number of people and very few shops. I am betrothed to a dear lady from Sunderland, a Miss Harle, and we hope to marry in a year or so.*

I hope this note finds you in good health and I look forward to the day when we meet again.

Yours affectionately

John

Chapter 22

Wellington was a most agreeable place to live, and through working in the mine was exhausting and often dangerous, our life over the following few years was mostly good. Our one eternal sorrow was the death of our dear son Padraig Michael. He was a handsome happy fellow, born about fifteen months after our wedding, but to our great anguish he succumbed to bronchitis and died when he was just three months old. We were distraught beyond measure. Our well-meaning friends and neighbours did what they could to help, and we slowly began to accept his untimely passing. We began to prosper and started to set money aside with the intention of one day buying a small farm. Although I never spoke to Bel about it, the haunting memory of the malevolent Kerrs never left me, but with the passing of time it began to fade.

Étienne, I wish I could tell you that Bel and I went on to live happily together for many years on our flourishing farm raising a fine brood of healthy children, sadly I cannot. It was the last day of June 1884, as usual I had gone to work very early accompanied by my neighbour and colleague Harold Arnold. We were working on level four of the Number 3 shaft at South Wellington Colliery. It was hard and often dangerous work as I knew only too well having suffered burns to my legs in a gas explosion two years earlier. You may contend, as did the mine owners, that gas explosions are one of the occupational hazards to be endured if you chose a life in the mines, but miners would tell you there is much that should be done to make mines safer if owners did not put profit before the welfare of their workforce.

That morning as usual we took the cage down to level four and made our way to the coalface to begin our toil. Like most days, I was working alongside Harold, timbering up the shaft, clearing out the coal and rubble into the carts for the Chinese workers to haul away, and drilling out the holes for the blasting powder, ready for Barney McGinnes the fire boss to come and fire the shot. We hadn't been working too long when we heard Barney yell 'oh my God boys what's coming at us now!'

We had little time to react before we felt a sudden gust of wind, and simultaneously a deafeningly loud report, and a surge of heat, all the lamps went out. Anticipating what might be coming, I had the foresight to dive into a slight alcove which fortunately was just large enough to protect me from the worst of the blast. I was to learn later that Harold had not shared my luck.

Étienne, I still have nightmares about that day. Following the explosion, the mine was so dark, so unbelievably dark. I couldn't see my hand in front of my face, but I was still alive and thankfully I seemed to be in one piece. I could taste the dust and feel it stinging my eyes. My heart was beating wildly, and my body ached in so many places. I coughed frequently in an involuntary effort to clear my lungs of the insidious dust. Frantically I fought against the feeling of panic that I had been blinded. Everything was silent except for the violent ringing in my ears. This all happened in an instant but at the time it felt like an hour had passed. I calmed down and I began to think what I should do next. I shouted to see if anyone was near me. My voice sounded alien to me, like some soft far away under water echo but I heard no answering reply. I frantically fumbled around on my hands and knees looking for Harold but there was no trace of him.

I tried to stand but the blast had left me feeling disorientated and dazed so the best I could manage was to crawl along the ground following the cart track hoping that the shaft wouldn't be blocked and that I was going in the right direction for the cage. I stumbled against a body, the flesh was warm, I couldn't feel a pulse or a heartbeat, but I could feel the sticky wetness of blood. I couldn't be certain, in that stygian darkness, but I guessed it was probably poor Barney. There was nothing I could do for him. I continued following the cart tracks, occasionally they were covered with boulders and rubble, but I was able to clamber over it. I passed by two more bodies. I examined them as best I could, sadly both appeared to be lifeless.

I kept going for what seemed like hours, I stumbled over a safety lamp but thought against lighting it in case I unwittingly ignited a lingering pocket of firedamp. I noticed the air seemed to be becoming stale; I guessed the pumps wafting fresh air into this part of the mine had been damaged by the explosion. I had no choice other than to keep going but that choice was soon taken from me when I was confronted by a rock fall. Probing for an opening seemed to be futile, each time I moved a boulder some more rock and rubble fell, and I was hampered by the absolute darkness. Overcome by despair I slumped down in the darkness and head in hands sat contemplating my sorry situation. My thoughts soon turned to Bel and how worried she would be. No doubt the colliery whistle would have sounded by now and the whole town would be aware there had been an incident at the mine.

I tried to imagine the activity that would be taking place above ground with off duty miners and others rushing to help in a rescue attempt and wives and relatives anxiously waiting for news of loved ones. Then my thoughts returned to my own situation, would anyone find me, and would there be sufficient air to sustain me until they came? I couldn't say how long I sat there dwelling on these matters, but I was jolted back to the present when I thought I heard the sound of picks or shovels hitting rock. I listened carefully for a while and then I was sure my deafened ears hadn't deceived me. I shouted as loudly as I could and banged hard on a rock with a stone. Then I stopped, they had heard me and the shouted something back in reply. Someone else much closer to me also replied, somehow, I hadn't found him earlier. I scrambled over the rubble to where I thought the sound came from. He was groaning constantly now. I spoke to him trying to calm him asking how badly he was injured. He replied through gritted teeth that his legs and one arm were trapped, and he couldn't move them. He was gasping for breath, and although I couldn't see, it was clear as I rummaged around that he was almost totally buried by the rock fall.

The rescuers were getting closer, there was a chink of light in the darkness and suddenly they were through the blockage. 'Glory be there's someone here,' cried a rescuer.

The first rescuer clambered through the gap shouting to his colleagues to shore up the opening. 'Thank god we found you how many are there? Are you hurt?'

Blinking with the arrival of their light I replied, 'there's two of us, I'm fine aside from aching all over and being a bit deaf, but there's another fellow other there in a bad way.'

He went over to the injured man telling me to get off to the cage. 'We were lucky the cage wasn't damaged by the blast, fortunately both cages were midway in the shaft when the blast happened.' one of my rescuers informed me as I made to leave.

Étienne I should tell you that in the mine shaft there are two cages operating side by side, and while one goes upwards the other descends. Had one been at the bottom, timber and rubble thrown up by the explosion may have made it unworkable, and I would not be here today. Anyhow, I got to the cage, another fellow was already there with a body wrapped in a canvas sheet, and we made our sombre ascent to the surface in silence.

I helped the rescuer, a man I didn't know; carry the canvas wrapped body from the cage out into the open to be greeted by what seemed to be a scene of chaos. Adam Ross a colliery foreman, was barking out instructions and men were running backward and forwards carrying out various tasks and fetching pieces of equipment for use in the rescue. Dr Jones the colliery surgeon, was tending to some fellows with injuries, and near to where he stood were a group of concerned families and neighbours anxiously waiting for news of their loved ones. We carried the body and placed it at the end of a line of eight similarly covered corpses. Two men were making their way along the row of bodies; they uncovered the first body no doubt seeking to try to identify the deceased. That task would not be easy, for all the deceased men I saw had such horrendous injuries they would be unrecognisable even to those closest to them. As we straightened up from laying the corpse one of the men turned and looked towards the body and quickly looked away. In that moment my heart sank for the man's face was familiar, it was unquestionably Hugh Kerr.

My first instinct was to run, but I composed myself and calmly walked away following my erstwhile colleague. I was sure Hugh Kerr hadn't recognised me, he had barely glanced my way and I doubted my own mother would have known me that day, dishevelled as I was, caked from head to toe in coal dust and grime. I had intended to join the queue to seek attention from Dr Jones as I had sustained burns and cuts to my face, arms and hands in the explosion, but instead I went back down the shaft to assist in the rescue.

Before long, the rescuers found two more poor souls who had perished. I helped take them to the cage and was going to return to the surface when one of the other men asked for my assistance with a third cadaver. The corpse was horrifically burned, nothing of his facial features remained and his fingers and lower arms were almost melted away. As I helped cover the body my partner remarked that it was to be hoped the man had his tags on him or they'd never be able to identify him. The cage returned, we carried him in, and my partner left me with the deceased. The cage began its ascent and at that moment I conceived a plan.

Alone in the cage with the cadaver; I uncovered the body and went through the grizzly task of searching it for anything that might identify him. There was nothing except maybe his belt and his metal tags which I removed and replace with my own. He was probably a little shorter than me and maybe slightly fatter but given his horrible injuries I didn't think anyone would notice. By the time the cage got to the surface I had him wrapped up again, and I shouted to one of the Chinese workers to help me carry him to join the other corpses. The colliery clock was striking eleven as we lay him down next to ten other bodies. As we left, I saw the Kerrs walking over to the line of corpses intending to examine the latest cadaver, but this time they didn't get to take a look for Adam Ross sternly shouted at them to go back.

Étienne, you ask what is the significance of the metal tag? You need to know that as far as the mining company was concerned a miner didn't have a name when he was at work, he was a number. He was given a collection of metal discs, or tags as we called them, bearing this number. That same number was also on his pick and lamp, and he would place larger tags on the carts he filled with coal, and when checking in for work he had to leave one hanging from a hook. So you see, it was his identification, and it was by these tags that the dreadfully injured would be recognised.

Wanting to keep well away from the Kerrs, and anyone else who might recognise me, I remained amongst the Chinese workers, and then later I hid out in the coal yard watching the proceedings from a distance. I had been fortunate so far that the men I had encountered had been miners from other shafts or workers from outside the colliery, and none of these men were known to me. By 9.30 that night 15 bodies were laid out to be identified and 9 more men were still unaccounted for and thought to have perished. Nearly half of the 50 men and boys who went down the shaft that morning would not be going home. It was harrowing to watch as they tried to identify the dead. I glimpsed Bel, grim faced and crying, in the midst of the crowd of family and friends waiting for news. After some time, a sombre faced overman read out a list of those men who had perished and those presumed to be dead, to unbridled shrieks and sobbing from the crowd of assembled wives and relatives, friends, and neighbours.

Benjamin Jose

James Donahue

Christopher Hoskins

Thomas Pettigrew

John Winders

John Eno

John Jones

John Gill

John Frear

James Coundley

Barney McGinnes

Daniel Evans

Harold Arnold

Michael Wilkinson

Martin Lowry

John Lowry

Vittoria Berdotti

Peter Traffo

Dominico Ricono

Bettoni Lazarro

Roberto Vergino

Rosetti Vergino

Milletto Domionico

I longed to go to comfort Bel and let her know I was alive, but I refrained from doing so for fear of putting her in danger should the Kerrs be watching. I remained in my hiding place till long after the grief-stricken crowd dispersed. There were a few wives, sons, and daughters, of those men not yet recovered, still lingering at the pit head waiting for news, but Adam Ross urged them to go home saying they would be told as soon as there was any word. By midnight the colliery was much quieter, some miners were below ground still seeking their missing workmates and at least one more body was brought to the surface. It was dark now, though in Wellington in early summer it is never truly dark, and I made a move to leave the colliery and make my way home. I was careful that no one saw me and got to our row of houses without discovery.

There was a light from our doorway, and I saw our neighbour Lizzie Fiddick hugging Bel and wishing her good night. I waited a good fifteen minutes, lurking in the shadows to make certain Bel was alone, before I ventured to our door. I entered quietly, closing the door softly behind me so not to frighten Bel, but my good intentions were in vain. Bel shrieked, then recognising me despite my acquired grime, ran to me sobbing and clinging to me fiercely said 'oh Michael, Michael, they told me you were dead. Oh my I can't believe you're really here, are you hurt?'

I tried to reassure her I was quite unscathed though truth be told my face and hands were stinging from the burns I had suffered. I quickly told Bel about the Kerrs showing up and why I had allowed everyone to think I was dead.

'Bel, I don't know how, but I wouldn't be surprised if the Kerrs showing up and the explosion are connected in some way, and they were trying to kill me.'

Bel didn't want to believe that and remarked, 'that doesn't make sense Michael, how could they have possibly arranged the accident just to kill you, and how could they have found us?'

'I don't really know Bel. Maybe they'd found out about our wedding in the newspaper or got to Tacoma and stumbled on someone who told them where we'd gone.'

Bel insisted I get cleaned up and brought me some water to bathe. I told her to burn the clothes I had been wearing for there must be no trace I had returned to the house. She brought me some food and I explained to her that she must act as if I was dead, she must play the grieving widow and hold my funeral and then afterwards when it was seemly leave Wellington and go back to her sister's house in Tacoma. My notion was to leave Wellington that night and get as far away as I could before daylight. Bel wasn't enamoured by my plan and said, 'Michael we should tell the police about them, they could lock them up and we'd be safe.'

I think she knew that was purely hopeful thinking, for we had no evidence the Kerrs had done anything untoward, and no ready proof that they were here to kill me. The only option was for me to leave Wellington that very night. Bel pleaded to come with me. I didn't want to leave her but I convinced her that if she suddenly disappeared the Kerrs would be suspicious and it would only be a matter of time before they caught up with us, but if she stuck to my plan we would be free of the Kerrs for good. Reluctantly she saw the sense of my argument and eventually agreed to go along with it.

About two hours after my resurrection, we embraced a final time and said an emotional good bye. I promised Bel I would write to her as soon as I was settled somewhere, and send for her to join me, and with a heavy heart I left our house for the last time about three hours before sunrise and began walking towards Nanaimo. It was still too early to meet any miners either coming home from work or going to the mine, for although Number 3 shaft was out of action the other shafts were unaffected by the explosion and work continued as usual. My intent was to go to Nanaimo and take the first train leaving for Esquimalt. I had taken some of the savings we had put aside for the farm, but nothing in the way of luggage. If anyone did see me, I wanted to give the appearance of someone who might be on their way to work not someone running away.

The first red glimmer of sunrise heralded my arrival in Nanaimo, and I made my way along Front Street passing the familiar sight of the imperious Bastion, originally built by the Hudson Bay Company to protect the population against possible attack by natives, gleaming in the nascent sunlight. I turned into Wharf Street walking past Jackson's Fish Market and the Fire Hall with its high hose tower and hurried past the Royal Hotel and on towards the railway station. I hung around outside the station for about forty minutes waiting for the Esquimalt and Nanaimo Railway ticket office to open, and then bought a ticket for the first train to Esquimalt. Arriving at Esquimalt I headed for the ferry and crossed the George Waterway and continued on foot to Victoria. I had decided my best course of action was to take a steamer somewhere and made my way to the harbour where I happened on the ticket office of the Pacific Coast Steamship Company. There were no ships leaving that day, but I was able to purchase a birth on the SS George W. Elder which departed at 9.00 a.m. the next morning.

That night I lodged at the Carrick's Head in Bastion Street and wrote a brief letter to Bel, care of Dr Elijah Collins, telling her of my journey and my immediate plans. After a mediocre breakfast I walked along to the Victoria wharf where I boarded the SS George W. Elder a two-masted iron ship with a single smokestack. On a whim I had purchased a ticket to New Orleans, a journey that was to take over four months. I remained below deck, keeping myself to myself, until we had left Port Townsend, our first stop on the voyage, not wishing to mingle with my fellow travellers in case someone recognised me, and news that I still lived found its way back to Wellington.

The sea was fairly calm, but I was not a good sailor at first and became quite ill, but happily by the time the ship reached San Francisco I had recovered from my bout of my mal de mer. Our next port of call was Valparaiso, a thriving port in the South Pacific. Here the George W. Elder docked at the Muelle Pra wharf for three days, while mail and other cargo were unloaded, and fresh supplies and more freight taken on-board. Having grown weary of the voyage I used the time to explore the old city. There were all manner of nationalities milling about and I listened to the babble of unintelligible languages with fascination as I walked the cobbled streets in the vicinity of the Iglesia de La Matriz del Salvador.

The stopover was a pleasant interlude, and we would not make landfall again until we steamed into Montevideo, but first we had to navigate the notorious Cape Horn. I had heard all manner of frightening yarns about the violent storms we might encounter rounding the Horn, but it transpired I needn't have worried for although the swell became wild, it was nothing like the experience I'd endured on the Pennsylvania. Our passage skirting the Cape thus proved to be relatively uneventful and by the end of October the George W. Elder had arrived safely in New Orleans.

Chapter 23

New Orleans was a fascinating city made more intriguing for me by the great mingling of nationalities that had chosen to call it home, but it was not to be my final destination. For my journey's end I had plumped for a place called Port Gibson in Claiborne County up in Mississippi, for no better reason than one of my fellow passengers Henry Gladders hailed from there and had sung its praises constantly since he had joined the steamer in Valparaiso. Gladders was a large garrulous fellow with bushy side whiskers and a deep voice, who had made his fortune during and after the War Between the States. He had been considered too unfit to join the army and told me he had remained in Port Gibson for the duration, witnessing some of the military action thereabouts. He recounted that Port Gibson was the location for several brushes between Union and Confederate forces, the worst of them being the Battle of Port Gibson in '63 which saw the death of over 200 soldiers. Henry enthusiastically told me the tale of him going out with friends to watch the skirmishes from what they believed to be a safe vantage point, and of being splattered with earth and shrapnel when one of the shells landed too close for comfort, wounding him in his right arm, and taking the eye of a companion. He proudly related that many of the town's historic buildings survived war because General Grant avowed the town to be too beautiful to burn.

Gladders was now an influential member of the community, a business man with many commercial interests in the New Orleans vicinity and a host of contacts in Port Gibson. He offered to share his coach to Port Gibson with me, however I chose to remain in New Orleans for a few more days to see something of the place. Before he departed, he enjoined me to look him up at his office next door to the Port Gibson bank, if I ever needed any help with finding accommodation or a job.

Later that night in my hotel room I penned a letter to Bel. I was anxious to let her know my situation telling her some brief details of my escape, that all was well with me and that I would write to her again once I was settled in Port Gibson. So, Étienne for once events seemed to be looking favourable, I had reached New Orleans safely, I was free of the Kerrs at last and could look forward to making a new life with Bel.

After so many weeks at sea it was revitalising to be ashore again. I enjoyed doing commonplace things like walking along the street and looking in shop windows, having a drink in a bar and sleeping in a bed that wasn't rising and falling with the motion of the waves, but my new found passion was dining in one of the city's many restaurants. After the bland seaboard cuisine I had endured for months, to have a wide choice of fresh well cooked food was indeed bliss.

I had left Nanaimo with no possessions and had scarcely had a change of clothes, so after my long sea voyage I was in dire need of additional clothing and some new boots, which I remedied on a visit to the

Lacroix Clothing Emporium in Carondelet Street, enticed inside by the legend displayed across the window, 'easy on the pocket prices which defy comparison.' After a week's sojourn in New Orleans, a place I never expected to visit again, I headed up to Port Gibson. I spent a week looking for work without success, then in desperation called on Henry Gladders.

'Michael my boy,' he bellowed, as I was shown into his office by an overly deferential clerk, 'good to see you, what can I do for you young fellow?'

I explained I was having trouble finding work and wondered if he could help. 'Why certainly, what would you like to do?' he asked.

I had been seeking labouring jobs but, on a whim, I blurted out that I had experience as a carpenter, so something along that line would suit me fine. Henry promised to see what he could do and told me to return the same time the next day. I duly returned the following afternoon and was again ushered into Henry's office by the same minion. Henry Gladders was sitting by his desk on a leather upholstered chair chatting to a tall, spindly, ancient looking silver haired fellow with a long horse like face and dark rheumy eyes.

'Ah, Michael good you could come. This fellow is Horace Cleaver, an acquaintance of mine. Horace here is in the funeral business, and it just so happens he has an opening for a carpenter. What d'you have to say to that?'

I replied, 'Mr Gladders, Mr Cleaver, I'd say I'd be more than happy to accept such a job, if the pay's agreeable.'

'Michael my boy there's no need to concern yourself with such trivialities. I've already agreed a generous remuneration with Mr Cleaver, at a rate of $20 a week, and what's more my boy, Mr Cleaver here has agreed to furnish you with room and bord, until you can find something more permanent. So, what d'you say to that?'

I was delighted with the agreement and gladly accepted the offer. $20 a week was almost double what I could earn as a labourer. Mr Cleaver gave a sickly sweet smile, revealing his long yellow teeth, stood up and limply shook my hand saying, 'Son welcome to the funeral business, you can start tomorrow at 7 o'clock sharp.'

As directed, I began work the next day, assiduously watched over by the ubiquitous Mr Cleaver, who is spite of my reservations, which were largely founded on his peculiar appearance and pernickety manner, proved to be a reasonable if somewhat taciturn employer. My carpentry skills, which I had used little since my time at the lumber yard in Port Clinton, were not challenged greatly and improved considerably over the next few months, and though I was able to put aside some money I was not yet in a position to set up a home for myself and my wife. I corresponded with Bel regularly and in her first reply she described my funeral service and sombre burial in Nanaimo's Public Cemetery and assured me she was once more settled, if not content, in her sister Maureen's household.

During the voyage on the George W. Elder I had shared with Henry Gladders my ambition to buy a small farm and, five or six weeks before Thanksgiving '85 I chanced upon him in J H Gordon's mercantile store. He greeted me like a long lost son, not having seen me for six months or so, and shaking my hand vigorously said, 'Ah Michael my boy I was going to come looking for you later, but you've saved me the trouble. You're still looking for a farm I take it?'

I confirmed that I was, and he continued, 'Well Michael I've got just the place for you. A fellow I know is looking to sell out Hermanville way, its 140 acres. I've knocked him down to a keen price and he's willing to take instalments, meet me on Saturday afternoon about two o'clock, and we'll take a ride out there.' He clapped me on the back and bustled out of the store before I had a chance to reply.

Étienne, I'll not weary you with a drawn out narrative of our journey to the farm or my subsequent negotiations, suffice to say Henry Gladders and I duly met with the owner one Charles Rowey, and a sale was agreed. A week later I was the new titleholder of a 140 acre stock farm, about 3 miles east of Port Gibson. Happily, the farm was in good order and initially there was little work to do as the only livestock was five chickens and a rooster. I sent off a long letter to Bel telling her of my good fortune suggesting she should travel overland to join me as soon as the worst of the winter had passed. I continued with my job with Mr Cleaver in Port Gibson and in my spare time I occupied myself cleaning out the farm house, fixing up the barn and I even bought a milk cow. As the weeks passed, I waited anxiously for a reply from Bel and eventually I received a letter from Tacoma, but regrettably it was not from Bel.

E.M. Collins M.D.
Pacific Street
Tacoma
November 15th, 1885

My dear Michael

It grieves me greatly to have to be the bearer of such distressing news but sadly there is no kind way to tell you that your beloved wife Bel passed away on November 9th. This will no doubt come as a grievous shock to you, as it did to Maureen and I, and you will question how a fit and heathy woman in the prime of her life should come to perish so unexpectedly.

I will elucidate the circumstances that led to Bel's untimely demise. You may remember our Chinese maid Anna? One morning she didn't show up for work and Bel was worried about her as she had never so much as been late before. Bel went over to Anna's house to see what ailed her and if she could help. She was greeted by an angry mob outside Anna's home urging her and her family to leave town. (You may have heard of the actions hereabouts to expel the Chinese community from our city?) Poor Bel beseeched the mob to disperse and when Anna's father opened the door to let her in, a hail of missiles ensued. One stone hit Bel square on between the eyes fracturing the poor girl's skull. Anna told us Bel collapsed immediately and notwithstanding the barrage and abuse she and her brother ventured out and carried her into their dwelling.

A bystander recognising Bel ran to fetch me. By the time I arrived the crowd had almost dwindled away. I took her home and did all I could to tend to her. Maureen sat constantly at her bedside tending her dearly and praying for her for four days and nights, but sadly dear Bel never regained consciousness and succumbed of her injury. I can reassure you that she was in no pain during her final hours, and she passed away peacefully with Maureen and I by her side. Her funeral service was conducted a few days later by Father Hylebos at St. Leo's and many friends and neighbours attended. Maureen visits her grave daily.

Michael, I realise that there is nothing I can write to help ease your pain, but Maureen and I want you to remember you that you are family and always welcome in our home. It seems insensitive and inappropriate to mention this now, but Bel left a few hundred dollars which she told us you were saving to buy a farmstead, if you care to send me details of your bank, I will arrange for the funds to be transferred to you.

Yours in sorrow

Elijah M. Collins

I read Elijah's letter again and again trying to comprehend the appalling news. My beloved Bel cruelly snatched from me and buried, while I her husband, knew nothing of her ordeal. I was overcome by feelings of utter despair and loss and began sobbing and howling as I had never done before or since. I cannot clearly remember how I got through those first desolate weeks, but I do remember the interminable sleepless nights, the sorrow, the anger, the longing, the hurt and the grief assaulting me without respite, like furious storm waves relentlessly crashing on a beach.

Étienne, even now as I recall those grim hopeless days, I still feel an overwhelming deep sadness, a sorrow only tempered slightly with the passing of the years. I had no plan or direction in those grim days, and looking back, it seemed as if my life had been suspended. I couldn't, and I didn't want to face a future without Bel. For weeks I had no desire to venture from the farm; in fact for maybe two months, I hardly ever left the house, aside from stepping out to feed the chickens and the cow. Somehow our dream of owning a farm felt pointless now that Bel was gone, and I had no inclination or desire to stay in Port Gibson.

The loss of my dear Bel was not my only sorrow at that time, for I received a letter from my brother John informing me that our father had passed away on the very same day Elijah Collins penned his letter. I had no capacity for additional grief and continued pretty much as before. Henry Gladders and Horace Cleaver came to visit me to see why I hadn't been going to work, and although I was in no mood to receive them, I related my unhappy circumstance. They tried to comfort me, each man in his own way, and as they left uttered the customary bromides offering their help should I need it.

There must have been some small spark deep within me that drove me to persist, and as the warm days of summer advanced, I rallied for a while, sold off my livestock and a few belongings I had no further need of, and returned possession of the farm to Charles Rowey, then with just a valise and a few dollars I left Port Gibson for ever. I had no idea where I was going or what I would do when I got there, I only knew that I had to get away. I had journeyed a great deal and maybe travelling was now in my blood, but this time was different. Previously there had always been a sense of purpose, somewhere to run to, promising excitement and a future, but now I was simply running away with nothing to look forward to.

For the next year or so I wandered aimlessly from town to town, taking work where I could, a temporary handyman, a labourer or farmhand, I didn't care, it was just a job to earn a few dollars to tide me over. Sometimes I had a roof over my head, but often when the weather was good and occasionally when it wasn't, I slept in the open, and nothing seemed to matter. I never stayed anywhere more than two or three weeks. Maybe I didn't want people to get to know me and trespass on my sorrow, or perhaps I kept moving on because I was hopeful life would be better in the next place. I was always disappointed.

It did occur to me that I might go home to England, but I dismissed the notion, I wasn't in any state of mind to contemplate planning a sea voyage, and besides I reasoned with myself, would my life really be any better back in the old country.   Though I wasn't knowingly aware of it, my solitary travels were inexorably taking me south, passing down through Natchez and working my way to Baton Rouge and many other places on the way, I eventually ended up in uptown New Orleans.

Unhappily, my state of mind did not rally on reaching the city. I continued my ritual of moving from job to job, frequently changing my accommodation, and I began to find some solace in alcohol. At first a simple drink or two after work seemed to ease my mind and help me to sleep, but to my shame it did not stay like that. I began drinking more heavily; at first drinking helped me forget Bel or at least the pain of losing her, but I would awaken in the early hours and the grief was intensified, so I drank a little more from the bottle I now always kept by my bedside. After a while instead of me quitting a job, I ended up being fired after a few days either for lateness, incompetence (drunkenness) or both. As work became more intermittent and money scarce, I was often turned out of my lodgings for not paying the rent and lost most of my few remaining belongings in the process. I was finding it difficult to get new accommodation in the same area such was my reputation, so after a few nights sleeping on the streets I moved to 2nd Ward just a few streets away from Canal Street, which was then the dividing line between the American uptown and the French influenced downtown.

Chapter 24

When I woke the sunlight was bleaching in through my unshaded window. I was lying on the floor, an empty whiskey bottle clutched in my hand. At first I didn't recognise my surroundings and then I recalled I was in my new lodgings. My head throbbed and my eyes ached. I turned over pulling a crusted old blanket across my head as I did so. I wasn't ready to face the world right now, and besides, I didn't have anywhere to go, having been fired from my latest job the previous day. The oblivion of sleep was the only thing I desired. Sometime later, possibly late afternoon, but maybe early evening, I woke again, this time I had to get up to relieve myself. I trekked downstairs on unsteady legs heading for the privy in the yard. It was then that I heard a sound that took me back to my youth and happy times spent with my brother John fishing on the river, it was the sound of someone playing the cornet. I stood in the yard for a while enjoying the music, it was the first thing for months that had made me feel better. The melody was unlike anything I had heard before but all the same it was a good sound. Then it stopped, I waited for the musician to resume but there was no reprise, the unexpected concert was over. I traipsed back up to my dingy room and ate what little food I had, opened another bottle and eventually went back to sleep.

Étienne this is how sad and wretched my life had become, but I hadn't reckoned on the three Norns with their relentless weaving adding yet another piece into the tapestry of my existence. The next day or maybe the day after, or it could have been a week later I woke again to another sunlit afternoon, I stretched and groaned with the effort, and then I heard that cornet player again. Something within me spurred me to get up and seek out the origin of the music. I hurried out of the room down the stairs and into the street, running towards the source of the sound. I sprinted across Bienville Street and into one of the streets leading off it. The music was getting closer, I ran along the road looking up at the windows hoping to find the player. I felt I was close to my goal then the music stopped, I waited for it to start again, but it did not. Exhausted by my recent exertion I slumped down against a house wall, about five minutes later a young fellow of African background came out into the street. He was carrying a cornet. I got up quickly and putting on my friendliest smile asked if he was the cornet player I had just heard. He was a little suspicious of me no doubt because of my unkempt appearance and maybe because of my almost feverish interest and backed away.

'Hey I don't mean any harm son. I really enjoyed that tune just now and I just wanted to hear you play again.' I used to play the cornet myself a while back, but I never played anything like that. I was just curious how you did it.'

The boy relaxed and admitted he was the player and bringing the cornet to his lips played a few bars of the tune.

'Some folks round here don't appreciate good music,' he replied, 'it's kind of nice to come across someone who does.' He thrust his cornet towards me, saying 'here mister let's see what you can do.'

I took the instrument and played the beginning of one of the tunes old Jacob taught me, the Ballard of Jone O'Grinfelt.

The boy grinned then said, 'well mister that's a fancy tune and you sure know your way round a cornet, but you got a lot to learn about how to play.'

I replied hopefully, 'I'd be mighty grateful if you could teach me to play like you, I could pay you a couple of dollars.'

The boy smiled, probably thinking I didn't look like the sort of fellow who had a couple of cents let alone dollars, but never the less he agreed and we shook hands on it. 'The names Charles Joseph Bolden but folks generally call me Buddy. See you here tomorrow about noon?'

The next day I arrived early for my meeting with Buddy. It was the first time I had been early for anything for months. Noon came and went but there was no sign of him. I hung around for about an hour and deciding he wasn't coming I set off down the street. I hadn't gone far when a voice shouted after me, 'you sure is persistent, you coming back for your lesson? I was waiting to see how long it would take before you took off and mister you just passed the test.'

I smiled and Buddy led me up to a dingy room. 'The neighbours don't take too kindly to me playing much before noon but they seem to appreciate an afternoon concert. 'He went over and opened the windows. 'I was thinking about that tune you played yesterday, it needs loosening up a bit.'

He picked up his cornet, and to my surprise played the chorus of the Ballard of Jone O'Grinfelt, varying the tempo and adding new beats. He finished and grinning at me remarked, 'see now it's got the makings of a grand tune. Now let's hear what you can do.'

Buddy listened to me play, I was more than a little rusty, but I soon got into the way of playing again. 'Well I'll be, you're a natural cornet player, but mister what you got to do is loosen up more and improvise.'

He took the cornet from me and to illustrate his point, played Jone O'Grinfelt all the way through, in an upbeat way I'd never heard that tune played before. We met two or three times a week for the next seven months and my cornet playing improved immensely. I was nowhere near as good as Buddy, but I had got to grips with playing in something like his style. A couple of times Buddy took me to some clubs, where musicians were playing his kind of music, which he called jass, and such was his standing that he was invariably invited to play with the performing band. Buddy had a lot of demands on his time with his playing commitments and juggling the competing demands of a string of admiring lady friends. Our meetings gradually became more infrequent, and after a lesson towards the end of October Buddy told me he was going away. The band he played with had got work up in Baton Rouge and then they were going on to Memphis. 'Michael, I got something for you by way of a parting gift,' he said sheepishly, and with a glimmer of a smile on his face, going over to a cupboard, he produced a cornet. 'Here I want you to have this; it's the first cornet I ever played.'

I said I couldn't accept such a generous gift and refused gracefully, but Buddy insisted I take it, telling me that he had found it in the street, as if to make it seem less significant. Thanking him profusely we shook hands and parted. I never saw Buddy again.

Meeting Buddy and my renewed interest in music had a remarkably favourable impact on my life. It added some structure and enjoyment to my previously erratic and dismal existence and importantly it helped me curb my drinking. For the first time since learning of Bel's death I was feeling more positive about life. I had stopped constantly moving around and I was holding down a regular job, but a spur-of-the-moment action was to change my life further.

Since meeting Buddy, I occasionally visited the Rampart House Club on the corner of Bernadotte and Bienville Streets, to listen to Papa Jack's jass musicians. One evening, I was sitting up close to the band, and I became aware of some hubbub taking place. The club manager was anxious that the band hadn't started playing, and Papa Jack was trying to placate him. The other musicians were clearly uneasy, and the audience was getting restless with the waiting. Then a fellow with a cornet under his arm, and a broad smile on his face, came staggering up to the band. Papa Jack was clearly angry with the man, and I could hear harsh words being exchanged. The latecomer climbed up on to the low stage helped by a fellow musician, and the band made ready to play.

At a nod from Papa Jack the clarinettist began the opening chords of a tune and then the cornetist promptly stumbled off the stage landing in a heap on top of my table. The poor fellow was very much the worse the wear from imbibing too much drink and Papa Jack losing his patience yelled that he was fired. The manager signalled to a couple of burly fellows to throw him out into the street. His cornet lay by my feet and on an impulse, I picked it up and began to play a tune Buddy taught me, a one he called 'Funky Butt.' To my surprise the rest of the band joined in. At the end of the song the bandleader asked me if I knew any other tunes. I rolled off the names of a couple of tunes Buddy taught me, he beamed expectantly and asked me to join in.

At the end of the night as I was leaving, Papa Jack tapped me on the shoulder and asked if I'd consider joining his band. I said yes without thinking. He told me to turn up at the club at 8pm the following evening, adding as an afterthought, did I have my own cornet as the one I had been playing belonged to the fellow he fired. The next night with my freshly polished cornet and my best clothes I met the rest of the band. I can still remember their names, there was Alphonse Picou clarinettist, André Boulanger alto horn and Nicolas Brunet string bass, a couple of French speaking Creole fellows from Louisiana with little English, Tom 'Red' Brown on the Trombone, and the bandleader Papa Jack Laine on drums, Felipe Vasella a Cuban fellow who played Tuba and finally Abrah Taylor a resourceful confrère who could play banjo, piano and pretty much anything else if he had to.

George Vital "Papa Jack" Laine was well known in jass circles, and his band was in great demand. I guess I spent the best part of two years with the band. Most of the time we played clubs and bars in New Orleans, but such was the reputation of Papa Jack's band that we were booked to play all over southern Louisiana and even drifted up as far north as Baton Rouge from time to time. When we were working the money was good, we generally had plenty to eat and most of the fellows in the band were good company. The band membership frequently changed during my time, but André Boulanger and Nicolas Brunet remained stalwarts throughout and we became close friends, initially because I was the only other member of the band who was fluent in French, but Papa Jack didn't hire musicians to talk, he hired them because they could play and because they could quickly pick up any tune by ear.

There was one recurring issue that sometimes caused enmity when we played, the Jim Crow laws imposing racial segregation. Papa Jack skated round this by only recruiting lighter skinned men of colour for the band and priming them to say they were Mexicans or Cubans if asked. My time with the band was a happy period for me, and although I wasn't able to forget the pain of losing Bel, nor did I want to, at least I began to be able to live with it, and even enjoy living again. However, as so often happened in my life, as soon as my path seemed settled, something was about to occur that would change my course again.

A few weeks after Christmas '92 we were in New Orleans playing in a new venue on Bernadotte Street about half way between Canal Street and Lake Pontchartrain. We'd been booked to play there for a week, and this was our last night then we had a rare lean spell of about six weeks coming up with little or no work to speak of. We'd just finished our first set of tunes and were taking a short break when one of the waiters approached me telling me, 'There's a fellow in one of the booths near the back of the hall wanting to buy you a drink.'

This wasn't anything unusual, appreciative followers sometimes bought drinks for us or wanted to talk so I thought nothing of it and went to join the man. The back of the hall was rather shadowy, and I couldn't see his face clearly, he had a bottle of brandy on the table and poured two generous measures. I never took more than one drink a day now, and after thanking the man I took a small sip. 'That's mighty fine playing Mike,' he said, we could've stood some of that at Dutch Sam's cabin that winter out in the Bitterroots.'

I squinted in the half-light to get a better look at the fellow, could the man sitting opposite me be my old friend Luc Beauséjour? He was stouter than I remembered, his hair was thinner, and he was certainly much better dressed. Seventeen long years had come and gone since we'd parted, but most definitely it was my steadfast old friend and travelling companion Luc Beauséjour.

Chapter 25

Hugh Kerr viewed Michael Wilkinson's interment from a distance. He could see the widow Bel dressed in black weeping at the graveside and it gave him some comfort. Even though he'd seen Michael's death reported in the July 1st edition of The Victoria Daily British Colonist, Hugh had been suspicious that Wilkinson had somehow escaped the blast, but Bel was certainly acting like a grieving widow should. Nonetheless he decided to stay around a bit longer just to be sure. His brothers had gone off on a job he had organised for them in Boise Idaho, and they were not due to meet up again for three months, which Hugh Kerr thought would give him plenty of time. In the weeks following the funeral he kept watch on Bel's home, but he saw nothing untoward. Helpful neighbours coming and going, and then the widow packing up to go back to her sister's place in Tacoma. Tacoma wasn't far out of Hugh's way, so he went there too, watching Dr Elijah Collins' house just as diligently and anonymously as he had Bel's. Nothing seemed amiss, Wilkinson was truly dead, he had had his revenge, and soon he and his brothers would go after James McParlan.

***

Hugh carefully counted the money his brothers reluctantly passed over to him. He mused to himself, 'the boys have had a profitable few months, and at least if they hadn't kept out of trouble they hadn't been caught.' John and Tom waited expectantly for a share of the money. They were disappointed. Presently Hugh spoke, 'I met a fellow a few days ago who would appreciate our help. It seems there's a stagecoach hauling out of a place called Mountain Home carrying a bundle of money this fellow would like to have, and we're the boys who's going to help him get it. We're going to travel on down towards Mountain Home and meet this fellow in a week. It should be an easy couple of hundred dollars for you boys.'

The brothers grinned guilefully at each other; this sounded much more like their line of work, not the dust and drudgery of the cattle herding work they had just finished.

The Kerrs met up with George Mahoney and his partner Jim Pringle at Castle Rocks a couple of miles off the Rocky Bar trail. Mahoney was agitated, 'you boys are late I was expecting you yesterday. You weren't followed out here?'

Hugh insouciantly dismissed the other man's concerns, 'Just took longer to get here than we planned, Tom's horse lost a shoe and we got slowed down till we got it fixed. You worry too much George.'

The men sat around Mahoney's camp fire and Hugh helped himself to some coffee. Mahoney was eager to talk to Hugh about the stagecoach, but Hugh puckishly kept digressing. Eventually Hugh tiring of his game, remarked, 'So you say the stagecoach will be out here in two days, and your man told you there's gonna be over

$2000 of easy pickings on board, just waiting for us to help ourselves?'

Tom and John grinned at the thought.

'Yes, that's the story,' said Mahoney. 'I though you and your brothers might like to ride out tomorrow and see the place I reckon we can stop the coach without them being too suspicious.'

The next day the Kerrs and their new partners set out on the Rocky Bar road to view the holdup site. Mahoney proudly explained why he'd chosen this place for the robbery. 'See the trail narrows and cuts through those high rocks and suddenly comes up on that sharp bend. They can't see round there and what's more just round the bend the trail is mighty steep. So they'll be going real slow, and that's when we bushwhack them.'

'George that sure is a mighty fine plan, but what if we just arrange a bit of a rock fall on the uphill side of that bend. Then they'll stop for sure, and the money's all ours for certain' Hugh replied.

Hugh made sure Tom and John understood the plan, painstakingly going over it for the third time. Jim Pringle was on look out, he'd signal when he saw the stage coming, so all they had to do now was wait. It was a cloudless day and the men relaxed in the warm sunshine. There had been three or four riders and a wagon along the road earlier, but they'd taken cover and hadn't been seen. An hour or so after noon Jim Pringle gave the signal the stage was coming and clambered down from his rocky vantage point. Tom and John set to work loosening the rocks that they hoped would block the trail. Then the five men climbed on their horses and waited for the stage to arrive. They could hear the horses trotting slowly up to the bend and the whip calling to them to slow down even more, in anticipation of the steep slope. Hugh and his companions already mounted, drew their guns and covered their faces in readiness. As the stagecoach rounded the bend they heard the whip shout loudly, 'whoa, whoa, easy there gals, whoa! Lord, what's this come upon us?'

As the stage came to an abrupt halt, Hugh and the other men surrounded it, George and Hugh aiming their rifles at the whip and shotgun, while their confederates did likewise with the passengers. George shouted, 'throw down your guns, nice and slow and there'll be no one hurt.'

The men complied and Hugh gathered up the weapons. Tom was yelling at the passengers to come down from the coach while John kept his gun at the ready. George bellowed at the shotgun to throw down the treasure box. Hugh shot the lock to break it, and hurriedly transferred the banknotes to the robbers' saddlebags. John Kerr ordered the passengers to toss any weapons to the ground, whilst Tom briskly searched them to make sure none were foolish enough to disobey. As Tom quickly unloaded the cache of weapons, Jim Pringle was more concerned with divesting the six passengers of their money and jewellery, causing a poor woman to piercingly scream in agony as he roughly helped her shed a stubborn wedding ring. A man rushed forward to defend her, but he was quickly discouraged when Tom fired a shot which stuck the ground just inches in front of his left boot.

Satisfied the passengers had no more wealth about their person, Jim climbed into the coach and rifled through their carpet bags hoping to find more plunder. He came out smiling; he had uncovered a wad of bills and a fine silver pocket watch. Jim shouted, 'I think were about done here boys. I'd like to thank you lady and gentlemen for your forbearance and generosity.' Hugh and George had already tied the bulging saddlebags to their horses. Hugh unhitched the stagecoach horses and scared them off. The five thieves, well satisfied with their work, mounted their horses. As they were about to depart, George warned the whip to stay put for at least an hour after they'd gone. They knew the stage horses wouldn't travel too far away, but in the time it took the shotgun and whip to round them up and then clear the boulders from the trail, the raiders would be well on their way. By the time the stagecoach reached Rocky Bar and the law there raised men for a posse the robbers would have at least four hours head start over any pursuers and maybe even five if the whip had waited an hour before resuming the journey.

The bandits rode hard for three hours before they stopped. They had been travelling in the direction of Rocky Bar but deviated from the trail after an hour to avoid the expected pursuit. George and Jim were Boise men and wanted to head back that way and the Kerr boys intended to go east. They were a happy bunch aside from Jim Pringle who was looking worried; he knew one of the stage passengers and was concerned the man may have recognised his voice. George Mahoney, who had been counting the stolen banknotes, belittled his concerns saying, 'If I'd been that fellow I'd be far too troubled with saving my hide and my money, to give any heed to who might be robbing me. Anyhow boys there's close to $2,000 here, and another $600 we took from the passengers, so that's half for Jim and me and the same for you boys just like we agreed.'

'Or,' said Hugh Kerr suddenly pulling his gun on George, 'me and my brothers here could just take it all.'

Jim Pringle went for his gun, but Tom was faster, shooting and fatally wounding Jim in the chest. George went for his weapon, but Hugh fired first, killing the other man, 'no point in leaving any witnesses boys'.

Tom and John laughed as Hugh retrieved the stolen pocket watch from George's body. The Kerrs had had a good day. They travelled eastwards towards Salt Lake City, Hugh Kerr still burned with a desire to take his revenge on James McParlan but for now they needed to put distance between themselves and the bodies of their erstwhile associates. They had a good few hours lead over any pursuers and Hugh felt confident any posse wouldn't be able to track them down. Hugh decided they would spend a week or so in Salt Lake City where his brothers could spend some of their recently acquired wealth, then they would take a train east and see what pickings they could find.

Their sojourn in Salt Lake City was incident free and the three brothers boarded the Denver & Rio Grande Western Railroad train for Pueblo in good spirits. Hugh

Kerr had no particular reason for choosing Pueblo except that they'd never been in that neck of the woods before, so they were unlikely to run up against anyone who knew them. The brothers took rooms at Mrs Phillips' boarding house at 209 West Seventh Street and Hugh wasted no time securing employment for Tom and John with the Colorado Coal and Iron Company, for he knew from former experience that if he didn't keep his brothers occupied they'd most likely run into trouble. They complained bitterly about having to deliver coal six days a week, but Hugh mollified them by promising his brothers they could keep their earnings, less deductions for room and board, and by occasionally doling out a little extra from their robbery haul. However, Hugh's largesse was to prove ineffectual in keeping his brother out of trouble.

A month or so after arriving in Pueblo John and Tom discovered Pollards' Saloon on Santa Fe Avenue, a popular gambling den. The brothers soon became frequent patrons. They were consummate gamblers and although they enjoyed a drink they imbibed very little when they were gaming for they needed their wits about them as they had a penchant for not strictly playing by the rules. Hugh had warned his brothers to stay out of trouble while they were out in town. He seldom went with them and trusted John to keep their impulsive younger brother in check. His trust had held up for the two months since their arrival in Pueblo so when John and Tom went out one September night Hugh had no particular reason to feel concerned.

John and Tom were playing cards and drinking at one of the tables, with a couple of fellows who worked at the smelter yards. They had had deliberately lost the first few hands to encourage the others to wager more heavily, then the brothers had a winning streak. As their money dwindled the other men became surlier and more argumentative, but John and Tom stuck to their game plan. John was dealing a card to Tom when suddenly one of the men called John a cheating swindler, accusing him of dealing from the bottom of the pack. The fellow, who was named Bill Dodds, jumped up and grasping his chair with both hands picked it up to throw at John. Tom whipped out his pistol from his jacket pocket and pointing at Dodds shouted, 'Mister you don't want to do that,' but the other fellow jarred Tom's hand and the pistol went off. The bullet harmlessly passed by Dodds hitting the wall behind him. An onlooker grabbed the chair from Dodds, who ran for cover behind the bar shrieking 'murder, murder'.

John quickly got hold of Tom and tried to take him out of the saloon, but Tom was struggling violently, and Dodds' companion began punching John about the head knocking him to the ground. Suddenly freed from his brother's grasp, Tom began firing wildly towards the bar, seemingly not caring where his bullets went. The saloon customers were all on their feet by this time hurriedly seeking cover or running out into the street. Most of Tom's bullets hit the walls or the ceiling but one grazed the bartender's cheek, and another passed through the thin wooden bar lodging deep in the thigh of the cowering Dodds. John was striving to get free from his erstwhile assailant, but the man was tenacious and would not let go. John managed to unsheathe his knife and succeed in wounding the man in his hand and neck as he feverishly tried to break free to restrain his brother.

Pueblo's Marshal Jack Smith, who had been passing nearby, heard the ruckus and entered the saloon, his colt -44 at the ready. Seeing Tom with his gun drawn and aimed at the hapless Dodds he ordered Tom to put down his weapon. For a moment it seemed as if Tom wasn't going to comply, but he realised he was trapped and meekly surrendered throwing down his pistol. Marshal Ben Hall had arrived moments after Marshal Smith and the two men took the Kerr brothers off to Pueblo's Central Jail. A doctor arrived to examine the injured men, the bartender had a deep gash on his cheek exposing his teeth but was not otherwise hurt and Dodds, who had lost a lot of blood and was screeching in pain, was taken to the Sisters of Charity hospital where the bullet was successfully removed. A couple of other fellows had sustained some cuts and bruises in the melee and subsequent stampede, but all were expected to make full recoveries.

Hugh Kerr didn't visit his incarcerated brothers in Central Jail, but two days later at their trial he watched the proceedings and sat stern faced and infuriated as the Judge passed sentence. Tom having been found guilty of a more serious crime was given five years six months imprisonment, while John was to be locked up for three years and nine months. Both men were to serve their sentences in Colorado's State Penitentiary forty miles away in Cañon City.

Chapter 26

Colorado State Penitentiary was a three story stone building occupying twenty five acres on a hillside outside Cañon City. The prison had been built from local stone hewn from a quarry to its rear and the whole site was surrounded by a high stone wall. Hugh Kerr sat on his horse outside the Penitentiary's main gate, it was early morning, but the June sun was already warm. Hugh was waiting for John. He hadn't spoken to his older brother since his arrest three years and nine months earlier, but today was the day of John's release and Hugh wanted to be there. Soon after his brothers were imprisoned Hugh had gone home to Schuylkill County. He hadn't settled there easily, there were too many painful memories and too many old feuds still simmering, but he'd used his time well. He'd patched up some quarrels, settled some scores, made a number of useful contacts and earned some easy money. Then he'd journeyed to Philadelphia to find James McParlan. Hugh had watched McParlan for two months, but the Pinkerton man was so obsessive about his security that Hugh never managed to get anywhere near enough or secluded enough to take his revenge. As John's release date drew closer Hugh had been drawn back to Colorado and his brother, like a salmon instinctively returning to its ancestral spawning grounds, there was some force within him driving him to reunite with John.

There would be no such reunion with Tom. The Kerr brothers had been sent to the same prison, but circumstances meant they spent very little time together. There was little time for prisoners to socialise and besides talking was not encouraged. Meals were taken in silence. The prison had a strict policy of rehabilitating wrongdoers by introducing them to the benefits of hard work, so after their captivity John was detailed to labour in the prison laundry and washhouse, while Tom was ordered to join the gang of inmates who worked in the stone quarry. Work began after breakfast and by 6.30 the brothers would be busy at their onerous toil. John rarely got outside the prison walls, but each day Tom and a party of other convicts dressed in their black and white striped prison uniforms, would be marched in lock step out of the prison westwards to the stone quarry. Once there and closely overseen by armed guards as they laboured, they were tasked with breaking rocks for use in building. Aside from their usual grumbling which was always quickly quelled by the guards and an occasional injury the workday in the quarry usually passed without incident. One day was to be different.

The prisoners had been working for two to three hours, when suddenly one of them dropped his tools, and grasping his face in his hands began screaming raucously that he'd been blinded by a flying stone fragment. With the attention of the guards momentarily distracted, this was a pre-planned signal for four of his fellows to scramble for freedom. The guards were quick to react, one firing his rifle over their heads as a warning, and others shouted at the men to stop, while levelling their guns ready to shoot if the men continued with their escape. Three of the convicts stopped running almost immediately and hastily raised their hands up high in the air, but Tom forever defiant, kept on running, his eyes unwaveringly fixed on the distant mountains. The other prisoners cheered him on but made no attempt to escape. Once more a guard shouted at him to stop but taking no heed, Tom ran on. The guard aimed his rifle and fired. Tom dropped to the ground stone dead.

The prison gates opened, it was 6am, John walked out a free man. Squinting in the bright Colorado sunlight, he walked up to Hugh and gratefully mounted the horse Hugh had brought him. The two men rode side by side in silence. After about ten minutes Hugh questioned his brother, 'why did you let him do it?

John replied, 'Hugh, he didn't confide in me. It seems only some fellows in the quarry detail knew of the plan. If he'd told me I'd have tried to talk him out of it, but you know how headstrong he was?'

Far from mollified by John's response, Hugh spurred his horse to a gallop and John hurried after him. The two brothers rode east towards Cañon City, finally Hugh spoke, 'It's good to see you John. You're getting fat, must be all that wholesome prison food you've been having.'

John laughed, 'brother its solid muscle got from pounding away in the prison laundry six days a week.' Now Hugh's mood seemed to have improved John ventured another question. 'So, where're we heading?'

Hugh didn't answer immediately. 'Well brother while you were on vacation, I met a fellow in Denver who has a job for us over in a place called Creed, it's about four days ride from here, but you'll be pleased to hear were going by train.'

Feeling plucky, but not wanting to anger his frequently volatile brother, John responded cautiously, 'well I hope it's not washing laundry, herding cattle or hauling coal and iron, I've had a bellyful of that kind of work.'

Smiling roguishly Hugh replied, 'I think you'll like this job. You're gonna be sitting all cosy in a saloon playing cards with a bunch of fellows with money to lose, and I'll be there watching over you to keep you from being shot if you get caught double-dealing.'

John celebrated his release with a few drinks that night, but Hugh had him up early the next morning to get him sober enough to take the noon Denver and Rio Grande Western Railroad train into Creede. After years of enforced abstinence John was reacting badly to the excesses of the previous night. He'd had little to say during the journey but became more animated as they neared their destination. 'Some of the fellows in the pen were saying that there's a mighty lot of silver being mined in Creede and cursing their luck for being locked up instead of getting rich.'

'You've no need to worry on that score brother,' Hugh responded, 'you'll not be getting your pretty hands dirty, excepting when you're counting the money you're going to make for us from those miners.'

John was curious to know more about the work they would be doing in Creede but he was wary of questioning his unpredictable brother. Hugh would tell him when it suited him. People from all over the country and beyond were flocking to Creede. In the two years since silver had been discovered, it had grown from a town of around six hundred residents to a population of over ten thousand, with hundreds more arriving each day, all drawn there by the hope of striking it rich in the silver boom. Some were hoping to find silver, but others were looking to make their money from the influx of gullible miners and not always honestly. Hugh had found employment with one of the latter.

Creede was built in a narrow high walled canyon and the train stopped right in the centre of town. On leaving the station the brothers emerged on to Creede's bustling Main Street and Hugh headed straight for the Orleans Club. The Orleans club was housed in a timber framed building not too different from its fellows. Inside, along one wall, there was a busy bar and filling up the rest of the floor space were numerous tables and chairs, mostly occupied. Hugh went to the bar and after buying a drink asked the bartender to inform Mr Smith that the Kerr brothers had come to see him. The bartender spoke to a craggy bearded man propping up the far end of the bar and he went off upstairs. Some minutes later he returned and said Mr Smith would join them presently. He moved some fellows from a table and indicated Hugh and John should sit there and wait. A couple of minutes later a waiter brought over a bottle of whisky and two glasses telling them it was with Mr Smith's compliments.

Forty minutes later a sprucely attired man of about thirty years old came over to their table. Hugh stood up to shake his hand. 'Good to see you Hugh', said the newcomer.

'Pleasure to be here Mr Smith,' Hugh responded.

'My friends call me Jefferson or Jeff, and this is your brother?'

Hugh confirmed the relationship.

'Let's see if he's as good as you claimed?' John looked at his brother inquiringly. Jefferson Smith cut in, 'your brother told me you had a certain skill at cards, you are to put it bluntly, able to win consistently by not adhering to the rules of fair play and more importantly you do it without being observed.'

Seeing John hadn't understood Hugh interjected, 'what Jeff's saying is you're a gifted double-dealing cheat who doesn't easily get found out.'

John's expression changed to a broad smile as understanding finally dawned. Jeff sat at the table and signalled to two of his people to join them. 'These fellows work for me, now let's play cards and see what you can do.'

With Jeff and Hugh watching, the three other men started to play. They played for about an hour with John mostly successful. Jefferson finally stopped the game saying, 'well boys I've seen enough, he's a crafty player and even though I knew he'd be cheating I'm dammed if I can figure out how he did it. I guess he's hired.'

John smiled broadly and Hugh shook Jeff's hand again. 'You boys can start tomorrow. You can get rooms across the street at John Zang's Hotel, just tell him I sent you.'

Hugh and John went off to find the hotel. John was itching to ask his brother about their new employer but elected to stifle the longing for the time being. It was now late evening, but Main Street was still crowded, it seemed Creede never slept. They found John Zang's easily enough and John Kerr eagerly pounded the bell on the reception desk. After a brief moment a tall and exceedingly thin long haired man in his late twenties emerged from a door behind the desk. 'If its rooms you fellows are seeking, you're out of luck we're full to bursting.'

Hugh smiled at him serenely and said, 'that's not what Jefferson Smith told us just now. He said you'd be mighty glad to see us, and our accommodation would be waiting.'

The thin man who suddenly seemed anxious and eager to please smiled, 'ah, yes sure, sure I remember gentlemen. If you give me a few minutes, I'll just get your room aired. In the meantime please have a drink on the house.'

He produced a bottle of spirits and two glasses with lightning speed and hammered repeatedly on the bell. A burley wild eyed man arrived, and the thin fellow whispered something to him. The burley fellow ran up the stairs with surprising speed and a couple of minutes later a gangly man, looking terrified, came running down the staircase, suitcase in hand and pulling on his jacket, he sped quickly out of the front door. The thin man smiled obsequiously saying, 'gentlemen your room is ready now, number 6, left at the top of the stairs.'

Alone in their room John probed his brother. 'Your friend Jefferson, he isn't by any chance the racketeer Soapy Smith out of Denver?'

Hugh responded, 'yes he's the same fella, but I think he'd prefer to be known as an entrepreneur, and you'd do well to remember his friends don't call him Soapy. I met him in Denver a while back and we got to talking. He told me Denver had too many interfering do-gooders bringing in the law, and he was going to Creede to start over and to look him up if we wanted some work.'

'So,' said John feeling bold, 'what work will you be doing?' 'John you're asking a mighty load of questions.' John frowned thinking he'd angered his brother, but Hugh continued, 'since you're troubled, I'm gonna be toiling with the sheriff, keeping the roughnecks in order and watching over your hide.'

John almost choked with surprise, 'you're gonna be a lawman?'

'Sure, in this town the law is Jefferson Randolph Smith and Will Light the deputy sheriff is his brother in law. I'm gonna be working alongside Will taking care of Jeff's interests.'

Uncharacteristically, Hugh went on to explain that Smith had by various dubious means got hold of numerous low rent leases all along Creede's business district and set himself up as town boss, controlling much of the criminal activity, gambling dens and legitimate businesses in the town and even the law through Will Light.

John enjoyed his work, as never before; being paid to play cards and cheat without fear of retribution was his idea of a perfect career. He had a warm bed, good food and if he wanted it plenty of female company, and as the weeks passed even brother Hugh seemed more agreeable. Regrettably, the good life was destined to end sooner than John would have liked. Things had settled down in Denver and Smith had taken the opportunity to return to revive his former businesses, but before he left, he had become irked about a rival gambling den, Ford's Exchange owned and run by Robert Ford, the man who killed the outlaw Jessie James. A few days earlier, John overheard Smith vociferously complaining to a group of associates that Bob Ford had been a thorn in his side ever since he'd arrived in town, and Creede would be a better place without him. Hoping to win favour with Smith and reward for himself John conceived a plan to help his employer's wish come true.

On the night of 5 June after he'd finished work about 2 a.m. John decided to put his plan into action. Creede was still busy but most people who were out were too drunk or too busy scurrying home and paid no attention to him as he walked purposefully along Main Street. Instead of entering Zang's Hotel as usual, John walked on farther down the road until he reached Ford's Exchange. The saloon was closed, but John slipped into the shadows and waited. Twenty minutes later a light inside the building was extinguished, John waited another half hour, all remained quiet so unnoticed he picked the door lock and entered the building. He made straight for the bar and gathered up some discarded newspapers and bar cloths into a heap under the bar then soaked them with alcohol after first taking a large slug. Then he stacked up some wooden boxes around the heap and stuck a Lucifer and threw it down. The heap ignited with a sudden flash. John pleased with his work, added some wooden stools to the inferno and took another drink. It was a good blaze and it was time to leave. He left by the same door and waited for ten minutes, no one raised the alarm, it was time to head back to Zang's. When John got to his hotel flames were already billowing from Ford's Exchange and the inferno taking advantage of Creede's tinder dry wooden structures, had rapidly spread to neighbouring buildings. Before long there was a crowd of people on the street trying in vain to extinguish the blaze. The fire spread briskly, leaping across the narrow street, to engulf buildings on the other side of the road. People were banging on nearby doors to arouse anyone who might be sleeping. John bounded up the stairs in Zang's to alert his brother.

Hugh was already awake, fully dressed and packing some possessions when John burst into the room shouting, 'Hugh we gotta get out of here the towns on fire, it's almost reached the hotel.'

The brothers hurried from their room down the stairway and out into the street. The fire had spread rapidly, all the far side of the street was ablaze including the Orleans club. The brothers ran down the road to the livery stable and took two horses and saddles. Hugh released the other horses and drove them out into the night. 'Come on brother ride,' shouted Hugh, 'it's time we got out of here.'

They rode down to the creek and settled by the bankside, safe from the firestorm they left behind. Hugh had done his good deed for the day by releasing the horses; he had no intention of helping the townspeople fight the blaze. They went back to town the next morning, the whole business area was smouldering, not a building remained untouched, but away from the devastation work was already underway constructing a tent town, life had to go on. Bob Ford's place may have burnt down but the man still lived and he was already setting up his business in tent town.

Three days later, on June 8, while Bob Ford was getting ready to open his tent saloon a fellow named Edward O'Kelley came in brandishing a shotgun hollering, 'hello Bob.' Ford turned round to acknowledge his visitor. O'Kelley fired his pistol shooting Ford in the neck killing him outright. Rumours quickly spread around Creede that Jefferson Smith had ordered Ford's death but O'Kelley never disclosed why he killed Bob Ford. The brothers waited a while to see if Smith would return but he was too busy in Denver and Hugh decided it was time they moved on. John never told Hugh he had started the fire.

Chapter 27

Hugh and John followed Jefferson Smith to Denver and for the next couple of years earned a comfortable living, but their good life was destined not to last for Colorado's State Governor Davis Waite, ordered that all of Denver's saloons, gambling dens and bordellos must close. After some resistance, the Governor's ruling prevailed. Jefferson Smith's fiefdom began to disintegrate, and Smith and his associates moved on. Hugh and John no longer having employment decided to return to Creede. They were well known there and without Jefferson Smith's protection they couldn't risk going back to their old profession, so for once Hugh acceded to his brother's persuasion and agreed to go silver prospecting up in Deerhorn Creek. No one had found silver in that location, but John was adamant there was plenty of sliver to be found. They worked their claim for a season without success, and by then Hugh had had enough.

John was disappointed at their failure to get rich, but Hugh was undaunted. People were still flocking to Creede in the hope of a better tomorrow, and Hugh making outrageous assertions about its potential profitability, was able to sell their claim to an unsuspecting Easterner. In addition, Hugh sold the credulous man all their mining equipment and a couple of worn out burros for an exorbitant price, telling the naïve fellow he was getting them for much less than they were worth as the brothers had had a bellyful of mining and just wanted to sell up quickly and go home.

It was a few weeks after selling their claim that Hugh happened to be reading the Creede Candle and saw an article that immediately seized his attention, James McParlan was living in Denver having been appointed the Pinkerton's Denver Office Assistant Superintendent a year or so earlier. His old enmity returning, Hugh resolved to go there and seek his revenge on McParlan. John desperately tried to talk his brother out of the venture, but Hugh was resolute. He would have his retribution. Hugh's latent animosity towards McParlan had resurfaced and he started to regret giving up on the man back in Philadelphia. The brothers travelled to Denver a couple of days later.

Hugh began watching the Pinkerton office located in the Opera House Block at Sixteenth and Arapahoe Streets, noting the comings and goings and in particular scrutinising McParlan's routine, from his room in the St James' Hotel just across the street. On occasion Hugh would follow McParlan the short distance from his office to his residence at 1256 Columbine Street where he lived with his second wife Mary, always looking for a way to strike back at his quarry and finally avenge his wronged cousin Jimmy. For five weeks Hugh carefully followed James McParlan's every move, hoping to conceive of a way to finish him off without getting caught, but nothing came to mind. Hugh had soon ruled out trying to kill McParlan near his office, there were just too many Pinkerton detectives around. Similarly, the journey to his home was short and McParlan was scrupulous about his safety and always escorted.

Hugh then concentrated on McParland's home. It was a handsome brick built house in a quiet residential street, but it differed from its neighbours in two ways, there was a tall brick wall engulfing it, and it appeared to have iron bars on all the ground floor windows. John who had cultivated the acquaintance of a delivery man, who often called at McParlan's residence, revealed to Hugh that the fellow told him McParlan always had a gun in his hand if he happened to answer the door. He also divulged that the woman who cleaned the McParlan house had told him McParlan had an obsession about being assassinated and kept a loaded pistol in every room. It dawned on Hugh that maybe McParlan would suffer far more if he let him live, such was the turmoil of his mean existence. The more Hugh thought about it the better he liked it, yes, he'd let McParlan live with his demons, he was done with him and with Wilkinson, he could finally let his cousin rest in peace.

There was nothing to keep the Kerrs in Denver and Hugh was eager to move on. He had a hankering to go and try their luck in Wichita. The Kerrs were heading east and as they were in the vicinity Hugh decided they should take advantage of the Wells brother's hospitality. Joshua and Amos Wells were acquainted with the Kerrs from their time Creede but they didn't expect them to show up at the family farm in Kansas. Joshua Wells was three years older than his brother Amos and did most of the talking and most of the thinking for both of them, the trouble was he wasn't very smart. Back in Creede he had picked a fight he couldn't hope to win with one of Jeff Smith's associates and uncharacteristically Hugh had intervened, saving Joshua's hide. After that episode Joshua had come to look up to Hugh Kerr and was happy to do his bidding. Hugh had quickly found a use for Joshua and his brother, planting them as shills in John's crooked Three Card Monte games in Jefferson Smith's Orleans Club. While Hugh watched out for trouble, John would quickly set up the game placing three cards face down and ask if anyone wanted to try their luck. John would show the target card, the Ace of Spades, and quickly place it face down and rearrange it and the other two cards. Amos Wells pretending he didn't know John would come forward to play while they waited for a likely victim or mark to chance upon the game.

While John and Amos were playing cards Joshua would look out for a likely mark and casually begin a conversation saying how easy it was to follow the ace card and how he couldn't understand why the fellow playing didn't win more often. Then as if to prove a point Joshua would join in and win two or three games in a row before retiring and starting up the conversation again, encouraging the mark to have a go. If it went to plan the mark would step up but he'd never win, for if by chance he picked the right card Amos would bet higher, but usually so skilful was John's sleight of hand that the mark had no chance of winning. While Three Card Monte was a profitable side line for Jefferson Smith, who paid Hugh a percentage of the takings, there wasn't much left over for the Well's boys.

Joshua and Amos had never taken to the farming life, and when they left the family farm behind hoping to get rich in Creede's silver boom, they hadn't envisaged returning. Like many others the Wells boys didn't get rich. They'd lost what little they possessed in Creede's fire and almost broke had reluctantly returned home to Barclay Kansas soon afterwards. Their widowed father had gloatingly taken them back and set them to work on the farm, daily berating them for their uselessness and lack of fortitude. A month after their return, annoyed by his father's constant barbs, Amos had rallied against the old man pushing him backwards out of the hay loft. The resulting fall had damaged the old man's spine leaving him permanently housebound and barely able to rise from his bed unaided. With their domineering father incapacitated Joshua and Amos had little inclination to work the farm and let it slip into decline.

Then the Kerrs came calling. Joshua was pleased to welcome his visitors seeing their arrival as an opportunity to alleviate the boredom of life on the farm. He could soon tell Hugh wasn't enamoured by the frugality of the place so eager to impress, Joshua shared with him a plan he had concocted to hold up Atchison, Topeka and Santa Fe passenger express which passed by just a couple of miles from the farm. Joshua had picked out a location for the robbery, a place where the train slowed to take a sharp bend in the track, and where he thought it would be easy for two or three men to climb on board while the fourth rode alongside with their horses. Joshua had heard that the express car generally carried a lot of money on the last Wednesday of the month, which just happened to be the following

Wednesday. Train robbing was a new venture for Hugh Kerr, and after viewing the location he cautiously ruminated over Joshua's scheme before concluding that with a couple of tweaks it might just work.

Hugh wasn't sure the train would be travelling slowly enough for the gang to ride alongside and climb aboard so he had come up with an idea to make sure they could slow down it. Shortly after midnight on the Wednesday morning before the robbery, the Wells brothers broke into the Atchison, Topeka and Santa Fe Railway's tool-house in Barclay to get hold of some sledgehammers, picks and spike pullers. Their task was successful, and they rode out of town for two miles or so and met up with Hugh and John Kerr near the hold-up spot. A freight train due forty minutes before the 4 a.m. passenger express, steamed by on time, then the Wells-Kerr gang quickly set to work. The four men walked along the track to a point where it met a sharp curve on a ten feet high embankment, and with much effort pulled the spikes from one of the rails, then they removed the fish plate joining it to the next length of track and shifted the rail out of place. They could hear the train approaching in the distance and hid well away from the track so they couldn't be seen. As expected, the train slowed slightly as it approached the curve and when it reached the point where the rail had been moved there was a mighty crash as the engine slew down the embankment taking the passenger cars with it. The leading cars tumbled off the track one falling on top of another. The would-be train robbers were horrified, many of the crew and passengers had surely been killed. They had expected the train would merely be derailed and come to an abrupt halt in the ballast, they hadn't anticipated the carnage that now confronted them. Without a word the four men took to their horses and rode off back to the farm, stunned by what they had done.

Back at the farmhouse Joshua Wells was panicking, clearly still shaken by the harrowing experience. He supposed the Osage County sheriff and an armed posse would be riding in to arrest them at any moment and shouted at his brother to pack up and get ready to leave. Hugh and John managed to calm him by convincing him that no one could have seen them and that there was no evidence to associate them with the train crash. For the next two days the Wells boys set about tending the farm as never before and there was no sign of the sheriff. Hugh wasn't greatly concerned that they'd be discovered, but to put his mind at ease he decided to ride into Barclay, telling the Wells boys he was getting some much needed provisions, but in reality, seeking any information on the derailment and possible pursuit of the perpetrators.

Arriving in Barclay in the Wells' buggy, he pulled up outside the general store keeping his ears open for any news. It wasn't long before he was rewarded; as he waited at the counter, a woman in front of him struck up a conversation with the storekeeper. The fireman, engineer and two others had been killed and twenty five people had been injured. The store keeper said that the sheriff believed the train had been derailed by robbers, but they rode off without getting the payroll. Hugh interjected asking if they knew who they were. The store keeper said he didn't know but the sheriff was out with a posse looking for clues. Hugh completed his purchases and headed back to the farm.

Joshua was quick to ask if Hugh had picked up any news in town. Hugh related his conversation with the storekeeper adding that it looked like they were in the clear. That evening Hugh persuaded Joshua it was best if he and John move on so as not to draw unwanted attention to the brothers, saying that strangers are often the first to come under suspicion when there is a crime in the neighbourhood. The Kerrs left Barclay early the following morning, telling Joshua and Amos to carry out their business as normal. In the circumstances Hugh decided they wouldn't go to Wichita, they would ride to Kansas City and from there catch a train to St Louis, where Hugh Kerr reckoned there'd be plenty of opportunity to make a few dishonest dollars.

Chapter 28

I was taken aback at meeting Luc out of the blue like this, the last time I'd heard from him he was in San Francisco. 'It's good to see you Mike, we've got a lot of catching up to do,' he said standing up to shake my hand, both of us beaming like schoolboys.

I replied, 'Luc, we certainly do but I haven't got long to talk right now, I've another set to play and I'll have to get back to the band soon.'

We finished our drinks over some small talk and agreed to meet at the close of the show. At the end of the evening Papa Jack paid off the band and gave us instructions for us to meet up back at the Rampart Club for a rehearsal in a month. Luc was waiting for me, 'You ready for that chinwag now,' he asked, 'I suspect it might be a long night, how about you come back home with me, it you've got nothing better to do?'

I agreed and we emerged onto a chilly Bernadotte Street where almost immediately a horse drawn Hanson cab came to a halt outside the club. The driver quickly climbed down and opened the door for Luc and me to enter. Once inside Luc called out for the driver to take him home and we trotted off turning into a tree lined Canal Street, passing the renowned Krauss store, heading towards the river. The coach stopped on the waterside in front of a Mississippi Riverboat. Luc gestured towards the steamer proclaiming, 'Mike, this is home.'

In the darkness I couldn't fully take in the riverboat, other than to make out its outline with its twin smokestacks and white painted sidewheel. Luc ushered me up the gangway, and acknowledging a crewman, steered me into his luxuriously ornate stateroom. We sat on red velvet covered chairs. Luc lit a cigar and offering one to me, remarked, 'I guess you're thinking this is a lot different from Sam's log cabin?' I agreed that it certainly was and asked Luc if he owned it. 'Well Michael that's a sore point. The fact is that it was left to me by my late brother a few years back, but the problem was he was in debt to his bank and things haven't got much better since, so I guess you could say truthfully it mostly belongs to the bank and various other creditors. However, I have plans in hand to change that, but enough about me, tell me what you're doing in this neck of the woods and where is the lovely Bel?'

I still had difficulty talking about Bel, but Luc had a way of putting me at ease and soon the whole unhappy story came tumbling out. Luc, who was clearly shocked by my telling of Bels' demise, offered his sincere commiserations and I went on to describe how I arrived in my present situation. 'Well, you've sure enough had more than your share of bad fortune my friend,' Luc remarked. We chatted for a while then Luc declared, 'I've a proposition to put your way, if you're interested,'

I nodded and Luc continued, 'in three days' time I'm taking the old Jacques Pinsoneau here up to Vicksburg. There's a fellow up there who's mighty interested in buying this boat, and if I can sell it all my money worries will be lifted. I need to make a good impression, and I've had the crew busy fixing it up and painting so it looks in good shape, but I reckon to hook him in I could do with adding some atmosphere, so what about you and some of your fellows from the band coming along for the ride. Playing in the saloon for their keep, all free accommodation and food and some pay at the end of it? And it would give us a chance to catch up at our leisure. I guess the ride there and back will take a couple of weeks. Well what d'you think?'

I didn't need time to think and said yes straight away, adding that I was sure some of the band would be pleased to come along. 'I'll see who I can persuade tomorrow, but I'd have to speak to Papa Jack first to check he has no objection.' With that issue settled we conversed long into the small hours until finally we said goodnight and Luc showed me to a stateroom.

The next morning a steward arrived with my breakfast and a message that Mr Beauséjour would be along presently to show me round the Jacques Pinsoneau. Some twenty minutes later Luc arrived. He was wearing a well cut dark blue suit and seeing him in the daylight I noticed his appearance had changed slightly in the last seventeen years, his hair was darker than I remembered, thinning slightly, but neatly cut and combed back, he sported a thin moustache and he'd gained at least sixty pounds, but he still exuded the same sense of humour and undimmed optimism. 'Good morning Michael, ready for the grand tour?' he asked, gesturing that I follow him out on to the deck.

As I tailed Luc down to the main deck, which is the lowest deck in a steamboat, he informed me that the

Jacques Pinsoneau was a wooden hull sidewheel packet boat weighing some 1,417 tons, having four boilers and two engines. Those four boilers produced 2,300 horsepower. The boat could accommodate 8,400 bales of cotton and sat only 6 feet 9 inches deep in the water when fully laden. I couldn't help but notice there were no cotton bales in the hold. Luc remarked, 'there's my problem Mike since the war most of the freight goes by rail. It's cheaper and quicker and the railways can carry freight inland well away from the river. To stay competitive, I've had to keep my charges down, and I've still got to pay the crew, and there's high insurance costs so my profits are thin.'

We continued the tour, heading up to the boiler deck. 'We've got fifty-four luxury staterooms taking up to a hundred and eight first class passengers and as many deck passengers as we can cram in, but trouble is a lot of them are using the railroad too.' We reached the Pinsoneau's saloon. Luc continued, 'here's where you and your fellows will be playing, I hope it's agreeable. If you need it there's a grand piano you can use over there.'

Étienne the saloon was magnificent; it must have been two hundred feet long and at least sixteen feet wide. It had expensive carpets and curtains, and highly polished mirrors and decorative paintings adorned the walls. The wood carved ceiling was a work of art itself. It was painted white and highlighted with gold tinted acorns and oak leaves, with the occasional cherub and elegant cut-glass chandeliers thrown in for good measure. In addition to the saloon Luc told me the Pinsoneau had a ballroom, four bridal suites, a bar and even a barber's shop.

We moved on up to the Hurricane deck and finally settled in the Pilot House facing the twin red painted smokestacks. As the river boat was at its moorings the Pilot House was deserted and we sat and talked without fear of being overheard. Luc confided that he was deep in debt owing more than $500,000 and selling the boat up in Vicksburg was his chance to get out of a pickle. It transpired that it wasn't just the bank he owed; he had a number of other creditors who were pressing to get their money. 'The truth is Mike, this boat wasn't doing too good when I inherited it. My brother had been losing freight contracts and passengers to the railroads for years, and soon after I took over the boat it hit a snag in the riverbed and almost sunk. I had to borrow money to get it repaired as the insurance didn't cover the cost, then a couple of years later flying sparks from the furnace set fire to some timbers stacked too close by. The crew managed to put out the flames, but we lost a number of cargos while the damage was fixed, and I was faced with another large bill, and I had to borrow again. So, when I found this fellow who seemed keen to buy, I jumped at the chance. It all hinges on what he thinks when he sees the boat. We're picking him up at Vicksburg on our scheduled trip up to Greenville and then I've got to convince him to buy before we return to Vicksburg. The Pinsoneau cost $375,000 when it was built, and if the sale goes through I'll have about $120,000 after I've paid off the crew. I can go back home to Canada, leaving this dammed boat and my debts behind. But Mike, and this is just between you and me, I've told my creditors I'm planning to go back to San Francisco, and I'll be settling my debts from there, just in case they come after me looking for their money.'

Étienne, I can tell you I was a little shocked at the brazenness of Luc's scheme, but I felt it was not my place to interfere in his business affairs, so I said nothing to gainsay it. My tour of the riverboat was concluded, and Luc and I made our way back to his stateroom. Over coffee, we reminisced some more about days spent in the Bitterroots and our ensuing journey to Tacoma. Presently Luc reluctantly declared he had some business to attend to ashore and he would have his coachman drop me off at my residence, but I was welcome to return later and make the Pinsoneau my home till he sold it.

Later that day I met with Papa Jack who gave me his blessing to take some of the band on the river. I managed to recruit Felipe Vasella, Abrah Taylor, and Nicolas Brunet, but the other musicians either didn't want to come along or were committed to play elsewhere. I was short of a drummer, but Nicolas recommended a fellow by the name of Louis La Roca, and when he accepted my offer my band was complete.

Two days later I arrived back at the Pinsoneau with my fellow musicians. Luc was ashore when we boarded but he had left instructions with the ship's Captain that we were to be well looked after. During our journey to Vicksburg, I spent quite a lot of time with Luc, usually taking breakfast together. I often passed the rest of the morning rehearsing with the band and when we didn't rehearse, I invariably spent time watching the world drift by, taking in the changing Mississippi vistas as towns and villages, farms and plantations, bayous and woodlands appeared and vanished as the riverboat inexorably travelled northwards. That was my only free time as afternoon and evening my band played in the saloon.

The riverboat was far from crowded when we reached Vicksburg, but Luc had tried to improve the situation by allowing some crewmen's families to travel for free as deck passengers and by instructing off duty crewmen to masquerade as patrons. On reaching Vicksburg Luc vacated his stateroom to make it available for the arrival of his prospective buyer Mr Charles Naismith from Bossier City. Charles Naismith was a wealthy entrepreneur, with diverse business interests, whose family had made their early fortune from cotton. I was struck by his amazing resemblance to Abraham Lincoln which was only palliated by the fact he was much shorter and almost totally bald apart from a tuft of ginger hair arching above each of his ears. I saw little of Luc during the rest of voyage up to Greenville and back to Vicksburg as he devoted his full attention to charming Charles Naismith and his accountant as he endeavoured to wheedle them into buying the Pinsoneau.

Luc's intensive inveigling assisted by some creative accounts worked and the sale was done. Charles Naismith disembarked when we returned to Vicksburg and Luc with his financial worries about to dissipate was a mightily relieved and contented man. Luc's new found ebullience soon spread to the crew and their mood was much relaxed on our return journey. Even my fellow musicians picked up on the changed atmosphere and we played some of our best music as we headed downriver towards our next stop, Natchez, where we docked for two days on account of The Pinsoneau taking on board a rare cargo of cotton bales destined for New Orleans.

Sitting out on the Hurricane deck the day before we left Natchez wharf, Luc asked me if I'd considered my future, reasoning that as far as he could tell, there was nothing to keep me in New Orleans other than my commitment to Papa Jack's band. I hadn't contemplated making changes to my life and replied I would most likely continue playing with Papa Jack. Luc asked, 'Mike, why don't you come up to Canada? I'll be up there in a couple of months once this boat is sold, and I've given my creditors the slip. There's my late grandfather's farm at Sainte-Rose near Montreal, you could live there, run the farm and start a new life.'

'That's a tempting proposal Luc, I might just take you up on it, but can you give me a few days to think it over?'

'Sure, but don't think too long, the Pinsoneau's sale will be completed two or three days after we get back to New Orleans, then I'm going on a little trip, so I'd like to know before I leave.'

Luc then shared with me his plan for his exit, which to me seemed quite thorough. He had told his associates and creditors he was going back west to San Francisco, even hiring genuine San Francisco lawyers as a conduit for settling claims against him for outstanding debts, but Luc, and his money, would be nowhere near San Francisco, he was flitting to Europe on a sentimental trip to visit Équemauville, the birthplace of his great grandfather, before returning to begin a new life in Canada.

Chapter 29

The first night after leaving Natchez my band had been playing in the saloon. We had received a good reception from our audience and at the end of the evening I was relaxing in the bar with Abrah Taylor, and Nicolas Brunet, the other band members having long since gone to their beds. Abrah and Nicolas were accomplished drinkers and leaving them to their accustomed practice, I bid them goodnight and trundled off to my stateroom on the now deserted boiler deck. It was a dark night, there being no moon, but the deck was well lit. It was quite late; I was weary and looking forward to my bed. I put the key in the door lock and was about to turn it, when I felt the sharp jolt of a pistol against my back and a voice harshly commanded, 'no noise if you know what's good for you.'

Another figure appeared from the shadows and the first voice ordered me to move slowly away from the door and turn around and face him. 'Well, what d'you know; it's Michael Wilkinson, come back from the dead.'

I looked into the fulminating face of my accoster, it was Hugh Kerr. John Kerr quickly searched me but found no weapons. Hugh Kerr motioned for me to walk ahead of him as John enthusiastically grasped me by the arm. We walked noiselessly towards the stairs to the Hurricane deck, the pistol rammed hard against me all the while. Hugh Kerr spoke, 'I always suspected you'd somehow escaped us at Nanaimo, but your widow was so convincing I doubted myself. Such a touching funeral, I was there, it's a pity you weren't.' He continued. 'I never thought to see you again and then tonight there you were in the saloon playing your dammed trumpet, and in a few minutes you'll be dead.'

John laughed at this utterance and spat contemptuously on the deck. We climbed up the staircase to the deserted Hurricane deck, John in front of me and Hugh close behind me. Hugh guided me towards the stern, all the while keeping his pistol firmly pressed against my back. We stopped walking, I glanced at Hugh, his eyes were radiant with malice, and that night I believed I was surely going to die.

'Here'll do. John, take his arms and hold him steady'. I braced myself as John gripped me tightly, he sneered, 'it would have been better for you to have stayed dead.'

'Sorry to disappoint you,' I responded defiantly, only to receive a forceful blow to my stomach from Hugh's boot. The wind was knocked out of me and I began to retch. Hugh Kerr unsheathing his Bowie knife walked towards me no doubt meaning to slit my throat. I was petrified with fright and breathing heavily.

'Well Wilkinson,' Hugh mocked, 'it's been a long time coming but your death has truly been worth all the waiting.'

I desperately struggled to break free, but John held me fast. I braced myself as Hugh grasped my hair, forcing my head back, and lifted his knife towards my exposed neck. Suddenly out of nowhere a gunshot cut through the night sending the knife in Hugh's hand flying through the air. Taking advantage of this unexpected intervention I stamped hard down on John's foot and struggled free, running wildly along the hurricane deck while frantically looking for somewhere to take cover. Two more shots were fired, one thudding into my thigh, and the other hitting John Kerr. The riverboat's pilot Zebulon Carrick was shouting at me to keep down, there was more gunfire and I saw John Kerr fall. The commotion had awakened some of the crew and passengers and I was aware of a few brave or foolhardy souls arriving on the deck, and then I fell into unconsciousness.

I stirred to find Luc leaning over me. It must have been some hours later and at first I wondered why I was in Luc's stateroom, and then the memory of my hostile encounter with the Kerrs came back to me. I became quite agitated, and Luc called for the Pinsoneau's doctor who mopped my brow and listened to my heart and asked me how I was feeling. Strangely it was only then that I was suddenly aware of the horrendous pain in my leg. The doctor told me I had been shot in the thigh but luckily it was a flesh wound. The bullet had lodged close to the femoral artery, and it had proved difficult to extract. I had lost a lot of blood before he had managed to staunch the flow. The doctor gave me morphine for the pain, and I drifted off to a drug induced sleep. I remember little of the next day or so as further doses of morphine caused me to be very lethargic, but by the time we returned to New Orleans although still in much discomfort, I was stoically refusing any further attempts by the physician to administer morphine.

As the effects of the drugs dissipated and my thoughts cleared, I became anxious for news of what happened to the Kerrs after I lost consciousness. Luc told me I had been fortunate that Zebulon Carrick had been looking out from the Pilothouse. He had seen me being abducted, and when he saw Hugh Kerr brandishing a knife at my throat, he had fired at the Kerrs, which surely prevented my death. John Kerr had been shot, and it seemed Hugh had also been wounded, but probably not seriously as he picked up his injured brother, and they both escaped by jumping overboard. Luc and some of the ship's crew had quickly launched the ship's wooden yawl to see if they could find them, but there was no trace, so either they drowned or made it to the shore.

We discussed whether we should inform the law, but Luc convinced me that there was little they could do, arguing he was reluctant to invite unwelcome attention to himself given his imminent intention to deceive his creditors. He concocted a tale that the gun fight was a dispute between two disgruntled gamblers who had mistaken me for someone else. I was still worried that if Hugh lived, he would easily find me when I returned to New Orleans, and Luc suggested that I accompany him on his clandestine trip to Europe.

My fellow musicians, concerned about my wellbeing, had regularly trooped by to see me. On the day we arrived back in New Orleans I confided in Nicolas that I was going to Le Havre so wouldn't be returning for Papa Jack's rehearsals. I asked him to let Papa Jack know what had happened and to go to my room on Murat Street, settle my rent and bring me back some belongings. Two days later the sale of the riverboat was concluded. Luc had his money and that same day shortly before midnight a Hanson cab was waiting at the Pinsoneau's wharf to take us on a brief journey further along the waterfront to where a ship destined for Le Havre was anchored. Our ship was the Compagnie Générale Transatlantique's SS La Bretagne, a four masted vessel with two funnels, which Luc enthusiastically enlightened me, had twin triple expansion steam engines driving a single screw propeller and could achieve a speed of 17 knots.

Étienne, I must admit at that time I showed little interest in the finer points of the ship's design, for Luc's description meant little to me and my leg was exceptionally painful, all I wanted to do was to go somewhere quiet and sit and rest. I was unable to walk without assistance and Luc inveigled the coachman to carry me up the gangway onto the SS La Bretagne and into his first class cabin. I made myself as comfortable as I could under the circumstances, while Luc checked that his luggage had all been brought safely on board. La Bretagne sailed at 5.00 a.m. by which time I was fast asleep.

Our voyage lasted just over sixteen days which included a twelve hour stopover at New York's Morton Street Pier to take on additional passengers, fuel, and supplies. While I convalesced, in my more pensive moments I sometimes reflected on my previous Atlantic crossing and pleasant times spent with Padraig and Bel and pondered how our lives might have been different had the intrusion by the Molly Maguires and Pinkertons not occurred. Alas Étienne what occurred in the past cannot be changed, and I tried not to dwell on such thoughts for fear my demons would resurface. My leg was healing and although still painful I could walk a few steps unaided. Towards the end of the voyage, I resumed playing my cornet and even composed a few mediocre tunes. Happily, this crossing was free of incident, the sea had been mostly calm and in the early evening on the sixteenth day after leaving New Orleans the port of Le Havre was in sight.

We spent little time exploring le Havre for Luc was eager to press on and get to Équemauville, the birthplace of his ancestors. We passed our only night in Le Havre in a comfortable but slightly downtrodden inn not far from the ancient Chapel of Saint-Michel of Ingouville. Luc was up early the next day, and by the time I had stirred myself and had breakfast he had hired a coach and driver to take us on to a ferry boat which took us across the river Sein. After crossing the river our next stop was here in Honfleur where we spent the night at Lucien Colbert's inn behind Place Sainte Catherine. It would be a cliché to say I fell in love with Honfleur, but I certainly would've liked to have tarried longer. Luc however, was keen to press on, and we set out for Équemauville the following day. For nearly two weeks we searched the environs of Équemauville for any traces of Luc's great uncle's elusive family. Finally, Luc had a breakthrough of sorts when he encountered an elderly cleric who recalled burying a man named Georges Beauséjour, the same name as Luc's great uncle. This Georges Beauséjour had died some fifteen years earlier, but the cleric recalled that his son, also named Georges, had been a baker in nearby Touques.

Étienne it is very late so I will not detain you with unnecessary details of the Beauséjour family reunion, suffice to say it was at least initially not a great success. It seems Luc's grandfather had left Équemauville under somewhat of a cloud, absconding with a sum of money that allegedly belonged to his younger brother, and not only that he was accompanied by his brother's fiancé. Georges, Luc's second cousin, had been brought up on this tale, and he was in no mood to forgive, until that is, Luc offered to repay the money, a sum of about one hundred and twenty francs, and family harmony was miraculously restored. Georges had two brothers who lived nearby, Luc visited them all and I suspect he made similar recompense to them.

Soon afterwards Luc and I were to part company. He was eager to explore Paris and then maybe go on to Geneva, Venice, and Rome, before returning home to Canada. Luc asked me to go with him, but I'd had enough of wandering, and told him I wished to remain in France. I was anonymous here and felt safe. Luc did his best to change my mind, but here in Honfleur we parted, and I have not seen or heard from him since that day.

There was something about Honfleur that drew me to it and made me feel at ease. Étienne I know this may sound ridiculous, but for the first time in many years I felt I was at home. The rest of my story you know, for later that very same day I came limping up to you in the harbour asking where I might find work and shelter. I said you know the rest of my story, but Étienne, that is not quite true, for I have still to tell you what happened to me last night.

Chapter 30

'Étienne I have shared with you the mysteries of my past and you have sat good-naturedly listening to my lengthy discourse, but I can tell by the expression on your face that you are eager at last to ask some questions.'

'Michel if you only answer one question, pray tell me what became of the man Hugh Kerr, was he drowned or is he pursuing you still?'

Sighing deeply, I responded in a quiet voice, 'would you like to meet my tormentor Étienne? Come follow me.'

I got up and taking a lantern led a nonplussed Father Étienne downstairs through my shop to the storeroom . Pausing briefly to light a candle to better illuminate the room I turned to Étienne and throwing open the storeroom door said, 'behold my pursuer.'

There on the floor lay the body of Hugh Kerr. Étienne crossing himself, walked forward and knelt down by the body, no doubt to offer religious succour or possibly to check for signs of life. I declared, maybe somewhat harshly, 'do not trouble yourself Father, the man is quite dead.'

Father Étienne was clearly shocked, but he observed the scene calmly. I could tell his mind was racing with more questions as he stared at the bloodstained chest of Hugh Kerr. 'Come back upstairs my friend for it is cold down here and not conducive to conversation.'

We retraced our steps to the living room. Étienne sat down while I refilled our wine glasses and began to relate my final encounter with Hugh Kerr. Just before closing my shop last evening, I was sweeping the floor as usual. I had my back to the door, and I turned around when I heard someone enter. At first, I didn't recognise his disturbing but familiar face, but when I glanced into the intimidating wild eyes of the customer instantly the memories came flooding back, I knew who he was and that my past had suddenly become my present. He looked much older than I remembered. It had been a long time since we last met but what struck me most was his changed appearance. He was clearly dishevelled as someone who had been on the road might be, but more than that he had an air of wretchedness or melancholy. He was much thinner than I recalled and moved slowly as if every step required a great effort. I also observed that his face was deathly pale.' 'You're a hard man to find Wilson or Wilkinson or whatever you call yourself these days, but I know who you are and that....'

Étienne, at this point whatever Kerr was about to say was interrupted by a coughing fit. While he recovered, he produced a pistol and aimed it at me. 'Well as I was saying you've led me a fair dance but now it's almost time for us to say a final farewell.'

He ordered me to close the shutters and bolt the door.

'That's better, we don't want our reunion to be disturbed', he uttered. 'I've been watching you these last few days and I know you live alone.'

Nodding towards a door at the rear of the shop he asked me where it led. I told him it was my storeroom. He mumbled during another coughing fit, 'it would do,' indicating that I enter first.

Keeping his gun trained on me Hugh Kerr went to sit on a chair next to the table I use as a desk. 'As I was saying you're a hard man to find, all these years and I've never stopped looking for you, never stopped wanting you dead. You probably don't know or even care that my brother John died that night after we jumped from the riverboat. I sat there on the riverbank holding John in my arms and watched him die, slowly suffocating on his own blood and there was nothing I could do to help him. After I buried him, I got down to New Orleans as quickly as I could, but you and your rich friend were gone. So, hearing a story your pal might have gone to San Francisco I travelled out there and when I didn't find either of you, I headed back over to New Orleans and after months of scratching around a fella told me Beauséjour had gone to Quebec. I thought maybe he'd taken you with him, so I headed up there, but no one knew him. I thought maybe you'd skulked back to Tacoma, but that weasel Collins and his stuck-up wife claimed they'd not seen or heard from you since '85 and feared you were dead. I didn't make them any the wiser, made my way back east and after fruitless years traipsing up and down the Mississippi, I got lucky and came across your old friend Nicolas Brunet. He had a very bad memory and claimed he didn't know you, but it's amazing what the threat of hacking off a musician's fingers can do, and he suddenly recalled you telling him you were skulking off to Le Havre with Beauséjour.'

Another coughing episode interrupted his lengthy diatribe. 'So, I shipped out to Le Havre and spent the next two years searching for signs of you or Beauséjour. Eventually I was directed to a baker called Beauséjour in Touques who suggested I take a look in Honfleur and here I am.'

'I've imagined this moment many times. For years now every night before I go to sleep I've planned how I'm gonna kill you. For a while I'd half a mind to hang you so you'd suffer the same way poor Jimmy suffered, but now I'm thinking that's too much bother and maybe I'll just slit your damned throat, it'll be quicker and quieter, and you'll be just as dead.'

He started laughing at his remark but began coughing again and rasping between coughs demanded I bring him a bottle of wine. I did as he requested and passed him the wine. He took a long drink and said, 'here's to Cousin James and brothers John, Tom and Andrew, God rest their souls.'

He pushed the bottle at me and insisted I drink to their memory too, reluctantly I took the bottle and defiantly declared, 'and here's to my good friend Padraig O'Brien.'

Hugh jumped up surprisingly quickly given the state of his health, snatching back the bottle and hitting me on the head with it. Stunned by the blow, I lay on the floor. He grasped me roughly by the arm pulling me to my feet and pushed a knife against my throat, puncturing my skin as he did so. 'No,' he rasped more to himself than me, 'that's much too quick, you have to suffer more.'

He pushed me down on to a chair, his exertions setting off a violent coughing fit causing him to drop his knife. He bent to retrieve it, I seized my chance and rushed at him kicking the knife away. He managed to draw his pistol, but I grabbed his wrist before he could get off a shot. We grappled for the gun, sprawling over the table and onto the floor. We rolled over a couple of times and somehow managed to get back on our feet. In spite of his wasted appearance and another coughing episode Hugh was surprisingly strong and I needed all of my strength to thwart him.

We thrashed around the room, neither one of us able to gain an advantage, and then we crashed against a wine shelf sending bottles tumbling to the floor. Sliding on the spilled wine and broken glass we fell on to some flour sacks and still clasped together fighting to grasp the pistol, we rolled off the sacks landing heavily on the floor. All the while Hugh was trying to get his gun into a position where he could shoot me and I was doing all I could to prevent him from doing so. I was tiring and I sensed Hugh was gaining the upper hand but then unexpectedly the gun went off. Hugh's resistance ceased and he fell limply to the floor.

Cautiously I examined his body; there was no obvious sign of a bullet wound. It seemed it wasn't the shot that subdued him, the effort of our struggle had been too much for his consumption riddled body. His chest was covered in blood from his coughing fits. Shaking from my exertions and the shock of my encounter with Hugh, I looked to see if he still lived. As I bent over him, I was certain he was dead, and then something on his waistcoat flickering in the shadowy candle light caught my eye. I retrieved it and unable to believe what I saw held it to the candle, it was the same silver and jade shamrock brooch Bel had given me many years before.

Hugh Kerr my long-time nemesis was dead. I had been hiding and running from him most of my adult life but now at last it was over, I felt relief and a strangely uplifting notion that in spite of all I had endured his passing was a death worth waiting for. So, Étienne those three Norns I often talk about had played out their game and it came to pass that for the first time since I was a young lad fleeing to America, I no longer had any reason to be a man who is ever watchful.

Chapter 31

On a cold snowy morning two days later the church bells of Sainte Catherine's were tolling. Father Étienne had just concluded a funeral. Aside from the celebrant, Michel Londres, and the pallbearers there were no mourners at the funeral mass. An unknown vagrant had been found in the snow, huddled beside a log store in the backyard of Michel Londres' shop. A doctor had been called and he certified death was caused by consumption most likely exacerbated by the unusually cold weather. Michel Londres had agreed to pay for the funeral. Hugh Kerr was laid to rest and Michael Wilkinson was finally at peace.

Epilogue

Michel Londres lived in Honfleur for the rest of his life. When he was 56, he married the widowed Madame Agathe Levasseur whom he had known for many years, and they lived happily, for the most part, until she died nineteen years later. Michel never did go home to Northumberland, but he was visited by his brother John in 1914, four months before the outbreak of the Great War. John visited twice more after the war before his death in 1930. During John's first visit Michel handed John the equivalent of £30, so fulfilling his promise to pay his brother back for the money he had borrowed to run off to America so many years before.

Michel continued to work in his shop, helped by Agathes' grandson, until he was incapacitated by a stroke when he was almost 87 years old, he died three months later and was buried in Honfleur communal cemetery just metres away from his nemesis Hugh Kerr.

Father Étienne made a long awaited pilgrimage to the Vatican six years after Hugh Kerrs funeral. He passed away peacefully in his sleep a week after his return to Honfleur.

Luc Beauséjour returned to Canada after travelling around Europe for nearly three years. His creditors were unsuccessful in locating him. He met and married the youngest daughter of a wealthy Montreal department store owner, some fifteen years his junior. They went on to have three children. In 1916 while crossing Montreal's

Ste-Catherine Street Luc was run down and killed by a motor car.

As for Samuel van de Beek no one knows what became of him. In the summer of '91 his cabin was found abandoned and in good order but there were no clues as to where Sam had gone.

Dramatis Personae

(In order of appearance)

Fictional characters

Father Étienne – *catholic priest in Honfleur and friend of Michael Londres.*

Madame Vernier – *Father Étienne's housekeeper.*

Monsieur Guillaume – *store owner in Honfleur and Michael's employer.*

Rector William Wildblood– *Church of England priest, and Michael's Headmaster.*

Albert Charlton*- *school bully and Michael's childhood enemy.*

Mary Scott* – *Michael's childhood school friend and later Albert Charlton's girlfriend.*

George and **Harriet Scott** – *parents of Mary and proprietors of the Shakespeare Tavern.*

Old Jacob Armstrong – *Napoleonic war veteran, boatman and friend of Michael and John.*

Hannah – *Old Jacob's daughter.*

Sir James Alexander – *wealthy landowner and entrepreneur, whose life is saved by John Wilkinson.*

Sean Padraig O'Brien - *Michael's friend and protector from Kilmacow County Kilkenny, commonly known as Padraig.*

Bella/Bel O'Brien – *Padraig's sister and later Michael's wife.*

Ciaran, Dara and ***Orla O'Brien*** – *Padraig's and Bel's siblings living in Ireland.*

Maureen O'Flahavan – *widow of Brendan O'Flahavan and sister to Padraig and Bel. Mother of* ***Nail*** *and young* ***Padraig O'Flahavan***. *Owner of general store and lodging house in Port Clinton. Later moves to Pottsville where she married Dr Elijah Collins and they moved to Tacoma.*

Elijah Michael Collins – *doctor and second husband of Maureen O'Flahavan.*

Aaro and ***Eska Järvinen*** –*Finnish brothers and Michael's fellow passengers on the SS Pennsylvania*

Séamus Collins- *an associate of the Kerr brothers, and a lowly member of the Molly Maguires.*

Jackson – *mine supervisor and lodger at Maureen O'Flahavan's, killed by the Molly Maguires*

Mrs O'Regan- *elderly lodging house owner and illicit whisky peddler.*

Klaus Weber –*purchaser of Maureen O'Flahavan's general store in Pottsville.*

Abe McClellan, John Webster, Anderson and **Jack Quinn** - *Pinkerton detectives charged with protecting Michael and Padraig.*

The Kerr brothers, *Hugh, John, Andrew and Tom - fictitious cousins of James Boyle and bitter enemies of Michael and Padraig.*

Zachariah Babington – *a purveyor of agricultural supplies from St. Louis and stagecoach travelling companion of Michael.*

Lieutenant Harold Garthwaite Brownbridge - *Ninth United States Infantry, a native of Quincy, in Norfolk County Massachusetts and stagecoach travelling companion of Michael.*

Luc Beauséjour- *a French-Canadian, a travelling companion and good friend of Michael's.*

M.C. Brown - *a defence attorney for Tom and Andrew Kerr in Laramie.*

Dusty McGregor – *an inmate of Wyoming Territorial Penitentiary.*

Ezekiel 'Zeke' Ramsey - *erstwhile trail guide and false friend of Michael and Luc.*

himíin 'ilp'ílp/ Red Wolf – *a young Nimipu (Nez Perce) warrior friend of Samuel van de Beek and fictitious nephew of Chief Joseph.*

Samuel van de Beek- *a trapper and solitary Mountain man also known as Sam or Dutch, rescuer of Michael and Luc.*

Pieter and **Tomas van de Beek**, - *Samuel's brothers who perished while serving in the Union forces during the Civil War.*

Toiréasa and **Rose Boyle** - *sisters of James Boyle and cousins to the Kerr brothers.*

Emma Bostwick- *Bel O'Brien's friend and wife of Dr Collins' medical practice partner Dr Harold C. Bostwick.*

Agnes - *Emma Bostwick's maid.*

Anna - *Maureen and Elijah Collins' Chinese maid.*

Charles Evans –*Bel's neighbour and son of a lawyer.*

Lizzie Evans and **Laura Clancy** – *Bel's bridesmaids.*

Dr Jones – *Wellington colliery surgeon.*

Lizzie Fiddick – *Bel and Michael's neighbour in Wellington.*

Henry Gladders – *a travelling companion of Michael's and an entrepreneur from Port Gibson in Claiborne County, Mississippi.*

Horace Cleaver – *an undertaker from Port Gibson and Michael's employer.*

Charles Rowey – *landowner near Port Gibson from whom Michael purchases a farm.*

André Boulanger – *a French speaking creole alto horn player in Papa Jack Laine's band.*

Nicolas Brunet – *a French speaking creole string bass musician in Papa Jack Laine's band and friend of Michael.*

Felipe Vasella – *Cuban tuba player in Papa Jack's band.*

Abraham (Abrah) Taylor – *African American piano and banjo musician in Papa Jack's band.*

George Mahoney and **Jim Pringle** – *criminal associates of the Kerr brothers from Boise.*

Bill Dodds – *a gambler who crossed the Kerr brothers.*

Ben Hall – *a Pueblo marshal who arrested John and Tom Kerr.*

Joshua and **Amos Wells** - *criminal associates of the Kerr brothers from Barclay Kansas.*

Louis La Roca - *a drummer in Michael's band. Friend of Nicolas Brunet.*

Charles Naismith - *from Bossier City, bought the Jacques Pinsoneau from Luc Beauséjour.*

Zebulon Carrick – *Pilot on the riverboat Jacques Pinsoneau.*

Lucien Colbert- *an innkeeper in Honfleur.*

Georges Beauséjour – *a baker in Touques and Luc Beauséjour's second cousin.*

Madame Agathe Levasseur – *a widow from Honfleur, Michael's second wife.*

Historical characters

Michael Wilkinson/*Michel Londres*/*Mike Wilson* - *in real life he was only known as Michael Wilkinson. He and his family emigrated to British Columbia from England in the 1860s. He was killed in the mining explosion in Nanaimo in June 1884, leaving a wife Isabell (nee Wood) and 8 children.*

John Wilkinson – *Michael's brother and in later life a successful businessman, magistrate and councillor.*

William Wilkinson – *Michael's youngest brother.*

Sarah Wilkinson – *Michael's sister.*

Sergeant Graham -*Coldstream Guardsman and hero of Hougoumont Farm.*

Sergeant Fraser -*3rd Scots Guards, fought at Waterloo.*

Captain Bradburn – *Captain of the SS Pennsylvania, lost at sea during a hurricane.*

Mr Sweetland -*SS Pennsylvania's first officer.*

Mr Ross-*SS Pennsylvania's second officer.*

Charles Rivers -*SS Pennsylvania's third officer*

Mr Blake -*SS Pennsylvania's first assistant engineer*

Captain Cornelius Brady –*Passenger and saviour of the SS Pennsylvania, after he took command of the ship during a storm in February 1874. The ship endured days of battering from high seas until the storm finally broke. Brady took the ship safely to Philadelphia. Having saved a $600,000 ship and its $250,000 cargo along with the passengers and crew from destruction, Brady felt insulted by the offer of $1,000 reward from the American Steamship Company. He sued for the full salvage value of the vessel, and in the subsequent court case was awarded $4,000 plus $200 expenses. Less than a year earlier the heroic Brady, then Third officer on the SS Atlantic, along with Quartermaster John Speakman, risked his life, in an attempt to save the passengers and crew of the Atlantic, when it crashed off Lower Prospect, Halifax County, Nova Scotia. His courageous action in personally establishing a rope from the Atlantic to the shore probably saved as many as 250 lives.*

Mr Williams - *SS Pennsylvania steerage steward.*

James McKenna/ James McParlan –*undercover Pinkerton detective in Pennsylvania's Schuylkill County and later the Pinkerton's Denver Office Assistant Superintendent*

'Big Pat' Dormer – *said to be a senior figure in the Molly Maguires and proprietor of the Sheridan House tavern in Pottsville.*

Muff Lawler and **John Kehoe** – *said to be senior men in the Molly Maguires*

Benjamin Yost – *a policeman allegedly murdered by the Molly Maguires.*

James 'Powder Keg' Kerrigan – *alleged to be a member of the Molly Maguires and to have been involved with the murder of Benjamin Yost.*

James Carroll, Thomas Duffy, James Roarity, Hugh McGeehan, *and* **James Boyle** – *all sentenced to death for Benjamin Yost's murder and alleged to be members of the Molly Maguires.*

Cyrus L. Pershing- *Molly Maguire trial judge.*

Robert Linden-*assistant superintendent of the Pinkerton's in Chicago, was installed as Captain Linden of the Coal and Iron Police.*

Jesse James – *(1847 – 1882) was an outlaw, bank and train robber and leader of the James-Younger Gang. He was murdered by Robert Ford.*

Sheriff Werner – *law officer in Pottsville.*

Reverends Welsh *and* **Beresford** - *James Boyle and Hugh McGeehan's spiritual advisors.*

Henry David Thoreau - *(1817 –1862) was an American philosopher, essayist and poet. He is possibly best remembered for his book 'Walden' published in 1854, where he reflects upon simple living in natural surroundings. Thoreau was passionately opposed to slavery and actively supported the abolitionist movement.*

Chief Joseph- *(1840 –1904) was a leader of the Wallowa Nez Perce people when they were compelled to leave their ancestral homeland by the United States Government and move to a reservation in the Idaho Territory. Joseph's band and other Nez*

Perce who resisted, attempted to seek refuge in Canada. Around seven hundred people led by Joseph and other Nez Perce chiefs were pursued by the U.S. Army, commanded by General Howard in a 1,170 mile action often referred to as the Nez Perce War. In October 1877, most of Chief Joseph's people were pinned down in northern Montana, about 40 miles from the Canadian border. Here Chief Joseph surrendered to the U.S. Army with the understanding that he and his people would be allowed to settle in the reservation in Idaho. However, Joseph was not sent to Idaho. During the ensuing years he was transported between various forts and reservations on the southern Great Plains before being finally relocated to the Colville reservation in Washington State, where he died in 1904.

Dr. Henry Clay Bostwick - *(1828-1916) was the first doctor in Tacoma, he also opened Tacoma's first bank in 1880 and opened a hotel in 1889.*

Harold Arnold – *from Pennsylvania, a colleague of Michael's at South Wellington Colliery, he had only been working for the colliery for 5 or 6 weeks when he was killed in the explosion.*

Barney McGinnes – *a fire boss at South Wellington Colliery, originally from the USA, also died in the 1884 mine explosion.*

Adam Ross- *a colliery foreman at South Wellington Colliery.*

Fr. Peter Hylebos - *was the first pastor of St. Leo's Parish Tacoma.*

Charles Joseph 'Buddy' Bolden –*(1877 – 1931) an African-American cornetist also known as "King" Bolden a key figure in the development of a New Orleans style of 'jass' music which later came to be known as jazz. His band was popular in*

New Orleans from around 1900 to 1907.It is generally believed there are no surviving original recordings of Buddy's music. His song Funky Butt is also known as, I Thought I Heard Buddy Bolden Say.

George Vital "Papa Jack" Laine – *(1873 – 1966) was musician and pioneering band leader in New Orleans from the mid-1880s to the early 1920s. He is recognised as being a leading influencer in the early development of jazz music.*

Alphonse Floristan Picou *(1878 – 1961) was a jazz clarinettist from New Orleans.*

Tom 'Red' Brown – *(1888 – 1958) a jazz Trombonist who played with Papa Jack.*

Jefferson 'Soapy' Smith – *(1860 – 1898) was involved in a number of criminal enterprises in Colorado and Alaska.*

Will Light – *Creede's deputy sheriff and Jefferson 'Soapy' Smith's brother in law*

John Zang –*a hotel owner in Creede, Mineral County, Colorado.*

Edward O'Kelley – *the man who murdered Robert Ford.*

***

*The murder of Mary Scott by Albert Charlton is to
some degree inspired by the real life killing of Catherine
Alice Baker by Alfred Etheridge that occurred in the
usually peaceful village of Sheepwash at 6.10 a.m. on
Tuesday 10th October 1911. Alfred Etheridge, a young
coal miner, murdered his sweetheart, Catherine Alice
Baker, shooting her with his shotgun and then killed
himself. Catherine aged 21, worked as a servant in the
Shakespeare Tavern and was one of ten children living
with her parents Francis and Jane Baker, in Pancake
Row, Sheepwash. The deadly early morning blast was
witnessed by local resident Thomas Patterson who was
about 90 yards from the pair when the fatal shots were
fired. At the inquest Francis Baker Jr. the murdered
girl's 14 year old brother, stated that when he had
returned home the evening before the murder Catherine
and Alfred had been sitting by the fire and he heard his
sister remark 'I'm not going to have anything more to do
with you,' to which Alfred replied 'I will shoot myself.
'Catherine then said, 'I'm going to get myself another

lad.' Alfred replied, 'I don't care,' and was then reported to have said several times he would shoot himself. Catherine, known to her family and friends as Alice, and Alfred were both buried on the same day at the nearby St Paul's Parish Church, Choppington. *The Morpeth Herald and Reporter, Friday October 13, 1911*, provides a full account of the murder and inquest.

Any similarity between the fictional characters of Mary Scott and Albert Charlton and Catherine Alice Baker and Alfred Etheridge is unintentional and purely coincidental.

ABOUT THE AUTHOR

 Shaun Beattie lives in rural north
Northumberland close to the Scottish
border.
His second novel Memorial is coming
soon.
email shaun.beattie@zohomail.com

Printed in Great Britain
by Amazon

12108234R00188